All Broke Down

Also by Cora Carmack

ALL BROKE DOWN

A RUSK UNIVERSITY NOVEL

Cora Carmack

WILLIAM MORROW

An Imprint of HarperCollinsPublishers

ALL BROKE DOWN. Copyright © 2014 by Cora Carmack. All rights reserved. Printed in the United States of America. No part of this book may be used or reproduced in any manner whatsoever without written permission except in the case of brief quotations embodied in critical articles and reviews. For information address HarperCollins Publishers, 195 Broadway, New York, NY 10007.

HarperCollins books may be purchased for educational, business, or sales promotional use. For information please e-mail the Special Markets Department at SPsales@harpercollins.com.

FIRST EDITION

Library of Congress Cataloging-in-Publication Data has been applied for.

ISBN 978-0-06-232622-5

14 15 16 17 18   DIX/RRD   10 9 8 7 6 5 4 3 2 1

For the Carmcats.

You guys are the best street team any author could ask for. Thanks for loving these characters, making Friday the best day of the week, and always being there in the middle of the night when I want to procrastinate.

Slow claps for everyone!

Chapter 1

Silas

The flash of a camera blinds me as I take my seat at the front of the room. I scoot in my chair, and the scraping sound grates on my nerves. A second flash. Then a third. Then I lose count. Sweat gathers at the back of my neck, and I struggle to keep my breathing slow and steady.

Fuck this shit.

I don't want to be here. I play football so I don't *have* to think or talk. As a general rule, I prefer to do my talking with my body whenever possible.

Football. Fighting. Fucking.

That's what I know how to do. Not this.

Coach has finally taken his seat, and I feel the tension in my spine lessen as he begins talking to the press. He's in the middle with me, Carson McClain, Jake Carter, and Mateo Torres surrounding him, the team leaders. Coach covers the niceties and starts talking about his plan for preseason camp, while I survey our group. Everyone looks calm but me. McClain is a freaking choirboy. He probably lives for this kind of shit. Torres has never met an argument he can't talk his way out of or a skirt he won't *try* to talk his way into. And Carter is so full of bullshit, he has no trouble spewing it to others. And me? My hands are shaking beneath the table like an addict in need of a fix.

If Coach weren't so strict and observant, I would have tried to calm my nerves with a little weed prior to this whole media day circus. But there's no way I could have slid that past him. And I've been trying to cut that out since Levi was busted. Coach has become like one of those sadistic teachers that love to give pop quizzes . . . only with drug tests.

"We've got a young team. McClain and Moore both still have two years of eligibility," Coach says, slamming me back into the present. "Torres has three. And though this is Carter's last year with us, we've got a solid group of linemen coming up. We've got our foundation, and I think we're going to surprise people with what we manage to build this season."

Coach opens up for questions, and even though I know what's coming, my body still locks up at the first one. "Coach Cole, your team was rocked by scandal last year with the arrest of starting quarterback Levi Abrams. The team snagged a few impressive wins despite that, but ultimately things fell apart in the latter half of the season. Mentally, where is your team at right now?"

"Last season, we had to do a lot of learning and discovery on the fly. And unfortunately, we had to do that while also trying to win games. But I'm proud of the season these boys put up." His expression goes hard, and I'm glad I'm not the only one scowling. I resist the urge to pick up the bottle of water in front of me and lob it at the reporter. "I don't think they fell apart at all actually. The last half of our schedule was certainly more demanding with bigger and better competition. But win or lose, *the team* never fell apart. They played through to the last second every time, and I feel confident that they gave it all they had. As for where their heads are at now, I can't say for certain. I know where they better be, though."

Laughter rolls through the room and the same reporter says, "Carson McClain, care to comment?"

McClain leans up to the microphone and says with perfect ease, "The team is focused. We've kept our heads down and worked hard this summer. We're all ready for camp to start. As a whole, I think we're pretty determined that any conversation about us this year happens because of what we're doing on the field, not off it."

A new journalist jumps in. "Silas Moore, you were close with Levi Abrams. You were redshirted together as freshmen. What's it like playing without him?"

Better. Worse. Fucking terrible. I don't know.

I can't talk about Levi. It twists up my head to think about him. He had everything—a good family, money, scholarship, talent, brains—and he screwed it all up. I don't have half those things. It's a joke that I'm even sitting here. If he can't get by without fucking things up, what hope do I have?

My hand shakes as I reposition the microphone, and I curl it into a hard fist. "McClain is a good QB." The whole room pauses, and the reporter gives me this expectant look, and I realize they want me to say *more*. Shit. "He's driven and focused, and the rest of the team works harder because of him."

I leave it at that because I'm not talking about Levi. When the discussion moves on, my chest feels like a boulder has been rolled off it. I don't have stage fright or some shit like that. I just . . . I don't belong here. And whenever we have stuff like this, I feel like I've been shoved under a microscope, and if they ever get a really good look at me, they're going to see just how different I am from these other guys and take it all away.

Another reporter asks me if I think our offense has come together well despite our last tumultuous year. (Who the fuck says "tumultuous"?)

"I think we have."

Again, they wait for me to say more, but this time I don't give in to their looks. If they want someone to chatter on and on, they should have asked Torres. The reporter prompts me, "How do you think that came about?"

"Hard work," I say.

I only get asked one more question, and when I give another short answer, they begin ignoring me in favor of Coach and the other players, and I finally manage to relax a little. All I want to do is go home, and spend the weekend blowing off steam before preseason camp starts on Monday.

When the media session ends, I catch up with Torres, who took over the lease on Levi's room this summer.

I ask, "You cool if people hang at our place tonight? I'll text Brookes, and have him get out the word."

"Like you even have to ask. I'm pretty sure *party* was my first word."

"I don't think I like where this is heading," McClain says, stepping up beside us as we walk.

Torres groans. "Let us get our party on, man. Not all of us get to go home to the Coach's daughter."

McClain nails Torres hard in the shoulder, and I glance back to make sure Coach isn't in hearing range. He's not. He's caught up talking to a few press people. When I look back, Torres is circling his arm like he's trying to work out the pain.

"Damn, QB. If that's how you react to me just mentioning her, how am I ever supposed to lay out all the dirty jokes I've been stockpiling?"

Torres is kidding. We all know it, but McClain doesn't joke about Dallas. He's easygoing about everything else, but not her. Maybe it was the weeks hearing Levi mouth off about dating her in high school (and yeah, me talking shit, too). Or maybe it was the mess of rumors that screwed things up for them a little while last year. Either way, the guy is intense about her. More intense even than when he's on the field.

Which is pretty fucking intense.

"Make your dirty jokes about Carter's girlfriend," I say.

Torres scoffs. "Carter's relationships go bad faster than the food in our fridge. Like I'm gonna waste my comedy gold on that."

Carter just grunts in response.

"And you," Torres turns on me. "I'm not even sure you could get to the third syllable in the word *relationship* without having a seizure."

I roll my eyes and steer the conversation back where it matters. "I want to get shit-faced tonight. Doesn't matter to me whether I do it at home or at the bar. But poor Torres here is still underage; so really, I'm trying to be kind."

"You're a regular old Good Samaritan," Carson says. He sighs and adds, "Just keep it small. We just spent the morning telling all those reporters how focused we are. Don't let anything get out of hand."

His eyes land on Torres first, then me.

If he's trying to guilt me into being boring, he's barking up the wrong tree. I don't do guilty. I do what I want. Life is too short and shitty to do anything else.

"Oh, I'm getting out of hand, McClain. Plan on it. If you want to keep us out of trouble, I guess you'll have to show up."

Torres grins. "Yeah and bring—"

Carson hits him in the stomach just hard enough to cut him off.

He wheezes a few times, playing it up, and says, "I was gonna say chips, man. Bring chips."

THE PARTY IS already going when we get back in the afternoon. Apparently, I'm not the only one who could use a bit of relaxing. There's a Slip 'N Slide in the front yard, and girls parading around in bikinis. A few people are throwing around a Frisbee.

I head inside, ready to grab a beer and shove off the unease still clinging to me after the press day.

I keep waiting for it to go away. That feeling that the other shoe is about to drop. But with three years here under my belt, it hasn't shown any sign of lessening.

I grab a beer from the fridge, and just closing my fingers around the cold neck of the bottle makes me feel a little more in my element. The first time my brother stuck a beer in my hand I'd been ten, maybe eleven. That's my world. What I know. These days I have to concentrate to push that all away, to be the Silas Moore that people watch and respect and expect things from. To be the Silas Moore that matters.

I must not be doing a very good job because my roommate, Brookes, sweeps in beside me. One dark arm reaches out to grab a beer and he says, "You okay?"

Observant motherfucker. How he knows what's going through my head at just a glance, I'll never know. But I don't like it.

There's a reason I do my best to seem laid-back and easygoing. When you look like you don't give a fuck, people don't ask you questions about how you're feeling. They don't ask you questions, period.

"Yeah," I reply, using the edge of the kitchen counter to pop the cap off my beer. I take a long pull, clink it with the bottle in his hand, and head out of the kitchen before he gets it in his head to play shrink.

My phone buzzes with a text, the third in the last hour, and I almost ignore it. I know who it's going to be. It's why I'm doing a shit job of keeping my composure, the old me too close to the surface.

My best guess is that somehow the media stuff this morning put me on her radar. Maybe she happened to catch it on a local TV station or read an article online because the texts started an hour or two after the meeting with the press.

Maybe all absentee moms have Google alerts on their sons. Or mine just has a canny sixth sense that tells her when I'm worth her attention.

The last time she reached out was my senior year in high school when recruiters came calling. My coach ran interference then. She'd been out of the picture for as long as he'd known me, so he had no problem making sure she stayed far away from the whole process. And considering I spent most of senior year living in guest rooms of friends or coaches, it wasn't like she could just go home and find me.

Now, though, things are different. There is no one here to run interference because no one knows. Rusk is a private school. Expensive and privileged. People here tend to just assume that you come from a background like them, and I never bothered correcting their assumptions.

I make my way out onto the front porch to watch the festivities, and I fish the phone out of my pocket to see what she's said this time.

Only this text isn't from my mother.

It's from Levi.

Fuck.

I've traded one person I don't want to see for another. Another who shouldn't even have access to a cell phone right now because he should be in prison.

I lean on the railing that surrounds our porch, paint peeling and wood sagging, and I read the text.

I'm out fucker. Come get wasted with me.

He's *out*? I count back the months. He was caught selling pot, among other things, last fall, but it can't have been more than six months since he was actually sentenced.

Six fucking months?

If it had been me, I'd be rotting away in there for a few more years at least. Then again, I grew up in a trailer park. Levi was raised in a house with bathrooms bigger than my old living room.

When you grow up like I did, no one has to tell you the world isn't fair. You figure it out pretty fast on your own.

A body settles against the railing beside me, slim and petite, and I look over at Stella Santos. She says, "You look even broodier than normal."

I look around expecting to see her best friend Dallas attached to her hip. She's alone, though, which means either Dallas and Carson haven't showed yet, or the coach's daughter decided she didn't want to talk to me and made herself scarce.

Probably the latter.

I guess when you try to bed a girl on a bet, you're not going to be party buddies anytime soon.

"I thought girls liked broody."

She flicks her short, black hair out of her eyes and sips something out of a red Solo cup. Her lips are painted nearly the same color, and she purses them before she answers, "Depends on the situation. There's a fine line between broody and potential sociopath. Right now you're walking the line."

She tops that dig off with a sly smile, and I shove my phone deep in my pocket, ready to let her distract me from my mom, my ex–best friend, everything. She'd turned that same smile on me last year at a party, and I don't remember doing much brooding after that. Granted, I don't remember much of it, period, except that she was feisty, and she knew what she liked—two things I can always get on board for. I don't usually go for seconds on my hookups, but Stella is different. She won't try to make it into something it isn't. I don't know for sure because we didn't talk about it, but I just get this feeling that we're alike, that we both know a different side of the world than everyone else here.

My gaze dips down to take her in, and I nod my head at the Slip 'N Slide in the yard. "Where's your bikini?"

She rolls her eyes. "Oh please. I believe in leaving *some* things to the imagination. I'm not that desperate."

I smirk. "Who needs imagination when you've got memories?"

She shoves me. Or tries to anyway, and I laugh. The girl is so tiny she doesn't have a hope of moving me.

She glares at me, but her full lips are tipped up at the corners.

I nod at the T-shirt and shorts she's wearing and say, "You're wearing one underneath there, aren't you?"

She looks like she wants to shove me again, but she doesn't.

Instead she huffs and says, "Fine. Yes, I am. But I'm only mildly desperate. Like a tiny, tiny amount."

"You do realize you could have half the guys at this party with very little effort, don't you?"

"But the effort is the fun part!"

She says it with a smile, but I think she's dead serious. When you live a hard life, you spend years wishing for the easy stuff, but then when you get it, it never feels right. You get used to having to fight and claw for the things you want, and when you don't have to do that anymore, everything feels a little bit muted.

At least that's how shit usually feels for me.

I ask, "That why you keep stringing the manager along?"

The glare she turns on me now is no longer playful. It's harder. With an edge of something I can't identify. "I am *not* stringing Ryan along. We're friends."

"Riiight."

"Don't *Right* me, mister. Like you know *anything* about relationships."

That's twice today I've had that tidbit waved in front of my face. I might be offended if it weren't entirely right.

"I know fuck buddies when I see them."

"We're not," she pauses, checking her volume, before adding under her breath, "We're not *that*."

"Yet."

"I'm going to actually kill you. I'm going to wrap my hands around your throat, and then claim I got tetanus and was incapable of relaxing my muscles."

"I had no idea you were into erotic asphyxiation, Santos."

She shoots back, "I had no idea you knew what *asphyxiation* meant."

I turn, laughing, and lean my back against the railing. A slow smile spreads across my face. "Speaking of erotic . . . here comes your fuck buddy . . ."

A group of people streams out the front door, including Ryan Blake, the team manager and Stella's not-quite-boyfriend.

Stella says, "We're not . . ." then trails off, a blush forming on her cheeks as Ryan comes to stand beside her, bumping her shoulder with his. Behind him is McClain, his arm draped over Dallas's shoulder as her eyes flick between me and Stella. I give her my most charming grin, but her eyes only narrow in response.

"You showed," I say to McClain when he walks over.

"Yeah, well, someone has to keep an eye on you douchebags."

Torres jogs past then, pulling his shirt off. He yells, "Keep an eye on this, McClain!" Then he dives onto the Slip 'N Slide right after a curvy brunette, and the two of them end up a tangled mess of slick skin at the other end.

Neither of them looks like they mind.

Dallas checks her watch and says, "Hey. Torres is improving. He was here a whole fifteen minutes before he took his shirt off. That's got to be a new record."

He must hear us laughing because he lets go of the brunette and says, "Moore! Get your ass out here!"

When I don't move, Stella gives me a shove. "Go on. You heard the man."

"You're just trying to get me to take my clothes off, aren't you?"

"Been there. Done that. So many girls have seen it, you probably *should* make a T-shirt."

I shake my head and start toward the stairs. "The rest of you might as well go ahead and come. He's going to want to play—"

I don't finish my sentence before Torres yells at the top of his lungs, "SLIP CUP!!!"

"What the hell is slip cup?" McClain asks.

Begrudgingly, the whole group comes with me, and we crowd with the rest of the partygoers around Torres as he explains his Slip 'N Slide/flip cup relay game. Basically, you take off down the slide where you get wet and soapy, and then at the end, you have to chug a plastic cup of beer, and flip it over with one finger. When the cup lands perfectly facedown (not easy when you're all soapy or all drunk), the next person on your team can take off down the slide.

By some miracle, Torres persuades our entire group (and about twenty other people) to play. I watch in amusement as Stella strips down to her swimsuit, locking eyes with Ryan as he does the same. I shake my head and pull off my shirt. I'm not wearing swim trunks, but the athletic shorts I have on will work just fine.

Torres splits us all into teams, and gets another punch to the arm from McClain when he lingers too long near a bikini-clad Dallas.

By the time the game starts, people are cheering, and there's enough booze and boobs to make me completely forget that I'd ever been in a shitty mood. I'm waiting on the already tipsy girl in front of me to flip her cup before I can go. I start to lose patience somewhere between her seventh and eighth try, and I glance to the side just as a beat-up old town car pulls up next to the curb.

A girl climbs out of the driver's side, and I don't see her face, but she's got white blonde hair falling down her back and tan skin, and some dude I don't know behind me says, "*Damn.*"

I'm so busy looking at her that I don't even notice when drunk and ditzy manages to finally flip her cup.

The woman rounds the back of the car, and lifts a pair of dark sunglasses off her face. The guy behind me pushes at my back, telling me it's my turn to run, but I can't stop staring.

Not because she's pretty or wearing skimpy clothes or smiling right at me.

But because she's my mother.

Chapter 2

Silas

She wears ridiculously high heels that sink into the grass when she steps up on my lawn. She raises a hand and waves at me. And I'm not sure why, but that fucking wave is what does me in.

I ignore my team yelling at me as I stalk across the lawn. She looks just like I remember her. God, what has it been? Eight fucking years? She still dresses like someone half her age and wears too much makeup, but even so she's pretty. Beautiful maybe. The kind of face that always drew attention. Her whole life always revolved around her looks, so my brother's and mine did, too. When Mom looked good, when she had a guy, we had a place to sleep. If she didn't, *we* didn't.

But that shit is over. No part of my life revolves around her, and I'm not about to let her pull me back in.

"Get the fuck in your car and go," I say when I'm standing in front of her.

She doesn't reply. Just blinks her long lashes and studies my face for a few seconds that stretch into lifetimes. When I open my mouth to tell her to leave again, she reaches up and touches my face.

I grab her wrist and shove her hand away.

"Get in your fucking car."

"Baby . . ." she says.

"I haven't been your baby in a long time. And that's not changing, so you can leave."

Her lips pucker on a frown. "You'll always be my baby."

She tries to touch me again, and I step back.

"I was yours through all your shitty boyfriends. Through the first time you left, and the second. Hell, I was even yours for all those years you weren't around, while Sean and I lived with Grams or whatever family would take us. But I stopped being yours sometime around the time Sean went to prison, and you didn't even bother picking up a phone, let alone showing your face. So, *Megan*, I suggest you do what you do best. Get in your car and leave before I call the cops and make you."

She sucks her bottom lip between her teeth, and gives me these big, innocent eyes, and God I want to hit something. My past and my present are supposed to remain separate. But now she's set it all on a goddamn collision course, and that feeling of inevitability I've always felt? The pull of it is so heavy right now, it makes gravity feel like a joke.

When she doesn't move fast enough, I pull out my cell phone, and she holds up her manicured hands. "Fine! Okay. I'm leaving."

I don't put my phone up, but I let it drop to my side. She steps back off the lawn into the street. She wavers for a second on her heels, and then she turns and saunters back to her car, like she doesn't have a care in the world.

She opens the door and before she climbs inside she says with a smile, "Go back to your party, baby. We'll talk another time."

I squeeze my fist so hard, I'm surprised I don't crush my phone. She ducks into her car, and it sputters to life, old and rusted and completely at odds with the image she works to project.

Then she's gone, and it feels like everything I've built here is seconds away from crumbling around me. Like a house of cards destroyed by a simple breath. And all I can think is if things are gonna fall apart, I'm not going to stand here trying to catch the pieces.

I turn and most of the game is still going, but half a dozen people stand off to the side watching me. McClain. Stella. Brookes. Torres. A few more. I walk away from the curb, and Torres grins at me. "You been holding out on us, Moore? Who was that hot piece—"

"Say one more fucking word, and you lose your tongue."

He holds his hands up in surrender, but he's still smiling. They all are. Except Stella and Brookes. They're both looking at me like they, too, are waiting for my sky to start falling. Like they're the only ones who really understand what they just saw.

My phone buzzes in my hand again, and I'm ready to throw it until I see the text. It's from Levi again.

Come on, man. I need to blow off some steam. Get your ass to Trent's.

·

I stalk past the group, ignoring the looks I get, and pick up my shirt from where I'd tossed it on the grass. Then I run inside to grab my keys and switch out my athletic shorts for jeans. Because it just so happens I need to blow off some steam, too.

TRENT'S IS A dank, grungy, hole-in-the-wall place that most students pass over for the newer, popular bars in the campus bubble. The bell rings as I step in the door, and even though it's late afternoon, it's dark enough inside that I have to squint to find Levi.

He sits at the bar, a bottle lifted to his mouth and another sitting beside him that I assume is for me. The place is practically empty except for the bartender, and an old dude in a booth at the back.

For a moment, I hesitate. Something twists in my gut and my jaw clenches, and I don't even really know why I came here. Part of me wants to say fuck it all, get smashed with Levi, and give in to the inevitability of this shitfest. Another part, a bigger part, wants to lay into my old friend and work off what I'm feeling with my fists.

Somewhere in the back of my mind, I know I should turn around and walk back out to my truck. There are only stupid decisions waiting for me here.

But I've never cared all that much about being smart.

I stalk across the bar and slide onto the stool next to him. I tip back the beer and fix my eyes on the baseball game playing on the old TV sitting up beside bottles of liquor on the shelf.

"What? I don't even get a hello?" Levi says.

I ditch the hello and ask instead, "How was prison? You got out fast." Must be nice to have a lawyer for a dad. Hell, must be nice to have a dad in the picture, period.

Levi lifts his hands in a shrug and says, "Can't keep me down."

Sad thing is . . . he's probably right. Guys like him always get second, third, and fourth chances.

"What are you doing here, Levi?"

"What does it look like I'm doing? I'm having a drink, and then I'm gonna get laid. Priorities, am I right?"

"I mean . . . what are you planning to do here?"

"I thought I just covered that."

"You're just going to hang out here in town? When you're not allowed to set foot on campus? Are you even allowed to be in a bar right now?"

He shrugs. "I just can't be around drugs of any kind. Alcohol might count, but nobody's gonna find out." He gestures to the deserted bar. "And why do I have to figure out what I'm doing right now? I'll just hang out. It will be the same as it always was . . . but now I don't have to go to class."

"The same as it always was," I mutter and drain the rest of my beer in three big gulps. I wave down the bartender for another while Levi continues.

"Yeah, man. We should drive down to Austin this weekend. Go to Sixth Street. We'll get plastered. Maybe float the river."

"I have practice on Monday."

"You'll be back in time."

I shake my head. "I can't. We're supposed to be keeping a low profile."

He scoffs. "Fuck. Coach Cole is the worst. Soon you guys won't be able to do jack shit."

"It's not Coach. It's all of us."

"All of you?"

"Yeah. We want the team focused. McClain and I—"

"McClain? Are you fucking serious right now?"

"Yeah, I'm serious. You seem to be forgetting that you screwed us all over. McClain stepped up."

Levi scowls, a low, bitter laugh rolling out before he takes another drink. "That guy's nothing. Walk-on, junior college piece of shit."

I'd always felt more at ease with Levi than anyone else. He reminded me of my brother in ways. My brother was always kind of an asshole, too.

And with my past pressing in on me, I know I've got two choices. I can go the easy way, the way that comes naturally to me. I can stay at this bar, get drunk, get some girls, and ride out my time here at Rusk doing whatever the hell I want for as long as it lasts. That's how I've always lived—take the good you can get before the bad catches up to you.

But I actually feel sick at the thought of staying here with Levi. As easy as it would be, as many times as I've made that choice, it doesn't hold the same appeal now. It used to feel smart, like I was one leg up on the world, but now it feels like I'm running downhill because I'm too much of a pussy to turn and face the incline.

I stand up, take one last gulp of my beer, and throw some cash on the bar.

"I gotta go."

Levi moves, too, his stool scraping the cement floor as he pushes it back.

"What the hell, man? You just got here."

"I don't see much reason to stay."

"Are you shitting me?" Levi asks, getting up in my face. "I thought out of everyone you would have my back."

"I've got my *own* back." That's the one thing I've always known. I can't depend on anyone else but me. "The only thing I care about is staying on that team. You've already fucked up your shot. And I'm not gonna let you or anyone else do the same for me."

"*That team* will fall apart without me. Then what will you do? Run back to the trailer park you came from?"

That shouldn't sting. It wouldn't on any other day, but I can't help but think that it's only a matter of time before everyone here knows that about me.

I want to get right back in his face, turn this on him, make him feel like the worthless one. But I get the feeling that's why this is all happening. Maybe I'm not the only one feeling out of control today.

"Nah, man. You got it wrong. The team is better off without you."

I turn to walk away, and he shoves hard at my back. Stumbling forward, I collide with a few stools, toppling them, and barely staying on my feet.

I try to breathe, but my vision goes black around the edges, and that familiar need to hit something roars back. I clench my fists to rein it in and stand, my eyes on the door.

"You're nothing, Silas. You've already got has-been written all over you." I glance back, even though I know that's exactly what he wants. The bartender is pointedly ignoring us, polishing a glass that probably hasn't really been clean in five years. Levi continues, "Don't you fucking look down on me. I know you, man. I'm gonna be just fine, but you? It's just a matter of time before you fuck it all up. And then what will you have? Nothing."

And that one? That hits a little too close to home.

I get up in his face, nose to nose. "You *know* me? You don't know shit."

"I know enough. Brother's in prison. Mom's a whore. Trash is trash whether you dress it up with a scholarship and a uniform or not."

His face makes a satisfying crack when my fist connects. The jolt of pain in my wrist, the bite of broken skin on my knuckles . . . it dulls out my thoughts and sharpens everything else.

Satisfaction and anger and exhilaration burn through me, and the world sure as fuck doesn't feel muted anymore.

He's slow to recover and retaliate, and even though I see it coming, I let him get one hit in. He goes for my midsection, but he must still be dazed from my hit because it makes even less of an impact than I expect. I barely feel it. And I don't know why, but the piss-poor punch makes me even angrier.

"Come on, Levi. I might be trash, but you're pathetic. Lazy. Couldn't even play football without cheating."

He swings again, and I lean back enough that he only clips my jaw. The jolt is enough to sting and break the dam on my much-needed adrenaline. I grip him by the shirt and ram him into the bar on my right. A few glasses go sliding and crash onto the floor. The bartender yells something, but I don't listen, delivering my own hit to Levi's stomach, followed by a second.

He curses and shoves me back, and I stumble into a chair, sending a few more glasses shattering against the concrete floor. He comes at me, and I shift, using his speed to leverage him past me, tossing him forward into a table that topples and splinters under his weight.

He rolls onto his back, groaning, but I don't let him stay down. I need more of a fight than this. I drag him to his feet and make him look me in the eye. He swings and clocks me in the side of the head, but my blood is pumping so fast and hard that it's more obnoxious than painful. I don't know if I want to hit him again or just shake him as hard as I can. While I'm standing there thinking like a dumbass, he gets a good punch into my kidney, and my whole body locks up against the pain for a few seconds. Before he gets off another, I shove him into the wall. He hits hard, and only my hand keeps him from slumping down to the ground.

"You just couldn't leave it the fuck alone, could you?" I ask. "Spoiled rich boy is unhappy, so he has to drag everyone else down with him."

Levi is beginning to list to the side, and I'm sure if I let him go, he'd keep on leaning until he crashed. Whatever pain he's in, it doesn't hamper the angry look he gives me.

He spits and his bloody saliva lands on my shoe. I've got him pegged and he hates it.

"That's enough," I hear the bartender say behind me. "Walk away."

Levi laughs. "Don't pretend I dragged you down. You came here looking to fight. You work better down in the gutter."

"Maybe I do."

Then I clock him once more, and his expression goes slack, and he slumps down against the wall at my feet. His head droops toward his chest, blood dribbling down from his busted mouth.

Reflecting colored lights dance over the walls now, and I hear police sirens. And *fuck*, I think I might actually be jealous of that black, nothing world Levi's lost in.

How the hell did I go from walking away to this?

For the first time, I take stock of the bar around us. Broken glass. Broken furniture. The dude from the booth is long gone. A woman has her head poking past the kitchen door, watching me warily with her cell phone to her ear. The bartender is an older, chubbier version of Mr. Clean, and though he has a bat pressed beneath his palms against the wooden bar, he doesn't look ready to use it.

I turn and head for the door, but even before the cop steps inside, I know I've got no shot at walking out of here that easy. The cop asks me what happened, but there's no point in saying *he started it* like a little pansy. Not when you've got a juvy record. He gets the rundown from the bartender and the woman who called them. While a paramedic checks on a barely conscious Levi, I'm put in the back of a police car.

They say bad shit happens in threes, but I gave up counting a long time ago.

The bad seems to follow me. Or hell. Maybe Levi's right. Maybe it's me that follows the bad.

Maybe I don't know who I am apart from that.

Chapter 3

Dylan

The plastic zip ties bite into the skin of my wrists, and I wait, my shoulders aching from having my hands bound behind my back. My heart is racing, has been since I refused the officer's order to disperse from the protest and got arrested instead. I wonder how long my heart can beat this fast without giving out. Maybe I'll pass out soon, and then I'll get at least a modicum of relief from the guilt and fear gnawing at my insides.

The female police officer is finishing up my paperwork, while my friend Matt is being escorted away to the holding cell by another officer. He meets my eyes and makes a ridiculous face. I don't know how he's so calm. With his massive russet beard, he looks more scary than silly. He's got a good six inches on the guy who arrested us, and I don't blame the cop for looking nervous. Matty looks like he could go Sasquatch on everyone and bust his way out of here.

"Miss Brenner?" Officer Tribble stands in front of me. She's in her mid-thirties, dark hair, and frown lines around her mouth. She knows my father. Everyone knows my father. It's probably naive to think he's not already aware I'm here. My stomach twists again, and I hunch over in my chair, hoping it will make the aching worry go away. But I don't get much time to see if it works. She takes my elbow, her grip soft, and helps me stand, and then we're walking in the direction Matt was taken.

At the end of a hallway are two holding cells, one across from the other. Lined with metal benches bolted to the floor, the cell on the left contains three men. A middle-aged man in a ratty T-shirt lays passed out on a bench in the corner. On the other side of the cell, I see Matt in all his bearded glory. Despite the fact that there are several empty benches, he's seated on the one containing the third occupant of the cell. He's talking, but his cellmate appears to be ignoring him, which doesn't faze my friend in the slightest. He sends me a wink as Officer Tribble parades me past and stops in front of the empty cell across from Matt's. I breathe a sigh of relief. Despite my fear, when Matt tilts his head toward his cellmate and waggles his eyebrows suggestively, I laugh. The guy next to Matt looks up, and the laugh dies in my throat.

He sports a bruised jaw, bloomed purple over stubbled skin. His messy hair is somewhere between blond and brown and tumbles over his forehead, leading me to a set of hazel eyes that are astoundingly pretty and at odds with the rest of his hard appearance. His knuckles, too, look ripped up, and his eyes follow my progress with an intensity that has my stomach twisting with a fear that is altogether different from what I've been feeling for the last hour. Even so, I continue watching him . . . watching him watch me, really, as Officer Tribble cuts off my plastic binds and locks me in the empty cell.

I move to sit at the same end as Matt, so we can talk to each other quietly, but the intense-eyed stranger sits closer to the bars, blocking all but the wave of red hair that adds an extra two inches to Matt's already tall frame.

The guy is young, around my age, I would guess, and I wonder if the bruises have something to do with why he's in here or if they're just a separate part of his bad-boy mystique. Like *oops, I forgot to put on leather before I left the house today, better get a little bloody instead.*

Matt doesn't seem concerned that he might be dangerous. Then again, Matt is rarely concerned about anything. When he leans his bulky frame around his cellmate, I finally manage to tear my gaze away.

"You okay, Pickle?" he asks.

I'm going to thump him for using that nickname later. That is *not* a nickname to be used in front of beautiful people, even potentially criminal ones.

"Fine, Matty."

That's what I tell him, but I hunch over again. The worry is a physical weight in my belly, a stone that presses down on my gut, and I wonder how quickly one can develop a stomach ulcer.

"You don't look fine," my friend says. "You look like you're going to vom everywhere."

Lovely. As if I weren't mortified enough already by my actions today. But I can't be mad at Matt. If he hadn't stuck with me, I'd be here alone, which would be infinitely worse. "I'm sorry. This is my fault. I feel terrible that you stayed with me, and I got you into this."

He shrugs. "No harm, no foul."

Only Matt would call being arrested *no harm.* The guy is so laid-back, he's like the human equivalent of Xanax. I want that. I *need* that. All I can think about is what my father might say, and whether or not this will go on my record, and if it will affect my scholarship, and what Henry will say.

I stop myself there. I don't have to worry about what Henry will say because we're over. That should bother me. We broke up a week ago, and after four years together, I should be devastated. I should be moving right past shock and denial into the never-wears-anything-but-sweatpants stage.

I don't know what it says about me that I'm not. That I only think of him out of habit, nothing else.

I keep going, berating myself the way I wish Matt would. "We make plans for a reason, and I didn't stick to it. I should have walked away as soon as they gave the dispersal order. Next time I do something this stupid, don't you dare come after me."

"Nah. Next time I'll just clobber you over the head. Save us both the trouble."

I roll my eyes because we both know that would never happen. Matt's one of those guys who will always put themselves on the line for a friend. He could pretty much pass for a real-life Disney prince . . . if Disney made bearded, bisexual princes.

"Still . . . it wasn't cool of me. I don't know what I was thinking. I was just so frustrated, and tired of chanting while they ignored us. It made sense at the time."

"Yeah, well. You've had a lot on your mind lately."

I shoot him a glare. He thinks I'm behaving irrationally because of the breakup, but that's ridiculous. I'm not crazy. Matt, my mother, my roommate Nell—everyone keeps waiting for me to snap, to fold in on myself and just lose it because my boyfriend and I are no more. And maybe they're right. Maybe this is some weird emotional shock, and in a few weeks the hurt will hit me out of nowhere. But right now? The tiptoeing around the subject just makes me want to scream. "This had nothing to do with that."

Sure my life plan has taken a nosedive. And it wouldn't be unreasonable to freak out that the future I've been envisioning since Henry and I started dating four years ago has been blasted to bits.

But my boyfriend (or lack thereof) can't be the most important thing about me. So screw plans and futures and heartache and all of that. For the moment, I just need to focus on me.

Or I could keep doing crazy things like ignoring a direct order from police after a day of being ignored and derided for daring to stand up for the homeless population in town, which is about to lose one of only two shelters within twenty miles. Well . . . maybe

I went a *little* further than just ignoring a direct order. I might have handcuffed myself to a pole outside the shelter.

"Then what was it about? Why'd you do it?" Matt asks.

"Because I couldn't *not* do it."

"Yeaaaah . . . that explanation is going to hold up *really* well against your father."

"Next time I promise not to let my emotions get the better of me when handcuffs are involved."

The attractive potential criminal shifts, and when I look at him, his eyebrows are raised in interest. His eyes really are *far* too pretty for a guy like him. Dudes who look dangerous should just *be dangerous*. Period. The end. They should not be dangerous and beautiful all at the same time. It leaves the universe out of balance, and it makes me do stupid things like stare. At a guy behind bars. If ever there were a kind of guy I should *not* stare at, someone potentially going to prison definitely has to rank in the top three.

Matt stretches out his long legs and says, "Next time, just tell me you want to get arrested ahead of time. That way I can make sure we're prepared. Javier is going to be pissed. Unless, of course, you want to call daddy dearest to get us out."

I don't even have to glare before he's holding up his hands in surrender.

"Why would you *want* to get arrested?" The dangerous one speaks. His voice is low and smooth with a slight Texas drawl that stretches out his words and draws my eyes to his lips.

"Handcuff fetish," Matt says, and I go bright red.

I am going to thump him *so* many times.

I glare and clear my throat. "Getting arrested can sometimes be the most powerful way to draw attention to a cause."

He lifts an eyebrow. "A cause?"

"A political one." That eyebrow drops, and he nods, crossing his arms and turning his attention away from me.

I must still be cracked in the head because his complete dismissal reminds me of our protest today, of the way the city can just take away a sanctuary for people who have no other place to go, and not even bat an eye. It makes me want to do some more stupid things. I stand and grip the bars in front of me and say, "You know, it's youth like you that give our whole generation a bad name."

He leans back and surveys me with annoyance. "*Youth?* How old are you?"

I wave a hand. "Young people. Whatever. My point is everyone thinks that we're these ignorant kids who are more concerned with our phones than the state of the world, and it's because of people like you turning up your nose at the slightest mention of politics."

He stands to mimic me, only he's so much taller, and his shoulders are broad, and his arms too muscled to slip completely through the bars like mine do. "People like me? What the fuck does that mean? Poor? Uneducated? Trash?"

I jerk back. "*What?* No. I didn't say any of those things. I just mean the stereotypical young adults who—"

"Only care about their phones. Yeah, I heard that part. I'd rather be that stereotype than the pampered little rich girl who thinks it's *fun* to get arrested, to burn money so she can throw a temper tantrum about whatever thing in the world is bothering her this week."

"*Temper tantrum?*" I'm aware even as I speak that I'm practically yelling, and I sound just like the spoiled girl he's painted me as. "I'm *not* throwing a temper tantrum."

Matty, ever the pacifist, says, "Maybe we should all just take a couple of breaths."

I storm on, desperate to win at least *one* argument today.

"I am so sick of people thinking what we do is a waste of time. At least we're *doing* something, instead of sticking our heads in the sand while the rest of the world goes to hell around us."

"The rest of the world has been hell all along for some of us, princess."

That stops me mid-rant, and I'm staring again, opening and closing my mouth in a way that definitely isn't doing anything to prove my point.

Finally, I huff out a breath and some of my desperation breaks through. I'm not even sure if it's desperation for his approval or just for someone, *anyone*, to listen. "Haven't you ever wanted to do something that everyone tells you is impossible or pointless? Haven't you ever cared about something enough to sacrifice for it? Regardless of how stupid or unlikely it seems. Haven't you ever just wanted things to be different?"

He studies me for a few moments, his large hands lifting to curl around the bars. And when I expect him to make another crack about me being spoiled or naive, he surprises me.

"What exactly are you hoping to change?"

Matt snorts. "Congratulations, man. You've officially found a way to occupy however many hours you have left here. This girl wants to fix the whole world."

An officer comes then and takes Matt away to make his phone call. He glances at me and mouths, "Javi?"

I nod, and watch him leave.

I know he's prodding, hoping I'll give in and say we can call my dad instead. But I just can't. I know he could get us out faster, but I can't see him yet. Not until I've figured out some excuse. Not until I've figured out what crack in my brain made me behave so rashly tonight.

It's not because I'm upset over Henry, but I can't help but think it's all connected. My emotions are all out of whack, and the only thing I know is that today at that protest, I felt invisible.

And I didn't realize until I clicked those handcuffs into place that I'd felt that way long before we set up camp in front of that homeless shelter.

"So what were you trying to change?" he asks.

I feel weirdly shy now that Matt is gone, and I no longer feel the need to go into my ten-minute rant about the state of politics in this country.

I turn away from him so that I don't have to make eye contact, kind of like that whole don't look directly at the sun or you'll risk visual impairment thing. This was just a different kind of impairment. Like my ability to think straight. I wave a hand and explain: "The city is cutting funding for the homeless shelter downtown.

They're claiming budget problems, but really they just don't want their historic downtown blemished with the less fortunate."

He nods, but doesn't reply, and *why am I so damn self-conscious?* We stay silent for a while, and I wish Officer Tribble hadn't taken my watch because it feels like Matt has been gone a lot longer than the couple of minutes it should take for a phone call. And I can feel his eyes on me, ramping up my already frayed nerves. I've just given in to the urge to pace when he speaks again.

"So . . . Pickle?"

I spin and look at the cell across from me. The guy is staring, and I blanch. "Uh . . . no. I'm Dylan. That's just a Matt thing. Dyl Pickle. It's stupid."

"Dylan," he repeats. And I have never felt less invisible than I do in that moment with him looking at me.

"And you are?"

He grips the bar and leans back slightly, and he must be some kind of workout junkie because even with clothes on, his body is unreal.

"Silas."

I take a seat back on the bench and pull my knees up to my chest. "Sorry for yelling at you, Silas. I'm a little wound up."

"Getting arrested will do that to you."

So will a complete mental breakdown. Which I may or may not be having.

"Yeah," I answer absently, anxiety sweeping through me again. I lay my head down on my knees and try not to think.

Yeah, right. Like that's possible.

"I'm sure everything will be fine. It's not like you did anything too bad."

I wince.

"Did you?"

"Define bad."

He laughs. "I think our definitions of bad are probably very different."

If I wrote the dictionary, bad would just have a picture of him under it.

"Why are you in here?"

I don't really think through the question until the words are already out of my mouth, and his gorgeous eyes are narrowed on me. I'm pretty sure that there's some unwritten rule about not asking people why they're in jail while they're *still* in jail. And this may just be a holding cell, but the rule probably applies here, too. His tongue peeks out to worry at his swollen, busted lip, and I feel a wave of heat curl up my spine.

Totally inappropriate. Totally *psychotic* because he is way out of my league. Or I'm way out of his league, I don't know. Either way, someone is out of someone's league.

And more important . . . he's so not my type. At all. So, I'm not sure why I'm still staring at his swollen lip, wondering if he'd flinch if I touched it.

I rein in my thoughts. "Sorry. That's none of my business, I—"

"I got in a bar fight with a friend." He pauses and looks away. "Or someone who *used* to be my friend. Or something. I don't know. I wasn't really thinking."

I laugh. "Me either. Must be something in the water."

I want to ask what he fought over with his friend. Or his former friend. I want to know what makes a guy like him tick, what he cares enough about to bleed for. Because it sounds personal, not just the mindless, Neanderthal slugfest that I'd been picturing.

"Are you hurt?" I ask.

A flash of a smile has a field of goose bumps sprouting along my arms. "You worried about me, Pickle?"

I throw my head back and groan.

"I'm going to kill him."

Officer Tribble returns then with Matt, and she gives me a look at overhearing my last words.

I lift my hands and say, "Hyperbole. I promise. No actual plans to kill anyone."

As she lets Matt back into the men's holding cell, he raises an eyebrow.

"Who are we killing?"

"You," Silas answers.

Matt holds a hand to his heart and gives me a pathetic look. "I thought we promised to look out for each other on the inside? And now you turn on me for the first pretty face." Silas frowns at the assessment of him as a *pretty face,* and I wonder what expression he'd make if he knew Matt really did find him attractive. Though I'm willing to bet if you go through life every day looking the way Silas does, you probably get used to all kinds of people finding you attractive. "You're a hardened criminal already, Pickle."

Silas's frown is swept away by a low laugh at the name, and

I drop my feet off the bench and stand. I'm getting restless, and maybe walking around again will help me.

"Since you're already going to kill me, I guess it doesn't hurt to tell you that I couldn't get a hold of Javi. You can only call land-lines, and I guess he hasn't gotten back to the dorm yet. I left a message, but I bet he's already working on getting us out."

Javier is the president of our student activism group, Voice for Tomorrow. And Matt is right that he's likely to be pissed with me. Today was supposed to be a preliminary protest just to raise awareness. We were hoping that it combined with the petition we're compiling might be enough to at least get them to postpone the closing. Now I've made us look reckless and impulsive. Like troublemakers instead of informed citizens.

Maybe Javi is already working to get us out. Or maybe he's pissed enough to let us stew for a little while. I wouldn't be surprised.

I sigh. "I could leave a message for Antonella at the apartment, but I don't think she gets off work until midnight." I'm not exactly sure what time it is, but a ways off from midnight for sure.

"What about Henry?" Matt asks. "He'd come if you asked."

"I am *not* calling my ex, Matt. That's almost worse than calling my father."

"Then we might be in here until morning because if we have to wait for Antonella to come after midnight, I'm betting they won't get us processed until daytime."

I was almost willing to risk staying overnight. If it were just me, I would have, but I'd caused Matt enough hassle for the night. For the whole year actually.

Officer Tribble returns about twenty minutes later, and I move toward the cell door, expecting it's time for my phone call, resigned to contacting my father, but instead she turns her back to me and addresses Silas.

"Mr. Moore, you're good to go. Mr. Abrams has declined to press assault charges, and he's offering to cover the damages at the bar, so they're willing to let it go, too."

Silas scowls. "And what if I want to press charges? I told you guys that I didn't start it."

Officer Tribble fixes him with a no-nonsense look. "Both witnesses and Mr. Abrams say you threw the first punch."

"Well, yeah, but—"

"And you can choose to press charges, but then Mr. Abrams is likely to consider doing the same to you."

"This is ridiculous," he says, but he looks relieved when she opens the cell and ushers him out.

Matt pouts as he watches his eye candy removed from the cell, and there might be a similar expression on my face. I sigh and lean into the bars, and the events of the day swallow me again. I don't know what worries me more—the consequences or the cause. As Silas exits, he comes within a few feet of me where I'm standing at the cell door, and I get my first up-close look at him.

I *don't* feel like all the breath is knocked out of me. I *absolutely don't*.

He runs a hand through his shaggy hair, and his eyes dip down, starting at my feet and sliding up my legs. He lingers on my hips and waist and breasts for what feels like eternity, but in reality must be only the few seconds it takes for Officer Tribble to lock the cell door.

He still looks dangerous, but not nearly as dangerous as the effect his gaze has on me.

He turns away, hesitates, and then faces me again. His expression is inscrutable, but he leans a little closer and says, "Don't call your dad. I'll figure something out."

And then he's gone, and I'm so shocked that I wonder if I imagined his words, if it's just another symptom of whatever meltdown I'm having.

Because a guy like that going out of his way to help us? Definitely crazy.

Chapter 4

Silas

The cop returns my belongings to me—my cell phone and my wallet and my keys—and I'm still not sure why I told that girl I'd help her. She was just standing there with that oversized shirt hanging off one shoulder and these short fucking shorts, and she looked so completely out of place in that cell. She looked like she belonged on some beach or in some fancy European city or something—somewhere I've never been and probably never will be. Maybe it was all that bare skin. Or maybe it was the long, wavy hair that was too easy to picture skimming over my chest as she rode me.

That has to be it.

I've had a shitty day, and my dick did my thinking.

Sighing, I ask the police officer, "What's going to happen to those two?"

She shuffles through a pile of papers and says, "They'll get cited and released."

"How much is the citation?"

"One hundred and fifty for the girl. Fifty for the guy. Cash only."

Fuck. Am I really considering coughing up that much money for the *possibility* of hooking up with her? If the girl is even half as uptight as she appears, she'll probably spend the night preaching at me about the dangers of alcohol or something, trying to *save* me.

I'm suddenly in the mood to punch something again. I should just leave, but I don't. Something about that girl has gotten under my skin, and she doesn't deserve to sit in there for trying to help people.

"There an ATM near here?" I ask.

"Gas station across the street."

As I head out into the night, I don't let myself think about the fact that I'm about to do serious damage to my bank account. I don't work during football season. There's not enough time between that and school. Instead, I just bust my ass in the off-season and during the summer to save up enough to last me. I've already resigned from the landscaping job I worked this summer since camp starts on Monday, so there's no making this money back.

I punch my PIN number into the ATM and mumble under my breath, "She better be fucking worth it."

I could really go for a joint right about now . . . something to cloud my head and keep me from thinking about money and football and fights and Levi and home. There are so many fucking things I don't want to think about that it's impossible to block them all out.

Sex or pot. Those are my best options.

The party should still be going at my place. Maybe I can squeeze in both tonight. I think for a little while, and eventually decide to ask Carson if he can come pick me up and give me a lift to my truck at the bar. He answers on the second ring, and says that he and Dallas will come.

Yet another thing for the coach's daughter to hold against me.

Back at the police station, I tell the cop that I want to pay the citation for Dylan and her friend.

She gives me a skeptical look.

"You know them?" she says.

I shrug. "Nope. Just full of good deeds."

She looks around like maybe she's being punked, but in the end she takes the money and finishes processing their paperwork. I don't blame her for being skeptical. Hell, *I'm* skeptical. I spent the occasional night in a local shelter as a kid whenever one of Mom's relationships blew up and lost us our place to stay. So maybe that's part of it. Most of it is *her*, though.

Dylan is the kind of girl who would never fit in my old world. Maybe a night with her will pull me back where I'm supposed to be, anchor me here in this life.

The red-haired dude comes out first, and Dylan shuffles behind him, her head down. When she looks up and meets my gaze, she freezes. Her jaw drops a little, and I realize she didn't believe me when I said I would figure it out.

I don't know whether to feel satisfied or disappointed at her shock. The two of them talk to the cop a bit, are given a slip of paper each and their confiscated belongings, and then allowed into the general lobby, where I'm waiting.

Then she's standing in front of me, and that shirt is hanging off her shoulder again, and she's woven her hair into a long, thick braid that drapes over her shoulder and falls into the valley between her breasts. I can't decide whether I liked her hair better how it was before, or like this, where I can wrap the whole length of it around my hand to tug her head back.

"You didn't have to do that," she says.

"And be labeled a stereotypical, uncaring *youth* again? No thanks."

She scrunches up her nose and her lips twist to the side. "God, I was kind of a jerk tonight. I'm sorry."

I run a hand over the tender place on my jaw where Levi got me and shrug. "It happens. To some of us more often than others. I've got a friend on his way to pick me up. You two need a ride?"

The guy answers, "That would be great, thanks. I'm Matt, by the way. I didn't catch your name."

He reaches out his hand, and I shake it. When I go to reply, Dylan beats me to it. "His name is Silas."

Her friend gives her a look, and she swallows and casts her eyes at the floor.

"Well, it's nice to meet you, Silas. We'll pay you back the cash for the citations."

I shrug. I should probably be all polite and shit and tell them not to worry about it, but I don't exactly have money to throw around. I nod toward the door and say, "Let's go wait for my friend outside."

Matt goes first, and I hold the door open for Dylan. I catch the scent of her hair as she moves past me, and it smells so damn sweet that I want to bury my face in it, to breathe her in. I wonder where else she smells that sweet.

Matt offers to call their friend Javier to fill him in, and he tells Dylan to call her father. But when Matt walks a few paces away to talk, she doesn't reach for her own phone. Instead she looks up at me.

"Thank you. I don't really know what to say."

I shrug. It's not in me to play the chivalrous good guy, even to pretend. Instead, I tip my chin toward where her red-haired friend paces as he talks on the phone, and I get right to the point. "You two together?"

She'd mentioned an ex in the holding cell, and it sounded recent, but that doesn't mean she hasn't already hopped to the next guy.

She laughs. "Me and Matt? Seriously?"

From a few yards away, Matt covers the mouthpiece on his phone and shouts, "Hey, I heard that! Could you at least *try* to sound a little less incredulous?"

The two share a strange smile, and then Dylan looks up at me.

"No. Matt and I are not together."

Well, that certainly makes things easier.

"Good," I say.

She lifts her eyebrows in question. When I only smile, she dips her head, and her long hair falls across her face.

"What are you doing for the rest of the night?" I ask. A quick glance at my phone reveals we're just coming up on midnight.

She tilts her head to the side, and looks up at me from behind the veil of her hair. She shoots me a sly smile that I can picture her giving me in a number of other . . . *dirtier* scenarios.

"I'm not really interested in witnessing a bar fight," she says. "If that's how you spend your evenings. Not really my scene."

"No bars," I promise. "There's actually a party going on at my place. You and Matt are welcome to come."

Her head tilts even farther, and she's confused rather than coy now.

"Why were you at a bar if there's a party going on at your house?"

I shrug. "Was having kind of a shitty night and needed to get away."

"Doesn't sound like getting away helped on that front."

I look into her eyes and say, "Things didn't turn out so bad."

She laughs and smiles down at the ground again, and I'm feeling good about my chances.

"You're really hitting on me? After we just met in jail?"

"Is it working?"

She tries to look stern, but I can see the smile curling at the corners of her lips. I'm about to move in for the kill when Carson and Dallas pull up in Dallas's tiny little car. She's driving, and he leans over to kiss her quickly on the mouth before he opens the passenger door and jumps out to greet me.

"You okay?" he asks, eyeing the remnants of the fight that show on my face and hands.

I nod. "Fine."

"Levi look worse than you do?" he asks.

"A hell of a lot worse."

He bobs his head in a nod and says, "Good."

McClain might be the closest thing I've ever met to a saint, but the guy doesn't have an ounce of compassion for Levi. Too much history with Dallas for him to keep a clear head where our former quarterback is concerned. I'm still a little shocked that he's been as cool to me as he has. Dallas still hates my guts, which I guess I can live with.

"This is Dylan. We, uh, got acquainted in the holding cell."

Carson lifts an eyebrow, and I can see he's trying not to laugh. But he stays in control and holds out a hand to shake. "Nice to meet you, Dylan. I'm Carson. I'm a . . . friend of Silas."

It's the first time he's ever really used the word *friend* in reference to me, and I think he might be doing it just for appearance's sake. But then again . . . he did come get me. He could have blown me off. I wouldn't have been surprised if he had.

Matt returns then. He starts to say something, but stutters to a halt.

"*Holy shit.*" He looks at Carson, squints, and then looks back at me. He repeats the process a few times, and then says even louder, "Holy *fucking* shit."

Carson scratches at the back of his neck uncomfortably, and I add, "That's Dylan's friend Matt."

He's still staring, and he's begun shaking his head back and forth slowly. "Oh my shit."

I look at Dylan, and she's gaping at her friend. "Hey Matt, why don't you try saying hi instead of cursing out strangers?"

"That's Carson McClain . . ." He turns to me. "Which means you're probably Silas Moore. I am such an idiot."

Damn. This isn't going to help with the question I need to ask. I turn to Carson. "You mind giving them a ride, too? Just to my truck, and then I'll take care of the rest."

McClain looks like he'd rather eat dirt, but he smiles, always the Boy Scout. "Sure thing. Might be a bit of a tight squeeze in the back."

Matt says quickly, "I don't mind."

And the hero worship has officially crossed over into creepy territory.

Dylan coughs lightly, but I'm pretty sure she's hiding a laugh. "I'll sit in the middle. I'm small."

She coughs again, harder, when she sees the look on my face. Hell-fucking-yeah, she's sitting in the middle. If she tried to stick me by Carrot Top, I would flip my shit.

Carson leads us back to Dallas's ride, and I'm disappointed when Dylan goes to the opposite side of the car with Matt. Before McClain climbs in, he whispers, "Only you would pick up a girl *in jail.*"

"Only I *could*."

Or I hope I can anyway.

I pull my door open and sit behind where Carson is in the passenger seat. If I'd been thinking, I would have gone for the space behind Dallas because my knees are shoved right up against the back of Carson's chair. I put that out of mind, though, when Dylan slides in from the opposite side of the car. She moves in right beside me, less than an inch between us. Her friend is a big guy, though, and when he sits down she's pressed all the way up against me. Matt struggles to get his door closed well, and I shift, placing my arm along the bench seat behind Dylan's head to make more room.

The heat of her singes my side, and this close I'm drowning in her scent.

I don't mind. Not at all.

Matt whispers another *"Holy shit,"* and Dylan shoots me a quizzical look.

I shrug, and use the movement to run a finger over her braided hair.

"Is anyone going to explain what's going on?" she asks.

Matt seems to finally remember a few other words. "What's going on is that we're in a car with the quarterback and running back for the Rusk football team. *And* the coach's daughter. I feel like I'm in a reality TV show or something."

Dylan looks up at me and she's so close that her cheek brushes the inside of my arm. She tilts her chin up, bringing her lips a fraction closer to mine and surveys me. I wonder if this will help my chances. I wait for her to comment on my position on the team, but she doesn't. Quietly she says, "Sorry. Matt is kind of obnoxiously school spirited."

"Would it be weird for me to ask for an autograph?" he asks.

"Matt!" Dylan turns to smack him on the arm, and the move makes her shoulder slide against my chest.

"It's weird. Got it. Forget I asked."

Her shoulder is still against my chest, and she's leaning back into me, and I want to drop my arm down and lock us together. I reach out to trail a finger along her braid again, and it wouldn't take but a couple more inches to lay my arm across her shoulders.

I dip my mouth down to her ear and ask, "What's your spirit level like?"

She starts to turn, but when she realizes how close I am, she sucks in a breath and only angles her head toward me.

"Minimal. I'm not really into sports."

So, she's playing it hard to get. I can deal with that. It's not often that I care enough for the chase, but with her, I can make an exception.

Somehow, getting with her feels important, like it will prove I still fit here.

"You're just into getting arrested," I say.

She groans and throws her head back, and it leaves her leaning on my arm, so I drop it the rest of the way down to wrap around her shoulders. She lowers her head to stare down at her hands twisting in her lap. She stiffens a little, but she doesn't move my arm, nor does she stop leaning against me.

It's such a stupid thing. I've had my arm around more girls than I could possibly remember, but in this moment with *this* girl, who is so far above me I might as well be trying to scoop up the stars, it feels a little bit like a hard-earned first down.

Chapter 5

Dylan

've never hyperventilated before.

I'm not sure if this is what I'm doing, but I do know it's like my brain has forgotten how to perform the simple task of taking in and expelling air. How is it that I'm more anxious now pressed up against him than I was with my wrists bound in plastic zip ties? This is worse because it's not just nerves. It's a jumble of things—good and bad, and they're all fighting for dominance in me. And I have no idea which is going to win.

It doesn't help calm me down when Matt catches sight of Silas's arm around me and mouths *HOLY SHIT* another half a dozen times. I have only a second to be thankful that at least he didn't say those words out loud before I feel Silas's mouth at my ear again. "So what do you say? Come to the party at my place?"

I don't know what I'm doing. This guy is not my type at all. I can see his bloody knuckles from the corner of my eye, and as a general rule, I'm not *really* a bloody knuckles kind of girl. In fact, I'm kind of all-around antiviolence. I date guys in button-downs and ties who are studying to be lawyers or doctors or politicians. I date guys who are as interested and invested in politics and current events as I am.

I have never in my life been one of those girls who go gaga for athletes or actors or musicians. I've always thought having a good head on your shoulders is more important. Talent, money, fame—none of that automatically measures up to a good life. And that's all I've ever really wanted . . . a good life.

But then there's Silas.

If Matt's reaction is any indication, Silas has got the talent, and in sports, fame and fortune usually follow. But based on what I know of him so far, he's not at all the steady, stand-up guy I normally look for. He might not have a good head on his shoulders, but he has good shoulders, so that's close, right?

So he doesn't tick any of my usual boxes, but there's something in the way he looks at me. In his eyes, there's this strange kind of appreciation that is part attraction, part something else that makes me feel rare and precious and . . . *seen.*

Seriously, when did breathing get so hard?

"I should ask Matt," I finally say, even though normally I would have turned down a party invite in a heartbeat. "But I'm pretty sure he'll say yes." Normal doesn't appear to be on the agenda for the night.

Matt coughs next to me, and in his cough, I hear a not-so-subtle "YES."

Silas picks up the end of my braid and curls the dark blonde strands around two large fingers. "Good."

On a whim, I pick up his other hand, his right, and lightly run my finger across the back of it, just below his bloodied knuckles.

"And you'll let me help with this?"

"Trying to fix me, too?"

Jesus. That low, teasing tone is like a punch straight to the chest. Or the babymaker. Both, really.

"I'm just not a big fan of blood."

His lips are still at my ear, and he lowers his volume so that Matt won't hear. "I promise not to get you dirty. Unless you ask real nice."

I don't even . . . I can't . . . Oh my God.

I plant my elbow in his side and use it to pry myself a little space.

"You're incorrigible."

"You're gonna have to use smaller words with me, Pickle. Or better yet, no words at all."

The girl driving snorts, and I shoot Silas a look. "Does that ever actually work?"

He leans close to me, and this time the words are only for me, soft and seductive and almost vulnerable in my ear. "Am I trying too hard?"

I shrug. "Maybe. I can't tell if you're even serious."

His fingers tug on my braid, and his hazel eyes hold mine. He certainly *looks* serious. And I wish I hadn't said anything because a serious Silas is so much more intimidating.

He is a dangerous, *dangerous* boy, and I might have been better off if they had left me handcuffed to that pole outside the shelter. Then I think about what a guy like Silas could do with handcuffs, and I'm just gone. I can feel my face heating up, and I'm leaning closer to him, and even though all we're doing is touching, I feel . . . bad. Like I could do some terrible, irresponsible, *wicked* things.

And like them. A lot.

I stay silent the rest of the ride as Silas directs the girl up front to the bar where he'd left his vehicle. Every few minutes, Matt nudges me with a knee or a finger or an elbow, but I keep my eyes fixed forward because I'm scared that if I look at him, I'll start thinking again. About how I still haven't called my father. About the fact I've been single for oh, a whopping eight days. About all the ways in which this (like much of what I've done today) is an incredibly stupid idea.

Or a brilliant one. Still working on that.

But one thing is decided . . . I don't feel like thinking.

A few minutes later, we pull up beside a beat-up truck that's so rusted it looks as if it might crumble under the slightest pressure. In places it's a dark maroon, but where the paint has chipped away, you can see a layer of gray underneath. Add the rust to that, and his truck is three colors. Four, if you count the mud that the tires have splashed up around the wheels. Silas opens the door, and then reaches down a hand to help me slide out. I hesitate when I catch sight of the unhappy look the driver is giving Silas. I wonder what we took her and her boyfriend away from.

I take his hand, but before I duck out of the car, I tell the girl driving, "Thank you so much for the ride."

She sends me a smile that's very sweet, but almost pitying.

"You're welcome. Hope you get home safe."

I smile and nod, my stomach tumbling with nerves, and then let Silas pull me out into the warm night air. He keeps hold of my hand as he leans down to the passenger window to talk to his friend.

"You guys coming back to the house or heading home?"

"Home," the guy answers. "You'll stay out of trouble? Torres is pretty gone already."

Silas laughs. "What a lightweight."

"That freshman that Brookes invited, Williams, is already passed out on your couch, too. Ryan is still there. He'll try to make sure nothing crazy happens, but you know the guys will listen to you more than him."

"I got it, McClain. You've done your QB duty for the night." He shoots me a quick look over his shoulder and adds, "And then some. Thanks both of you. Sorry I dragged you out to take care of my ass."

"It's cool."

The girl's tight smile says otherwise, but I figure there's some story there that I'm just not getting.

He pats a hand on the top of the car, and then stands back as they pull away. He turns toward his truck and then shrugs at me.

"Sorry it's not much." He opens the door, and there's just one long bench seat, so it looks like I'll be squeezed in the middle again. The truck is tall, and I pause before climbing in, looking for a place to grab where rust won't rub off on my hand.

Two big hands settle on my waist, and Silas lifts me up and plops me behind the wheel. My heart turns over at the touch, but it's gone just as fast as it started. I slide over to the middle section, and I have to put one foot on either side of the old-fashioned stick shift that goes all the way down to the floorboard. The passenger door swings open, and both Silas and Matt slide in at the same time, caging me in with their big bodies.

"You guys have a ride you want me to take you to?"

Matt answers, "Nah. We carpooled with friends."

He looks at me then. "You still okay with coming to mine?"

I take a breath and hold it in for a few seconds. I wait for the flash of misgiving, the feeling in my gut that should tell me to go home, be reasonable, call my father. It doesn't come. Quite the opposite, in fact. I look up at him, and I feel that same insistent pull that made me disobey the dispersal order at the shelter.

Finally, I nod. He turns over the key, the engine cranking loudly, and then reaches between my legs to shift into reverse. He pulls the stick down, and it comes much closer to the seat than I anticipated, which means Silas's hand is between my thighs, his knuckles grazing my skin until I widen my legs another inch. He keeps his hand there as he backs out, and his forearm rests on my thigh. Goose bumps are popping up all around that point of contact, and I hope he doesn't notice. His arm rubs against me as he shifts into various gears, and even when he could return his hand to the wheel, he doesn't.

I wouldn't be surprised if he could feel my pulse from that touch because I swear I can feel it all over. But he doesn't do anything else. Just that simple, maddening graze of his forearm over the top of my thigh.

He turns onto a residential street that skirts the edge of campus, and I can guess which house is his by the cars lined up on the sides of the street. The driveway is open, though, and he pulls right in. His house is wooden and small and painted a cheerful green that seems an odd fit for Silas. It appears haphazardly built, like it's been added on to poorly over the years.

When he gets out of the truck, and I slide over to follow, I'm mortified to feel that not just my underwear, but my shorts are damp. If this is how my body reacts to a few touches, what will happen if he really touches me? Kisses me even?

I'm getting ahead of myself. Going to a party doesn't mean anything is going to happen. I throw both legs over the side of the seat, and Silas is there, his hands at my waist again. But this time he lingers as he puts me on my feet. His thumb brushes back and forth over a tiny strip of skin between my shorts and my shirt, running along the bone of my hip.

"You're sure it's okay if we crash your party?"

He stops the brush of his thumb, and grips my hip instead.

"I'm sure, Pickle."

Matt gives a whooping sort of laugh as he comes around the

nose of the truck, like he's just accomplished something by passing that atrocious nickname along to someone else. I'm still fuming when Silas loops an arm over my shoulder and starts maneuvering me toward the house.

And I proceed to *freak* out.

I have no idea what I'm heading into. I mean, Silas is on the football team, as was his friend Carson, who picked us up. So, I'm betting there are more players in the house, and what exactly do football player parties look like? Aren't they like the gods of campus or something? And what does it mean that one such football player has his arm around me? Is that like a *thing* thing, or just a thing that guys like him do? And do I want it to be a *thing* thing or just a regular thing? And what would a *thing* thing entail exactly? And dear God I'm going to lose my mind before we ever get to the front door.

Breathe, Dylan. He's just a guy. You're just a girl. Sure, he saw you for the first time wearing police restraints, but that's . . . whatever. Totally cool.

Totally not cool, and I might have a panic attack if I don't stop thinking about this.

I hear Matt clomping up the porch steps behind me, and his presence calms me a little. I am an intelligent, resourceful, capable young woman. I can compartmentalize. I can put all the craziness aside and this weird intense attraction, and just have a normal night out. I can talk to these people without saying something that makes me want to swallow my own tongue. I *believe* I can do that.

Silas pushes the door open, and a cry goes up like he's the freaking prodigal son returning to grace them all with his presence.

A handsome Hispanic guy stumbles forward, totally bare from the waist up. Just walking around a house full of people half naked like it's a normal occurrence. The guy has muscles like I've never seen before, and my jaw might be hanging a little loose.

"Moore! Where have you been? And what the hell happened to your face?"

The guy reaches out a wobbly hand to touch Silas's face, but in his drunken state, he can't seem to pinpoint exactly where Silas's face is and keeps missing. When he does come close, Silas bats his hand away and says, "Jesus, Torres. It's not even midnight. If I come out in the morning to find you bare-assed naked on the living room floor again, we're gonna have problems."

"What if I'm just mostly naked?"

Silas shakes his head, and nudges his friend toward a kitchen that opens up to our left. "Go drink some water and sober up a little before you embarrass yourself."

He holds his arms out, drawing my eyes to his toned body again, and says, "Who's embarrassed? Your girl there doesn't seem to mind my public display of perfection."

I flush, and resist the urge to duck my head when Silas looks at me.

He pulls me a little closer and tells his friend, "I'd take off my shirt, but then we both know that wouldn't be a fair fight. Besides, I wouldn't want to steal all that attention you crave." He gives

Torres a joking push, and this time the guy turns and heads for the kitchen.

I relax at his parting, only to freeze up when Silas leans down and brushes my ear with his lips. "If it's a display you want, maybe we can have a private one later."

I push down my nerves and think of this like a debate, a verbal battle of wits.

"Is being conceited a requirement to play football?"

My answer doesn't come from Silas, but from a petite Asian girl descending the stairs next to us.

"More like a requirement to live in this house."

Silas shrugs. "Brookes isn't that bad."

He doesn't even try to deny it.

The girl rolls her eyes. "Isaiah is plenty arrogant. You're measuring him against you and Torres. Everyone is humble compared to you two."

Silas doesn't reply, and the girl's eyes shift to me, specifically to the arm around my shoulders. She's petite and gorgeous with perfectly symmetrical features, and I feel like a mess in comparison. I haven't even looked in a mirror since I was handcuffed and hauled off to the sheriff's department.

She holds out a hand and smiles. "I'm Stella. You'll have to introduce yourself because Silas here wouldn't know manners if they bit him in the ass."

"Dylan. It's nice to meet you."

"Cute," she says. I don't know if she means my name, or me,

nor do I even know if it's a compliment. She asks, "Do you go to Rusk?"

"I do, actually. I'm a junior. Or I'll *be* a junior when classes start back up. I'm a journalism major, um, with a sociology minor. Potentially pre-law." Why am I still talking? Why am I telling this girl everything about myself? I grab hold of Matt and pull him up beside me. "This is my friend, Matt. He's social work. Big football fan apparently."

She tilts her head to the side and raises her eyebrows at Silas, and I just want to bang something into my face. Repeatedly.

"How do you all know each other?" Stella asks.

Oh you know. PRISON. Or jail. Whatever you call it when you don't actually leave the police station.

"Um . . ." I fish for a suitable explanation. "We met at a thing."

A thing. Really smooth.

Silas drops his arm from around my shoulder, and I've officially screwed this all up. Where is the nearest oven into which I can stick my head?

It's probably for the best. I'll let Matt do his thing, and then we can get out of here.

"You done with the third degree, Stell?"

She stands up straighter and shrugs. "No third degree. I'm just wondering how you leave your own party after . . ." She trails off, but not before giving Silas a look. "How you leave your own party and come back home with two strangers and a bruised face."

His expression has gone hard, but his words are still light. "What can I say? I make friends everywhere I go."

She rolls her eyes. "Right. And what exactly did your face make friends with?"

Silas drags a hand through his hair. "Jesus. We met at the police station after I got arrested for beating the shit out of Levi. So, if you don't mind, I'm not really in the mood to rehash my terrible day. Take your gossip and go."

He grabs my hand and pulls me into the living room.

Stella calls after him, but he ignores her. A younger guy vacates a recliner, and between one breath and the next, Silas has sat down and pulled me straight onto his lap.

Chapter 6

Silas

Spooked. That's the look in her eye as I curl a hand over her bare knee and turn her sideways on my lap. She already has big eyes, but now they're two wide blue oceans set in a heart-shaped face.

"Um, I think I'll find another seat."

I tighten my grip on her knee and say, "You see one?"

A frown pulls at her lips as she looks around the packed room. "I'll just . . ." She shifts like she's going to stand, but I stop her. I'm fucking this all up. Coming on too strong, pushing her too much. I know it's crazy. This one girl doesn't define my place here, but I can't take another moment today where my shortcomings are thrown in my face. I need this. Need her.

"I'll be good. I promise."

"I think we probably have very different definitions of good."

I laugh at having my own words thrown back at me. And I'm

a little puzzled at why she's still hanging in there with me. If she's actually as uptight and serious as she seems, she probably wouldn't have even climbed into my truck. The way she smiles at me from beneath her wild hair makes me feel like what I'm seeing is just what she wants me to see. Maybe I'm not the only one pretending.

"What's your last name?" I say.

She's worrying her bottom lip between her teeth, her eyes scanning the room uncomfortably as she answers, "Brenner."

Brenner. The name sounds familiar. Or maybe it's just that it flows right in my head. Like she's one of those people that you have to say their full name every time.

I watch her fingers tangling in her lap for a few moments, and I can see her closing herself up. I grip her hips and shift her forward until she stands. I do the same, and then push her back down into the recliner alone. Then I balance myself on the edge of the end table next to her.

"Tell me about yourself, Dylan Brenner."

She gifts me a smile that just might be grateful, and she shrugs. "You've already been party to my most mortifying experience—"

"Are we talking your arrest or that weird verbal diarrhea back there?"

"Oh God." She covers her eyes with her hands so fast, I can actually hear her palms hit her face. Laughing, I reach out to tug on her braid again. I don't know what the fuck my problem is, but I can't stop touching her hair. I don't want to stop.

"I'm kidding. Besides, it gave me *some* info. You're a junior, so that makes you what, twenty? Twenty-one?"

I slip my fingers down her braid, the texture smooth and complicated. She lifts her head out of her hands. "Twenty-one. Just turned in June."

Reluctantly, I let go of her hair.

"And what did *the* Dylan Brenner do for her twenty-first?"

"The Dylan Brenner?"

I shrug. "I figure people are going to call you that someday. After you've changed the world a few times. I'm just getting a head start."

She says, "I don't know that it's really possible to change the world."

"Then why go through all the trouble?"

She pulls her feet up into the recliner and balances her arms atop her knees. She did that in the jail cell, too, and I swear to God it's like she wants to torture me. I try not to stare at the gentle curve of her thighs, not while she's got this far-off, contemplative look on her face. She gazes just above my head as she speaks, like she's somewhere else entirely. Or like maybe she's explaining it to herself more than me. "Because once upon a time, someone went through the trouble for me. And I want to be that kind of person. The kind of person who fights for what I believe in even if I'm already beat. I don't think I can change the world, but I can change one person's world at a time. And that's something."

Her shirt still hangs off her shoulder, revealing the gentle slope up to her neck. She tilts her head to the side and shrugs, brushing off what she's just said. My gaze gets stuck there, on the sun-kissed skin of her neck and shoulder. She looks so soft. Her whole personality seems too sweet, too good to be real.

Or maybe that's my history. I only know how to expect the worst of people because it's all I've ever seen.

"I think *you're* something."

Her lips pull into a small smile.

"Something ridiculous?"

"Something special. Where I come from people are more concerned with changing their own worlds than someone else's."

"And that's bad?"

"It is when nothing ever changes. Each new scheme or plan always winds up just how you started. And all you've got is some messed-up cycle that does nothing but drain you a little more each time around. I think it would be easier to change the whole damn world than to change some people."

She lays her head on top of her knees, and those big blue eyes lock on me, studying and sizing me up like I'm her next save-the-world project.

Oh hell no. Enough about me.

"You didn't answer my question. What did you do for your twenty-first?"

She does another one of those deep-breath things where her whole body moves, and she looks out at the party, her eyes flitting between groups of people talking, drinking, and smoking. "Honestly? I went to dinner with my boyfriend." Her eyes flick to mine. "My ex now. We had dinner and then went back to his place. That was about it."

"No big party? No night out on the town with friends?"

She shrugs. "We weren't really party kind of people."

"You weren't? Or he wasn't?"

"You know," she laughs. "I don't actually know." Her laugh is this pure, perfect thing. Everything about her is light. She makes it seem so easy, like I could just toss off all the bullshit and live in a bright shiny world just because she's in front of me and that's the world she lives in.

I want to forget myself in her, and maybe help her do the same with me.

"Well, you're in luck, Pickle. Because you happen to be with an expert partier."

I stand and slip one arm beneath her knees and band the other around her middle before lifting her up. She squeaks and wraps her arms around my neck.

"Excuse me," I call out on my way to the kitchen. "Novice partier in the house!"

"Silas," she groans. I dig my fingers into her side, and she jerks, squirming and squealing in my arms. "Oh my God, stop!"

"No groaning then. At least not that kind."

She stills and the pink blush on her cheeks brings out her eyes even more, and who would have thought getting arrested would put me in a *better* mood?

I keep shouting until my way into the kitchen is clear, and then I sit her right onto the counter. People are staring, and I can see her noticing them all. Intent on distracting her again, I lean her knees and am surprised when her legs move to let me rest between them.

Not so nervous anymore, are you?

I end up being the distracted one, too caught up in how I like the feel of her knees pressing into my sides. It makes me want to really be between her legs, to be pressed right up against her. Up on the counter, she's the perfect height so that my head is just a few inches above hers. And if I tugged her to the edge, she'd be at the perfect height there, too. I plant my hands on the countertop beside her and lean in until all I can see are those wide, nervous, *excited* eyes.

"What's your poison, Pickle?"

She frowns. "What will it take to get you to stop calling me that?"

"Stop answering my questions with other questions. Tell me how you want to belatedly celebrate your birthday."

"I really don't think I should."

"Why not?"

"I just . . . alcohol leads to bad decisions. And I've already made enough of those today."

"So we'll get high instead."

Her mouth opens on a surprised inhale, and *goddamn* her lips are perfect. Curved and full, and I'm thinking of all the other ways I could make her lips part like that.

"I can't do *that*," she says.

"Your friend Matt doesn't have any problem with it."

I nod my head over to the kitchen table, where Matt is part of a group sharing a bowl.

She looks afraid, but she asks, "What's it like?"

I shrug. "It's different depending on the person and what you're smoking. Some stuff just makes you relaxed. Clears your head and calms you down. Some makes you happy and kind of light. Everything makes you laugh or seems really entertaining. It's like taking a break from the world, you know? The outside stuff just kinda melts away, and you forget to care about the things that are bothering you."

"Is that why you do it?"

I give in to the itch to touch her and start at her bare shoulder, dragging a finger along until I can curve my whole hand around the back of her neck.

"You're gonna have to stop trying to analyze me. I'm really not that complicated."

For a girl like her, analyzing is step one. Fixing me would be step two.

She leans her head to the side, and my hand falls away from her neck.

"Tell me about the fight tonight."

And so it begins. "Why?"

"Tell me about the fight. Let me clean up your hands. And then, I promise to let you teach me how to party. Or whatever."

I feel like I've just stepped into a courtroom, and am being out-negotiated.

"So we're making deals, are we?"

She smiles. "I suppose we are."

I reach up again, and this time she doesn't pull away when I curl my fingers around the back of her neck. I brush my thumb over her pulse point . . . feel that thin, vulnerable skin, and *fuck*, beneath that bossy exterior, I can see her nerves. But they're different now. She doesn't look scared or uncomfortable. Her heart is racing, blood pulsing fast beneath my finger, and she's taking these tiny sharp breaths. It turns me on in a way I don't even understand. Normally, the skittish, inexperienced types send me running. But the thought of teaching her anything makes my jeans feel too tight. I want her on her back in my bed, legs spread wide, eyes big and blue, lips parted, mouth babbling that nervous nonsense until I make her forget what she's saying, forget how to talk altogether.

I want to forget myself in her, too, steal some of her sunshine, and give this pristine, perfect girl a taste of what it's like to get a little dirty.

"Deal," I tell her. "But you'll have to come upstairs. All my first-aid stuff is in the bathroom up there."

She swallows, and I watch her long, delicate neck move.

Damn. Is there anything about this girl that doesn't turn me on?

I watch her think about it, and when she finally fixes her eyes on me and says, "Okay," I get the feeling that she's come to a bigger decision than just this.

I help her down, and on the way out of the kitchen, she stops to say something to Matt. He gives her a blissed-out smile, and takes another hit.

We exit the kitchen into the front entryway and cross over to the stairs that lead up to a meager second floor that only really consists of my bedroom and a bathroom. I feel a little like the big bad wolf as I follow her up the stairs, but when she reaches the top of the landing, she shoots me a look over her shoulder that makes me pretty certain that I'm not in any hurry to rejoin the party downstairs.

"Which door is the bathroom?"

"This one."

I twist the doorknob and open up the small room on my right. I let her go in first, mostly so I can get another look at her ass in those shorts.

"Medicine in here?" She's already reaching for the medicine cabinet behind the mirror, and when she pulls the latch open, a box of condoms falls out.

She mumbles, "Oh crap," under her breath, and rushes to replace the box, but it landed top down and when she picks it up, all the foil packets dump out.

She starts shoving them back in as she utters an apology. Or four.

Barely biting back a laugh, I decide not to help her and instead enjoy her flustered rush to throw the condoms back inside the box. When she's done, she returns it to an open shelf in the cabinet, closes the door, and then steps away from the sink until her back meets the wall.

She says, "I should let you find the first-aid stuff. It's your bathroom after all."

I step in front of her, not bothering to open the cabinet. I turn on the tap and let the cool water run over my hands. The water runs a little pink, mostly from the dried blood, and I rub at my skin with my fingers until the water runs clear again. I turn off the tap and shake out my hands a few times before presenting them to her. Still red and raw, but clean.

"See? We're all good. Now, let's go show you some fun."

I turn to go and she grabs my bicep.

"You're not going to bandage them?"

"Bandages would just be a nuisance. They'll heal up fine as long as I keep them clean."

She looks around the bathroom, and I can imagine she's thinking about the fact that college guys live here alone. How clean can things really be?

"At least put something over the worst scrapes."

"I think you're trying to stall."

"I am not. I just don't think it's a good idea to not put *anything* on it. Besides, our deal was that *I* clean up your hands, which means I decide how to treat them."

There she goes being bossy again.

"I'm going to leave this room with my whole hands covered in gauze, aren't I?"

Her lips twitch like she's trying not to smile. "Possibly. Now give me your hands."

I lay them on top of hers, our palms touching, and say, "Yes, ma'am."

Her eyes narrow. "Can't you ever just call me Dylan?"

I'll call her that when I'm inside her. When she's in my bed. When I've got my hands on that perfect ass. That's when.

"Maybe," I tell her. But I hope to God it's not a maybe.

She rolls her eyes, and after a few moments of her standing there, holding my hands, I raise an eyebrow and ask, "Would you like to know where the bandages are? Or are you going to heal me through touch?"

If anyone's touch could help, it would be hers.

She releases me and mumbles a quiet no. I have her open the medicine cabinet again, and this time the condoms stay where she put them.

"That little black bag on the bottom shelf should have whatever you need."

As she searches through the bag, I take a seat on the toilet and perch my elbows on my knees. She sets aside some ointment, gauze, Band-Aids, and tape. Then carefully, she begins, "So tell me about the fight."

She digs through the box of Band-Aids, looking at the different varieties. She looks almost uninterested. Almost.

"It was nothing." I direct my gaze to the floor.

"You said before it was with a friend. Or someone who used to be a friend."

"It was."

"Your friend Carson said the name Levi. That's the guy? Carson didn't sound like he liked him very much, either."

She comes to stand in front of me, but I keep my head down.

"Do you remember in the fall last year when there was a bunch of drama going on with the football team?"

"I remember people talking about it, but honestly I didn't pay much attention to what actually happened." I lean back to look at her, and she picks up my right hand. She's gentle as she rubs ointment across each busted knuckle. "But I'm listening now."

I tell her about Levi, about how we had a tendency to cause trouble together.

"He felt a little like a brother, you know? Doing stupid shit. Pissing each other off. Pissing *other people* off."

"Are you an only child?"

I laugh. "No, I'm not. But I don't really talk to my real brother anymore, either."

I tell her about those first few days after Levi's arrest. All the drug tests. Being questioned by the police, questioned by Coach. I don't tell her how it reminded me of when my brother was arrested. How the police searched our granny's house and found the stuff he stole. How I got taken in, too, because he'd given some of the stuff to me without telling me where it came from. Fuck, thinking about that shit used to feel like it was a different world I left behind. Now it feels too damn close. Like I walked right back into that world without even realizing my feet were moving.

Levi was supposed to be different. He was rich, smart, had a good family, but he ended up the same as the guys I grew up with, same as I would have ended up without football. I guess I understand better now why we worked so well as friends. Granny always said like sticks with like.

"You had no idea?" Dylan asks, switching to my other hand.

"I mean . . . he smoked on occasion, for sure. But I had no idea how far into it he was. That he was selling, too."

"So how did you end up fighting tonight?"

"Because I'm a fucking idiot." My tone is a little too hard. I'm still agitated about the whole situation, and that fight wasn't enough to clear the tension out of my blood.

"You're not."

"I am. I shouldn't have even gone to see him."

"Yeah, well. We all do stupid things sometimes."

Her brows crease, and I know she's worrying about her own stuff now.

"That's another thing we have different definitions of. Helping people doesn't seem that stupid to me."

"If only it were that simple."

"So why'd you get arrested? You could have backed off, yeah?"

"I should have. I don't know why I didn't. Except that . . . it felt right." Her eyes lift to mine on those last words, her thumb gently rubbing over my sore knuckles, and damn if *that* doesn't feel right, too. "Even as I was doing it, I knew the consequences. But I just didn't care. I wanted to *do* something, not because it was what I was supposed to do, but because it was what I *wanted* to do."

I think I get it then. That decision I saw in her eyes back in the kitchen. That's what this, what *I'm* about for her, too. I'm just another part of whatever rebellion she started earlier today. About doing what she *wants*, not what's expected of her.

"We're not talking about me, though," she says. "So you went to meet your friend, and then what happened?"

She keeps her eyes down as she picks up the gauze and begins winding it snugly around the knuckles of one hand, and then the other.

"He said the wrong thing."

"Which was?"

"Dylan." Now it's her that's pushing too hard. I didn't want to talk about things with my friends, and I won't talk about them with her, either, no matter how gorgeous she is.

"I'll guess. You were mad about what he did, and he wasn't sorry."

"This isn't middle school, Pickle. He didn't hurt my feelings. He said some shit he had no business saying, and it pissed me off. The end."

"But you don't think some of that anger stems from what you feel is a betrayal of your friendship?"

She finishes taping down the last of the gauze, but doesn't let go of my hand.

"I think you're analyzing me again. Making things more complicated than they are."

"And I think you're just a guy who doesn't like to admit he has feelings." She drags out the word, teasing me with some goofy smile on her face. I turn my hand over so I can clutch her wrist. I curl my other bandaged hand around her waist and pull her closer.

"I feel plenty of things."

The teasing stops. She swallows.

"I wasn't talking about *that* kind of feeling."

With her standing and me sitting, I'm eye level with her chest. I see the sharp rise and fall as she sucks in a breath. I want her in my lap again, straddling me this time.

"Doesn't mean we can't talk about that kind of feeling. Or experiment with it."

"Is that Stella girl an ex?"

I cough, surprised. My throat twists uncomfortably, and it takes me a couple of solid breaths to get a hold on myself.

"Ah, no. Stella and I have never dated."

"Have you—"

"Do you ever run out of questions?"

"Not ever." She turns playful again, and I'm done doing this the careful way. If she wants a rebellion, I'll be the one to give it to her. I want her against me, and I'm tired of waiting.

I pull her forward, insinuating my knees between hers, and her body naturally follows, settling across my thighs. Her lips part, but she catches herself before she gasps this time. I keep her steady with my hands at her waist and say, "I'll make you a deal. A question for a kiss."

Tentatively, she lays her palms against my shoulders. They rest there, her grip light and casual. She ponders my offer for a moment, and it drives me mad that she can do that while our hips are inches away from alignment.

"Okay then. Are you—"

I cut her off. "Not so fast, Dylan Brenner. I've already answered one question. We've got to settle up first."

I wrap her braid around my hand like I've been waiting to do all night, and I use it to pull her head back just enough that I can crush my mouth against hers.

Chapter 7

Dylan

'm going to shatter into a thousand pieces from the intensity of this kiss alone. His hand is on my cheek, turning my head, and it's so big that I feel like I'm completely at his mercy. In fact, he kisses me like he wants to own me. Not even that . . . he kisses me like he already *does* own me.

I want to feel put off by that. I want to feel disturbed by his dominance.

But I'm not.

I like that he wants me that much, that he kisses me hard enough to bruise, that he's holding on to my braid like a life-line. I like that he doesn't handle me like a breakable, naive little girl. The Brenners adopted me—their pretty little well-behaved orphan girl. Henry cherished me, kept me as a pretty little doll that would one day be his pretty little wife. Until one day that apparently wasn't good enough. Maybe I didn't play my part like I was supposed to.

Either way, I'm beginning to learn that I don't want to be a pretty little anything.

What I do want to be . . . I don't know. But I know that it needs to be something *I* want. Not what I think other people want me to be.

He tugs a little harder on my hair, pulling me back from my thoughts, and I gasp into his mouth. I bite down on his bottom lip in response, not because I've ever done anything like that, but because it seems like the thing to do. He groans, sliding a hand down my backside. So, I guess that means it was okay. He squeezes, lifts me forward and against him so that I can feel his hard length press right against the juncture of my thighs.

To quote Matt—*Holy shit*.

He keeps kissing me, his tongue sweeping past mine again and again, and it feels like a race to the finish line. Like if I can touch him enough, taste him enough, I'll reach a point where I'm so saturated by him that . . . that *something*. I don't even know what will happen then, but I know I want it. I dig my nails into his shoulders, and he groans into my mouth in response.

One of his hand slips down the waistband of my shorts, under the band of my underwear, and his fingers grip the curve of my behind. It's so mind-numbingly erotic that I lose pace on our kiss, overwhelmed just trying to catalog all that I'm feeling.

I pull back, struggling to breathe.

"That was more than just a kiss."

He shrugs, his smile downright devilish.

"Just another difference in definition."

His lips drift back toward mine, but I place a hand on his chest to stop him.

"Time for another question."

"Go ahead," he says, but he doesn't shift his grip on my ass; instead he tightens it and turns his attention to my neck. His teeth skate along my skin first, raising goose bumps in their wake. Then I feel the heat of his open mouth, the flick of his tongue, his hum of pleasure.

"When we, ah, um . . ."

Words. Letters together in patterns. Focus on the words, Dylan.

"Is there anything between you and Stella?"

His teeth nip at my collarbone and I jolt on his lap. He drops his head into the hollow of my neck and groans. His panting breath is hot against my skin. He uses the hand on my backside to mimic the surprised movement I'd just made, his hips rocking with mine this time, and he groans again, deep and low.

"Didn't you already ask me that question?"

"I asked if she was your ex, not the same thing as asking if there's anything between you at all."

He circles my hips over his, and oh God it feels so good, better than such a simple motion should. But between his erection and both our zippers, the friction is killing me.

"We hooked up once last year, but we're just friends."

I know that answer should make me pause, should make me

ask more questions, but his mouth has left my neck to explore my shoulder, and his free hand has found its way beneath my top, beneath the spaghetti strap shirt I'm wearing in lieu of a bra. He makes a noise of approval low in his throat when he discovers that fact, and his thumb draws circles around my nipple, teasing me with an almost touch for a few seconds before squeezing the tip between his thumb and forefinger.

I throw my head back, feeling relaxed and tense all at the same time. I want more, so much more, but I'm afraid to ask, so I bite my lip, arch my body, and grind against him, hoping that he can read what I want in my actions.

More. More please.

His lips return to mine, and all of a sudden, I have one of those weird out-of-body experiences where I'm not sure if this is even real. Being dumped by Henry. Getting arrested. Going to a party with a total stranger. Following my impulses without any concern for the consequences. This is not my life. This is not me.

The way his kiss feels . . . it's too good. The way kissing feels in a dream, like the complete sum of everything I want and need, and he's risen from my subconscious to give me the perfect fantasy. His touch is electric in a way that has to be my imagination because skin doesn't react like that, doesn't spark and heat and burn that hot. He has to be my subconscious reacting to the mess with Henry because he's the complete opposite of the guy I'd spent the last four years of my life with.

Henry was a plan, a future, 2.5 kids, and a backyard. Henry is everything I *should* want.

Silas is this moment only. A quick burst of adrenaline. The physical manifestation of want with no regard to logic or reason.

Silas is . . .

Oh God. Silas is touching me. Really touching me. My shorts are unzipped, and his hand is inside my panties, and one finger slides against my sensitive flesh.

Shit. Not out of my body anymore. I am firmly in my skin, and *burning up.*

"What happened to my bossy girl?" Silas says, and I don't think I can even form words to respond.

I just knot my hands behind his neck because I don't trust myself to hold on to his shoulders anymore for balance.

"No more questions?" he teases. "I thought you never run out of questions."

Oh, I had questions, but I no longer cared about the answers. I no longer cared about anything except what his hands were going to do next.

"I have a question for you then."

Just the tip of his finger dips inside me, and the heel of his hand is so close to where I'm dying for his touch.

"Do you want my fingers inside you?"

I swallow, wishing for another one of those out-of-body experiences. Because now I know this is real. It's too intense to be anything else, and I know he's going to make me answer. And I'm not sure if I like this kind of thing. It scares me how much I want to answer him anyway, how much I *need* him to keep going.

The heel of his hand grinds against my center just for a moment, and when he pulls back I cry out at the loss.

"Do you want me inside you?"

I squeeze my eyes shut and whisper, "Y-Yes."

His cheek slides against mine, and I shiver at the scrape of his stubble. His voice is a rumble in my ear. "One or two?"

"W-What?"

He slides one finger in, only to pull it all the way out. His teeth graze my earlobe and he asks again, "One or two?"

Please don't make me. I can't—

He pushes two inside, and it's just enough to ease the ache and simultaneously multiply it. It's just enough in every way. "Two," I answer before he can take them away again. "I want two."

His palm presses up into me as a reward, and I move against it, seeking more friction.

"*Fuck*, yes," he growls, stealing my lips for a quick, hard kiss. "Take what you want, Dylan. Ride my hand."

I whimper, and I don't know if it's in objection to his words or because they make something tighten in my belly.

"Come on. Move for me."

I kiss him. Maybe to shut him up. Maybe for courage.

As soon as his tongue slides against mine, I'm reacting on instinct, doing exactly as he asked. His other hand is out of my shirt, and digging into my braid, undoing it until hair starts to fall around my face and swing around me as I rock into his palm.

"God, yes. You're gorgeous like this. Keep going, baby."

Every time I tilt my hips, he pushes in sync, curling his fingers and hitting a spot that makes my arms and legs shake in anticipation. He pushes up my oversized shirt and his lips close over the tip of my breast through my camisole. He sucks hard, and my hips jerk, seeking *more*. I throw my head back because I'm so close.

So, so close.

He lets my shirt drop down and clamps his hand around the back of my neck. His grip is hard enough that it almost hurts. Almost. Instead it just adds to the frenzied pace of my blood rushing beneath my skin. With his hand at my nape, I have no choice but to look at him. His hair is mussed and wild, and I wonder when I ran my hands through it because I don't remember. I sink my fingers through the strands now, though, because that's something I want to remember, how it feels to hold on to him like that.

His hazel eyes are so dark and piercing, and that look alone brings me a breath closer to the edge. He pulls me into him, so that his hand is wedged between us with no extra space. I'm still moving against his palm, but when I rock hard enough, I'm pushing against his erection, too. I know when I've done that because I can feel his heavy exhale against my lips.

"I'm going to watch you, Dylan. Just like this. I'm going to watch you come apart around my fingers, and it might just be the hottest fucking thing I've ever seen."

My eyelids start to fall under the pleasure, and he twists his fingers inside me. I pull his hair on accident, and he growls in approval.

"Look at me, Dylan. Don't close your eyes. I want to see it. I want to watch you come for me. Can you give me that?"

"Si-Silas."

His grin is so wicked, so gorgeous. I just stare at him. I could stare at him all day.

"Feel free to say that while you come, too."

And that's it for me. I feel it building the second before it hits, like I can almost see the shadow of a wave cresting just behind me, and then it crashes over my head and I am . . .

drowning and

dying and

breathing and

perfect . . .

Everything is absolutely perfect.

Silas's lips touch mine, surprisingly soft, and I sink into him, boneless and exhausted and too undone to be embarrassed. My skin is buzzing, and my hearing is off, like I'm underwater. I can feel the delay between my thoughts and my movements, like my body short-circuited and is still trying to reboot.

"I was right," he breathes against my lips. "Hottest fucking thing I've ever seen."

He kisses me again, and that's when I realize . . . this isn't over. I've just had an incredibly intimate, incredibly *vulnerable* encounter with a relative stranger, in a bathroom, of all places, and though I had a (rather wonderful) *moment*, he didn't. And this was all just prelude.

Which is terrifying because that *prelude* was the scariest and most erotic moment of my life, and I might not survive more. And though I definitely *wanted* what just happened, my brain is still too fuzzy and disjointed for me to figure out what else I want.

He slides his hand out from under me, and I realize that we're both still fully clothed. Other than my soaked panties and unbuttoned shorts, you can't tell we've been doing anything more than kissing.

There's something even sexier about that, but at the same time, it wakes me up to a twisting sensation in my gut, something I recognize all too easily as guilt.

It's not like I'm against sex or anything.

But like this? When it's this . . . *impersonal?* I have no clue what I'm doing. It's as if I woke up today and completely forgot who I was, who I've spent my whole life becoming. And I don't know whether to be angry at myself for that or for feeling guilty about doing what I want. What feels right.

When is it okay for want to overpower common sense? And how do I know if this is just some phase, some rebellion? Or if it's me finally waking up, letting go of expectations and responsibilities and rules?

How do I know what to trust—what I feel or what I think?

I'm scared that whatever I decide, I'll end up regretting it.

I'm still straddling Silas when I ask, "You said you and Stella hooked up last year. That's what this is . . . right?"

He kisses me on the shoulder and helps me stand. "My room is right across the hall. Let's go over there."

He pulls open the door, but I plant my feet.

"This is just a hookup."

I don't phrase it like a question, but from the wary look he shoots me, we both know it is.

"What do you want it to be?"

I frown. "I'm not sure." I'm not really the one-night-stand kind of person, but I also can't picture myself having a relationship with Silas. I like him and the way he makes me feel, but that's not near enough to build a relationship on.

A holding cell meet-up and a few hot minutes in the bathroom is not exactly how I pictured my next romantic encounter.

"Can't we just leave it at that? Figure it out later?"

"No. I can't."

He leaves the door to cross over to me. He scoops my thick hair up and pulls it over one shoulder. Then he trails a finger down my cheek, and I'm relieved to note it's *not* the hand he recently had buried in my shorts.

"I think you're great, Dylan." He doesn't use any stupid nicknames. I guess that's another perk of the *activity* we've just done. "I like you. I like making you come. That's all I know right now."

I will not blush. I will not blush. I will not—

Damn that cocky smile.

I wish that were enough. I wish I could be fine with just worrying about right now.

"I don't ask questions to be a pain, Silas. I ask questions because I'm the kind of person who needs answers. I just am."

"What answer do you want? A relationship? Because that's not really something I do."

I don't think that's what I want. But I don't like that it's not even a consideration.

"How do you know? Do you have trust issues? Or you get bored easily? Or you've just never tried?"

He drops his hand away from my face.

"Dylan, I'm not sure what I want from you, but it isn't to be my shrink."

"I'm not trying to be your shrink. I'm just trying to get us on the same page."

"We were on the same page when you were straddling me. Let's go back to that."

"Silas." I know even as I say it that I sound like I'm reprimanding him. Like I'm already some angry girlfriend. And it's ridiculous because I'm actually tempted. God, as frustrated and wary as I feel, I'm *so* tempted.

"Okay. Here are the answers I have for you, Dylan. Yes, I like you . . . enough to bail you out of jail when I knew next to nothing about you. Maybe it's just a hookup. Maybe we'll see each other again. I don't know. I don't make promises because I'm not good at keeping them. You're either okay with that or you're not. And if you're not, that's whatever . . . fine. But I can't guarantee you anything. And if you're thinking of me as some project you can fix or change . . . don't. *That's* what I know."

"Thank you. That, um . . . that helps." And makes me feel a little sick to my stomach all at the same time. It's all well and good to act impulsively, to live in the moment, but I don't exactly have any experience dealing with what comes after.

"Should I go find Matt and take you two home?"

"No." I shake my head, my lips pursed tightly together. His eyebrows arch, and he curls a hand around the back of my neck. His mouth dips down close to mine, but I sidestep him and move toward the door. "I don't need you to take me home. But I think it's probably not a good idea for me to go into your bedroom. I'm in a weird place mentally right now, and I'm not sure I trust my decision making at the moment."

In fact, I don't trust myself at all. I haven't since I went out with Henry thinking he might be about to propose and got a breakup instead. Because . . . I think, I can't be sure, but I think when he ended it . . . I was relieved. And only minutes before I'd been prepared with the word *yes* on the tip of my tongue.

And that scares the holy hell out of me because I should know myself better than that . . . right? I should *know* who I am and what I think and how I feel . . . but I don't.

I don't know myself at all.

He swallows, and he must be gritting his teeth because his jaw is tight. He looks down at his feet and bobs his head in a nod. "I get it."

He looks up and asks, "You sure you don't need a ride home? It's not a big deal." But even though he's looking at me, he's *not* looking at me. His eyes are unfocused and just off to the side, and his expression is locked up tight.

And I feel so guilty, not just for what I did, but because this isn't fair to him. He's the collateral damage of my own indecision.

"Thanks. That's really nice, but we can walk. It's not far."

"Okay."

"Okay," I reply. I stand there stupidly for a few more seconds and then walk out the door.

I turn to say one last thing, and he's right behind me. He's looking at me now, and I can't read his expression.

"Sorry." I mean it to be an apology for all of it, but I'm scared he thinks it's just about nearly bumping into him, so I continue, "I'm sorry for being weird about all this. And thank you. For everything, not for . . ." I gesture in the general direction of where he gave me an orgasm. "*That.* But thanks for that also. Oh God. I'm going to go. Sorry. Thanks."

STOP SAYING THANK YOU.

I can feel his presence behind me as I flee, and I'm wondering whether it's worse to stay silent or to make some horrible, awkward small talk on our way down the stairs. Then I hear the door across the hall, his bedroom, click shut.

And I'm alone.

And I still have no idea what I want.

Chapter 8

Silas

find a joint in my room, and kill the whole thing in a few minutes.

Bad decision.

She didn't say it, but that's what she was thinking. She wanted to avoid bad decisions, and always, no matter what I do, no matter how far away I get from the trailer park and that shack of Granny's, I've got that written all over me.

The high comes on fast and hard, and I spend the next half hour, maybe more, staring at my ceiling. I'm fucking blank, barely even there. And it's perfect.

But when I start to level out, it all gets worse.

I'm horny as hell, and the weed only amplifies it.

Instead of clearing my head and relaxing me like normal, my thoughts turn dark, and I get stuck thinking about the past. I start thinking that there's no point. To football or classes or friendship or anything. I know where I came from, and I know where I'm gonna end up, and the longer I lie here, baked out of my mind, the more it starts to feel like those two things aren't as far apart or as different as I want them to be.

I start laughing, and I'm not even really sure why. Only that this all feels like some script I'm playing directly into. Like these first couple years at Rusk were just the setup, letting me believe I'd moved on, created something better for myself, only to have it all start falling apart, or rather falling back into familiar territory.

I laugh even though it's not funny, but what the fuck ever. I stumble down the stairs, and I must have been staring at my ceiling for much longer than half an hour because the party is over.

Torres is indeed passed out naked on the floor, and someone has balanced a throw pillow on his bare ass, and that seems so damn funny to me that I forget how to breathe through my laughing.

Torres doesn't stir. Neither does the new recruit asleep on the couch.

I make my way to the kitchen, but it feels like ages before I get there. Time never makes sense when I'm high. I blink, and it somehow feels like my eyes have been closed for centuries and seconds all at the same time. I load up on snacks, more weed, and a couple of beers. With my arms full, I turn to head back to my room only to find Torres standing at the entrance to the kitchen. He's pulled the throw pillow around front to block his junk, and he's looking at me through squinted eyes.

"Is it morning?" he asks me.

My chest bounces on a silent laugh, and I shake my head. He rubs a hand over his face and says, "What the fuck happened last night?"

He's the one laughing now, and my mood turns on a dime. All of a sudden things don't really seem that funny.

I can't shake the feeling that last night was the beginning of the end, and everything is downhill from here.

"Nothing good," I answer. "Nothing good at all."

Torres groans in agreement, and stumbles off in the direction of his room, while I head up to mine. I only eat a couple of handfuls of chips before I pass out for the night. Perfect oblivion.

I keep chasing that nothingness through the rest of the weekend, switching to alcohol when I'm out of weed and too lazy to go buy more.

Brookes comes in Sunday evening. He's the most stable in the house. He and Torres are best friends . . . both receivers. They're the jokers on the team, but really couldn't be more different. Torres clowns around for the attention. Brookes does it to put people at ease. He's also a fast motherfucker, which is why I barely have time to raise my hands before he's by my bed stripping back the sheets.

He's holding one of those jugs of water you buy at the grocery store. Throwing it on my bed, he says, "You've had your final weekend of fun or whatever the hell this was. Take a shower. Drink some water. Get it the fuck together. Practice starts tomorrow."

I groan, but I grab the water because he's right. I don't know what I was thinking.

Scratch that. I know exactly what happened. I've been trying my damnedest not to think at all.

It's not about Dylan. She's just a girl. A girl who is nothing like any other girl I've ever known, but still just a girl. It's all of it. All the things that have happened, and all the things that haven't, but inevitably will.

Because she was right. *Levi was right.* I'm bad . . . a bad decision, bad seed, bad blood . . . whatever you want to call it, that's what I am. And it's only a matter of time until it has me turning out just like Levi, cut off from the people I know and the only thing I love.

I peel away the circle of plastic around the mouth of the jug and pop it open.

"Isaiah," I stop Brookes as he turns to leave, my pale hand wrapped around his dark forearm. He flexes his fingers into a fist, and I let him go. He might be a little more pissed than I thought. "I'm sorry, man. It was just one of those weekends. I'm good."

He walks to the door frame and lightly raps his knuckles against it a few times. "I'm not really the one you're hurting, Silas. Just be glad we already took our drug tests when we reported on Friday."

Fuuuuuck. Yet another thing I hadn't thought of. The chances of Coach popping another drug test on us now are almost zero, but still . . .

He leaves, and I do as he says, starting with the shower. I drink the full jug of water and try to get some sleep.

Try being the key word.

I mostly lay there, resisting the urge to scream obscenities loud enough to wake the whole house.

I go for a run, but a hangover has already started creeping over me, and the nausea makes me feel like my organs are shifting with each stride. I call it quits and walk the rest of the way home, knowing I'm going to be a fucking wreck at practice in six hours.

I take another shower. I think about jacking off, but as soon as I picture Dylan draped over my lap, her hair falling out of that braid, the feel of her against my hand—a bass drum pounds in my head. I brace my hand against the tile, let the water pelt my face, and try not to throw up.

I chug some more water when morning comes, and think again how damn lucky I am that we did our drug tests when we reported on Friday. Not that there aren't ways to beat them. I learned plenty of tricks freshman year, but none of it is foolproof.

I remember Torres being scared shitless last year when his name came up for the random test. We taught him all the things that gave him a better shot at passing (which he did), and all the dude talked about for the week afterward was that he was scared the Midol we had him take was going to give him manboobs.

I'm sitting at the table, plowing through a mountain of toast, when Torres hurdles down the stairs.

"Look who's alive." He grins, grabbing a protein drink from the fridge. "Zay sort you out?"

Brookes enters the kitchen from the living room. "I just brought him water."

I finish my toast, have a little more water and a few pills. And that's as good as it's going to get.

I opt to take my own truck instead of riding with the disgustingly cheerful duo. I don't even make it to the locker room before a voice reaches me from the coaches' office.

"Moore!" It's Coach Oz, the team's strength and conditioning coach.

"Yes, sir?"

"Coach Cole's office. Now."

And . . . fuck.

Just fuck.

I could probably live the rest of my life only using that word and it would sum things up fine.

I step into the office and every coach inside turns to look at me. I nod at the first few, but then I'm stuck doing this stupid head bob that makes my headache worse. So, I give it up and head straight for the door to Coach's private office. The door is half open, so I poke my head inside.

"Sir?"

He looks up from his computer, looks back at the screen, and types for a few seconds longer.

"Come in, Silas."

And . . . another *fuck*. Coach only uses first names when shit is serious. I sit down, and the silence freaking swallows me. He takes a sip from a coffee mug, sets it back down, and waits another few seconds to look at me. Then he just stares. Straight face. Blank.

Almost expectant. This must be what it's like to have a parent around to piss off all the time.

"How was your weekend?"

Damn. Who told? I start running through the names and faces of who was at the party. No one saw me high that I know of, but they could have just told him about the party in general, and it was at my place.

"Fine, sir."

"Fine." He repeats, nodding. "Fine." He draws the word out a little longer the second time. "Then explain to me why I heard from a friend in the sheriff's office Saturday morning."

I close my eyes and drop my head back. I didn't even think about that. I'd assumed since Levi didn't press charges that I was in the clear.

Wrong.

"It was all taken care of, Coach. They only held me for a couple of hours or so. Nothing will show up on my record."

"I don't care about your record. What the hell were you thinking, kid?"

"I'm sorry, sir. Levi just got under my skin, I guess."

He stands up and plants a hard fist on his desk. "Then get thicker skin."

I nod. "Yes, sir."

He stands straight and paces behind his desk.

"You're a good football player, Silas. And I see it in you when you play . . . I know what this team means to you. But your grades are mediocre. You have a temper. You have a tendency to make poor decisions." Goddamn it, talk about a broken record. *I get it, world. I suck. It's pretty clear now.*

Coach continues, "I want to trust you . . . I do. You wield a great deal of influence over this team, and I want to make sure it's a positive one."

"I understand. I want that, too."

"Then stay the hell away from Abrams. He's banned from school property, but I don't want him poisoning this team from the outside."

"Done. I promise."

He surveys me, almost like he doesn't believe me.

"I need you to step up. I need you one hundred percent in this."

"I am. One hundred percent."

He crosses his arms over his chest and continues studying me.

"Then you won't mind proving it by getting a head start on practice. Get dressed. Coach Oscar will meet you on the field for sprints while I meet with the rest of the team."

Of course. Just what my body needs right now. Something else to make me feel like vomiting.

"How many, sir?"

"Until I feel confident that there will be no more calls from the sheriff's office."

In other words, until I damn near die of exhaustion.

THEY CALL THESE sprints suicides for a reason. You start at one end zone, sprint to the first ten-yard line, and back to the end zone. Then the twenty-yard line and back. Thirty. Forty. And on and on.

Coach Oz even has a little special twist he likes to add, in case you weren't already tempted to spill your guts all over the grass. He's one of the youngest coaches on staff, and as such feels the need to be a complete hardass so we take him seriously. So being the sadistic bastard that he is, he makes us do twenty push-ups every time we return to the end zone.

I'm already exhausted by the time I get to the fifty-yard line, and it feels like I still have an eternity to go. As I approach the end zone, Oz yells, "Pick it up, Moore! Looking slow today."

That's because I feel like I'm going to throw up my lungs, Coach.

I drop to do my push-ups and the constant up and down makes my nausea double. My arms are burning when I finish and drag myself to my feet.

"Move your ass, twenty-two!"

I'm still running when the rest of the team comes out on the field, and Coach Cole lines them up along the sideline to wait and watch as I finish.

I try not to get angry. I really do, but the humiliation gets to me. Might as well make me hold a sign that says I can't do anything right. Not even on the first day of practice.

I grit my teeth so hard I expect my jaw to break as I finish my last sprint from one end zone to the other. I drop for my push-ups and growl my way through them. When I'm done, I stand and face Oz. It's a dumbass move, but I'm pissed and not thinking straight, so I raise my eyebrows and ask, "Should I keep going?"

It's Coach Cole who answers. "That will do for now."

As I walk over to join the rest of the team on the sideline, I try to keep my breathing steady, but it feels like one of the linemen has been using my chest as a trampoline.

"Mr. Moore has just helped demonstrate our new discipline policy, gentlemen. When you skip a class, when your grades drop below the line, when your actions reflect poorly on this team, that's an infraction. For the first infraction, you run." He gestures back toward Coach Oz, and a few players groan quietly. "If you commit a second infraction or the problems persist, your entire position group runs with you." People start looking around at the players around them, the guys who now determine whether or not they're subjected to the will of Coach Sadist. "And if one of you is stupid enough to get in trouble a third time, you, your position group, and your position coach will run." He shoots his staff a sly smile, and I can tell this is news to them. And when they fix their eyes on the players, they definitely aren't screwing around. "We are a team," Coach yells. "We win and lose together. So, we'll screw up and get better *together*, too. It's not just your own ass on the line, it's everyone's."

Brookes catches my gaze, and I turn away. Like I don't feel like enough of a chump already.

"Any questions?"

Players and coaches alike shift, but no one says anything.

Then Torres opens his big mouth. "If we get in trouble a fourth time, do you run, sir?"

Nobody moves a freaking muscle. And I just know . . . we're

all gonna run for that one. But then Coach surprises me. He laughs and shakes his head, but when he speaks, he's serious again. "Mateo, you don't want it to get that far. It won't be pretty."

My new roommate never does know quite when to shut up, though.

"No, I imagine that wouldn't look pretty at all, Coach."

"Teo!" "Torres!" "Seriously?"

Every player surrounding him turns and lays into him. He covers his head with his hands and jumps back.

Coach blows his whistle, and we all snap back to attention. "It looks like you boys are beginning to understand what it means to be responsible for your teammates." He stares at Torres for a long moment and then looks at the team. "We'll let that one slide. Now, into your position groups. We'll start by seeing what you've retained over the summer."

A small whoop raises up from the crowd and as we disperse, Torres yells. "I love you, Coach! You're the best!"

"We'll see if you still feel that way when we're through. You know we don't do easy days here, not even first day back."

Chapter 9

Silas

I get my ass handed to me.

Multiple times.

By multiple people.

I'm focused. My head is in it, but my body just isn't. Between my binge weekend and my punishment at the beginning of practice, my legs are too fucking slow and my arms too weak to hold the ball as tightly as I need to. I keep making stupid little mistakes, and odds are that I'm going to leave practice with a damaged eardrum from all the yelling.

Coach is on me because he's still pissed about the fight with Levi. Coach Gallt, the running back coach, is all over me because he's taking over offensive coordinator from Coach Cole now that the team is settled. The entire offense is his responsibility now, which means my failures come down on him. So, he's coming down on me . . . hard. And some little asshat freshman (the same freaking one that passed out on my couch Friday night) is all keyed up trying to outdo me, soaking up every bit of praise like he's just won the freaking Heisman.

All of the noise just keeps swarming around me, and I can hear myself fucking panting for breath, and I'm melting in this heat, and I'm so damned frustrated I could scream.

"Damn it, Moore!" Coach Gallt yells. "I'm sick of watching you screw up. Is this what this season is going to be like? Because if so, Williams is gonna take your place in no time."

I don't even know who Williams is, but when I get a good look at the cocky grin on the freshman's face, I figure it out. His name is Keyon, or something like that. I don't give a fuck.

I rip off my helmet. To do what . . . I don't know. My head is about to explode, and I feel like I can't breathe with it on. I'm about to mouth off to Gallt when Coach Cole cuts in. "Go get some water, Moore. Shake it off."

I do what he says and head off to the sidelines. I gulp down a few mouthfuls of water and dump the rest over my head. It's so dry and hot out that the water feels like heaven. Or as close as I'm likely to get to it anyway. I go to repeat the process when McClain sidles up to grab a drink of his own. Unlike me, he's been killing it today. I had no fucking clue when Levi got kicked off the team that Carson would ever be able to replace him, let alone be better than him. But he did it . . . is doing it every day. Knowing him, he probably didn't take a single day off all summer.

"You all right?" he asks.

I wipe some of the water and sweat from my forehead and say, "Fine, QB. Just an off day."

"Yeah. Of course." He nods, but I can tell choirboy has more he wants to say. He doesn't wait long to get to it, either. "Listen, that lady who showed up at your party . . ."

Damn it. I knew this would come eventually.

"What about her?"

"Who is she?"

"Nobody," I say. "She doesn't matter."

"It's just . . . you seemed pretty freaked about it, and Stella thought she might be—"

I shove my helmet back on my head.

"I said she's nobody. Leave it alone, McClain."

"You took off so fast after she showed, and next thing I know you're calling me to pick you up from a police station—"

"Listen. I'm grateful that you came to get my sorry ass Friday night. I am. But I'm not Ryan. We're not gonna talk about my shit while we lift or whatever the hell it is you two do. You and I will just play ball, okay? That's how this friendship works. All you need to know is . . . I'm fine. I'm good. Same as I always am."

Or I will be. As soon as I get rid of this fucking hangover.

I spin to walk away, but not before adding, "And tell Stella to mind her own fucking business, too."

The rest of practice doesn't get any better. In fact, it just continues to get worse because now my head is as out of it as my body. When Coach blows the whistle calling it quits, all I want to do is hit the showers and get high again, but that would be the stupidest thing I could do.

Not that I'm above stupid. Stupid and I go way back.

And bad decisions are apparently what I do best. I sure as hell wasn't at my best in anything else today.

I'm only thinking about getting to the shower and getting out of here when I feel a hand on my shoulder.

It's the freshman. Keyon Williams. I might not have been sure of his name before today, but I know it now. He's shorter than I am, and a little bit stockier. The guy's got a pretty good sprint, but no real endurance. Not that I can really talk about endurance at the moment.

"What?" I bark.

"We didn't really get introduced at the party Friday. Just wanted to say hey. Tell you good practice."

I shrug his hand off. "Is that a fucking joke?"

He holds his hands up. "Nah, man. Didn't mean anything by it. We all piss the bed some days."

I lose it. Completely. I shove him up against the wall right outside the locker room and get in his face. "Listen, fish. You don't know shit about me." I said those same words to Levi, and now this asshat is fucking grinning, just like he did. It takes everything in me not to bash his teeth in. Carson steps into the doorway, and I catch his eye. I force out a breath and take my hands off the kid. Mouthy fucking freshman.

"Just stay out of my way."

I turn and head for McClain when the dick opens his mouth

again. "It's you that's in my way. But not for long. Not how you're playing. I'm sure you'll be heading Abrams's way before long."

I'm almost to the door, but those last words tug me back and his too white smile is all the extra motivation I need. I drop my helmet and ram him into the wall. He clips me on the healing bruise on my jaw, and my teeth rattle. But I hit him with a perfect uppercut, and blood starts pouring out of his mouth. He shoves me back and we both go tumbling to the ground. We struggle for control, rolling a few times, and just when I've got the upper hand and am about to lay into him, multiple sets of hands grip and pull me back.

I struggle for a couple of seconds, but there are at least three people holding me back. And now that I get a good look at the guy lying on the floor, blood all down the front of his shirt, I don't really feel the need to get back at him.

In fact, I don't feel much of anything except my stomach dropping to the ground.

Then the coaches are there. Gallt and Oz are down by Keyon, and Coach Cole slides into my vision. I've never seen him so livid. His face is purpling, and his eyes have that psycho look to them, like he might flay me alive. I brace for him to yell but he doesn't.

Instead, in this quiet, intense, fucking terrifying voice, he says, "My office. Right now."

I open my mouth to say something. An apology, maybe.

"*Now*, Moore."

My teammates let me go, and I turn to face them. There's Mc-

Clain, Brookes, and Carter. I wouldn't have expected Carter to jump in. He's usually one of the instigators, but I give them all a nod that will have to do for a thanks.

I shouldn't have let that dude get to me. I don't know why he did. It's not like I can't handle a little talking shit. When I was a freshman, I was the biggest asshole of them all. I head through the locker room, where everyone is silent and still, paused in the middle of getting undressed for their showers. They stare as I walk through the room and toward the lounge area that opens up into the offices.

For the second time today I enter Coach Cole's office, but this time I'm alone. The room is dark, and I don't turn on the lights. I just take a seat and bury my head in my hands, and I listen to the silence. I listen to it like it's going to tell me the answer, going to explain why I can't keep my head on straight. After a little while it starts to sound like music. The muffled sounds from the locker room, the ticking of coach's clock, the low whirring sound of his computer. There's a hell of a lot of noise to be found in the silence, almost as much as there is in my head.

The door opens, and I keep my head down. I hear Coach pause by the door, and I know he's looking at me. I think for a second that maybe he'll leave the lights off. That he'll let me get away with not looking at him during this. But then the moment passes, and he flips on the light.

He crosses the room and slams my helmet down onto the middle of his desk. He stands behind his chair and grips the back until his knuckles turn white.

"You better have a damn good explanation for what I just saw out there, Moore."

I sit up straight in my chair and face him head-on. I owe him that much.

"I don't, sir. I'm sorry."

Coach presses his lips together like he wants to yell and curse, but is trying to stay calm. He runs a hand roughly through his hair.

"Damn it, Moore. McClain filled me in. Told me what Williams said. He's a freshman. You know how this game goes. You've been there. You have thicker skin than this."

I nod because I do. I did, anyway.

"You've got to give something here, son. Help me understand."

How was I supposed to help him understand when I barely had my own head wrapped around it? All I knew was that something about Levi getting arrested had me all fucked-up. And Mom showing up had spun that tiny problem into a hurricane. There was my old life . . . living in the mobile home of whoever Mom was dating at the time, or in that rickety shack she left my brother Sean and me in when she split for good, always surrounded by people, never a moment of privacy, never having anything that was mine. There were my drunk uncles and cousins. People throwing punches over who did or didn't get groceries. My barely there granny who couldn't read or write, so I had to sign my own permission slips for football and school. There was Sean arrested for breaking into houses, leaving me alone with those people who thought of me as another brat running underfoot. That neighborhood was all about strength, about who was big and bad enough to fend everyone else off. I hated that neighborhood, hated what it did to my brother, but it was better than what came after. When Gram died, and my piece-of-shit uncle sold the house, and I had to beg people for a place to stay so I didn't get trucked off with some relative and torn away from my team. I fucking *hated* begging.

I'd let myself forget about all of that. Let myself believe it was behind me because my life here was so much better. I was part of a team. I had my own bed, my own room even. I had friends who had no idea what kind of life I'd had, and they just assumed I'd grown up like them.

Maybe I started believing it, too.

Then Levi got arrested and it was like my two worlds collided, and I could see that old life waiting just a layer below this new one, and I can't explain how that makes me feel.

There's just this word that keeps popping into my head.

Inevitable.

It's inevitable that I'll end up back there. I forgot to keep running, and now it's all caught up to me. That shit is in my blood, and there's no rinsing it out or diluting it with scholarships and classes and all the other shit I've been kidding myself with. I don't know how to be anything else but who I am, and who I am will never be good enough to make it in this place with these people.

I can't explain that to Coach because not saying it out loud is the only thing keeping it from being completely real. And if that's gone, I won't be able to hold it together.

Coach finally has enough of my silence and sits down at his

desk. He's back to that scary quiet that isn't the calm before the storm . . . it's the storm that destroys you because you think it's not a threat. "We've got enough battles to fight outside this locker room. I don't need someone starting trouble inside the team, too."

My stomach starts falling, and I wait for it to hit my feet, to drop through the floor. But it just keeps falling.

"I don't tolerate violence on my team, Silas. No matter how good you are. As of now, you're suspended. One week of practice, and the first two games of the season."

Impact.

But it's not just my stomach that's fallen. It's everything. My head. My heart. If it weren't for the chair, I know I'd have fallen to my knees, too.

"Don't you step back on my field until you've got your head screwed on tight. Because I've got to tell you, Silas . . . two games is a minimum. If I still think you're not good for this team, I'll cut you out like a cancer. It will hurt me to do it because I know what you've got in you. I know you can hack it, but I'm not willing to bet this team on you getting your act together. I've got too many other kids' dreams in my hands. So you better shape up and bet on yourself and prove to me that you're better than what I saw today."

He scoots his chair back, and I know the conversation is over, but I can't get up. My legs won't work. I can't piece together words.

If my present self is the top layer of skin and my past is the layer below that, football is every vital thing inside me that makes my body work. Muscles. Arteries. Veins. Organs.

I only work when I play football. Without it, I really am the trash I'm afraid of being.

Coach doesn't make me leave. He turns the lights back off and lets me sit in his office alone, and when I listen for the silence I don't hear music anymore.

I just hear what Williams said over and over again.

I'm sure you'll be heading Abrams's way before long.

And all I can think is . . . maybe he's right.

Chapter 10

Dylan

've put it off as long as I can.

Friday was my day of lapses in judgment. Saturday, I started cleanup. I started with apologizing to Javier about screwing up the protest. He was mad that I'd acted without talking to him. He's the leader of our group, and everything is supposed to go through him. He understood that I just got wrapped up in the moment, in the desperation to do something.

One apology down.

Then there is my father, whose persona is that of a man who *never* makes snap decisions. He does woodworking as a hobby, something I always thought was odd for a man with enough money to furnish a small country. But he's fond of saying that building things with his hands is no different from building a business. You plan, you design, you measure twice, and cut once.

Well, Friday I didn't measure twice. I'm not even sure I measured once.

I got lucky, though. Dad was called out of town on business, and since there were no major, lasting repercussions from my arrest on Friday, Mom convinced him that we could talk when he got back.

That's tonight. And since I'm not really sure how he will react (or if I'm still able to be grounded as a junior in college), that means today is the last day that I can go to Silas's and pay him back for bailing us out.

Something else I've been avoiding. Because he's the one thing I still haven't sorted out in my head. Every time I think about him, my mind goes right back to that bathroom, and the heat that sweeps through me burns away any coherent thought.

At first, I think no one is home because the driveway is empty, but then I see the familiar rusty tail end of Silas's truck parked across the street. I shake off the memories of what it felt like to be in his truck, his arm brushing against my leg, the thrum of excitement from being completely out of my element. A girl could get addicted to something like that.

In fact, there are quite a few things about Silas Moore that I could get addicted to.

I'm wearing a silky button-down shirt with no sleeves and a complicated bow tied at the neck. I've got my hair back in a long braid again, and a high-waisted skirt that goes almost to my knees and does a much better job of covering my legs than those shorts

I'd worn Friday. I made a conscious effort to dress for the way I need to behave today.

Appropriately.

I ring the doorbell, and then try not to think about the fact that I'm sweating through this stupid silky shirt and the strappy heels on my feet are monstrously uncomfortable, and I'm dying a slow, torturous death in the thong I wore to prevent panty lines.

Dressing appropriately sucks.

I wait a minute. No one answers, and I'm beginning to fear that I'll have to do this all over again later tonight or tomorrow after I talk to Dad, provided I'm still free to do what I want.

I ring the doorbell again, and then raise my hand to knock for good measure, but before my knuckles meet the wood, the door is ripped backward and I hear a gruff, "What?"

I hear his question, but my brain is a little stuck on the fact that Silas is wearing only a towel around his waist and is dripping water all over the floor. I open my mouth to say something, anything, but then I get distracted watching a bead of water slope down over one pectoral muscle. He has a massive geometric tattoo that starts on his shoulder and continues onto his chest. I watch that same bead of water cut through the black lines of his tattoo and escape into the valley down the middle of his abdomen.

Then it falls below the line of his towel, and I'm just standing there, staring at the one part of his body that's covered, and if there was an ounce of supernatural ability in me, that towel might have *accidentally* fallen to the ground.

But alas, I am not supernatural. Though his abs might be.

I'm still staring at his crotch when he asks, "You need something?"

"Oh!" I snap my head up, a blush exploding across my face. "I'm so sorry. I didn't mean to keep . . ." That's probably one sentence I'm better off not finishing. "I didn't mean to."

He lifts an eyebrow, and for the first time, I really look at his face. I expected the bruise on his jaw to be healing by now, turning ugly shades of green and yellow, but instead it looks even darker than it did Friday night, and bigger maybe. But that's not what really troubles me. It's his eyes.

They remind me of what my eyes looked like after Henry and I broke up, like I'd just found out that life was a game, and I'd been playing on the wrong board for years.

Not sad, per se. *Lost.*

"You okay?"

He raises his eyebrow again, grips the door with one hand, and resituates his towel with the other.

I don't glance down at the towel. Or his magnificently sculpted chest. Because that would be *awkward*. I absolutely don't . . . *won't* do that.

Aw crap, I'm awkward. For several seconds. Several *long* seconds.

"Dylan."

My eyes fly to his, and I expect an eyebrow, perhaps a cocky grin, maybe some dirty, dirty words.

But he looks tired.

"You're not okay," I say because I just know. This is not the same guy I met a few nights ago.

He takes a deep breath. "What do you need? Did you leave something?"

"Uh, no." I lift up the envelope in my right hand. "I'm just here to pay you back. And to say thank you again. So, um, thank you."

I hold out the envelope, and he stares at it for several long seconds, then his eyes raise up to mine.

"You want to come in?"

I hesitate. Because I want to. In the same way that I wanted his hands on me Friday night. The same way I wanted his mouth . . . the things it did and the things it said. I hadn't been able to *stop* hearing those words all weekend. I dreamt about it. I imagined what else he might have said if we'd kept going, and I woke sweaty and needy and so, so pissed it wasn't real.

I might not have taken measure of the situation Friday night, but I'd measured far more than twice since then. I'd thought about it almost constantly. But I still wasn't sure that was a bridge I needed to cross.

It's like there are two wills inside me, and each one insists the other isn't real. Part of me thinks that this is all just some emotional reaction, a self-destructive break of some kind. I need to go home, grovel at my father's feet, figure out what went wrong, so that I can fix my life.

The other half of me insists that I don't need fixing. That the reason things with Silas feel so right is that things with Henry never were. That I was just doing what was expected of me like I've always done.

But shouldn't I try to live up to people's expectations? I can't just let go of that. What kind of person would I become then?

As I stay silent, warring with myself, something in Silas's already weary expression starts to fray further, and I step right over the threshold just to make it stop.

Of course, a normal person says yes when they're invited inside. They don't step in before the person at the door has a chance to move back. Now I'm less than a foot away from that distracting chest of his, and with his hand braced on the door he's looming above me in a way that makes my girlie parts roll over and play dead.

I start to step away, and my heel hits the raised threshold, and I stumble back. I would have fallen on my ass right outside the door again if Silas hadn't reached out and caught my arm.

"Uh, thanks. And sorry."

He turns and heads into his kitchen. I don't think I've ever seen a back that muscled in real life. There are all these curves and slopes that I wouldn't have expected, and I have the sudden urge to trace them with my finger, feel where one muscle gives way to the next.

"I'm starting to think those are your two favorite words."

I come back into focus and close the door behind me. Then I follow him cautiously into the kitchen.

"You want something to drink?" he asks.

Tequila sounds appropriate for this situation.

"Just water is fine," I say. "Thanks."

He shakes his head and pulls two glasses down from the cupboard. "It's just tap. That okay?"

I nod, but he's not looking at me, so I voice my answer instead. There's not an ice machine in his fridge, so he grabs ice for my glass from one of those plastic cube maker things. He fills his own glass up with milk and then comes over to join me at the table.

He sets my water down and I ask, "Are you going to go change?"

Tilting his head to the side, he looks down at me. "Do you want me to?"

Oh God. How could I possibly answer that? Of course, I didn't *want* him to change. I'm not crazy. But I needed it if I was going to keep my head clear. I must take too long again because he sets his milk down and turns away. "I'll be back, Pickle."

And we're back to that again.

When he's gone I gulp down some water and then press the cold glass to the side of my heated face.

I don't know what it is about this guy that screws with my head so much. It's like he releases some kind of airborne toxin that melts all my sense. The Silas Virus.

He comes back not even two minutes later. He's still damp all over, his shaggy hair stuck to the sides of his face and the back of his neck. And he's *still* not wearing a shirt. He's swapped out the towel for a pair of gym shorts, which does nothing to make me any more relaxed. I suppose there's less chance of a wardrobe malfunction now, but he's still so very naked.

And nice to look at.

The legs of the chair scrape against aged tile as he pulls it out to take a seat. He demolishes half his glass of milk in one long drink, and my eyes stick on the way his neck moves. His Adam's apple bobs, and I notice how very defined it is. It's chiseled like his jaw and his muscles, and as weird as it is . . . it's kind of a turn-on.

If I can't even look at the guy's freaking Adam's apple without getting tingly, there's probably no hope for me.

He sets the glass down and wipes his mouth.

His mouth. Oh God.

"Water okay?"

I blink. "Hmm? Oh. Yes, it's fine. Thanks. I mean—"

"I think you're the most polite person I've ever met."

I shrug and trace a finger through the condensation on my glass.

"Strict upbringing."

That's an understatement. The foster home I'd been in before the Brenners adopted me was practically a military institution. We were out of bed at dawn, and had a full day of scheduled chores and activities. There was never a spare minute to just be . . . to play or imagine or discover something new. I was the youngest one in the group, and all the older kids were used to it, but I still only wanted to be outside lazing around in the sun, climbing trees, playing games.

I can't be too sorry, though. The Brenners had liked how well-behaved I was. At nine years old, I'd stopped dreaming that some family would come take me away. Or at least . . . I told myself to stop dreaming about it. Even then, I was practical to a fault. But they met me, liked how polite I was. They'd laughed and looked at each other every time I uttered "please" or "thank you" or "sir" in my high-pitched voice. And they picked me, just plucked me up and gave me a new life, and there are still days when my life before that feels like a dream.

So really, structure has worked out well for me most of my life. It's only the last week and a half that it's been crumbling around me.

Needing to do something to fill the silence, I push the envelope toward him and say again, "Thank you for helping me and Matt. That was a really nice thing to do."

"Nice," he mutters and lifts his glass to his mouth again.

"Yes. It was very nice. As was getting your friends to give us a ride and inviting us over to your place."

He clears his throat. "Trust me. My intentions were not nice at all."

"You were nice to me."

I see the first hint of a smile on his face since the moment he opened the door, and even though it's small, it nearly knocks the breath from my lungs.

"Yeah, well. That's the only kind of *nice* I know how to be."

I blush. Because I hadn't meant what he'd done to me, though that had been far more than nice.

"I mean . . . you were honest with me. You didn't get angry when I decided to leave. You offered me a ride home even though you probably didn't want to see my face again. You invited me inside today, and you didn't have to. I think that qualifies as nice."

He taps his fingers on the table and lifts those gorgeous eyes to mine. "I'm not sure my intentions are any nicer today than they were then."

I swallow, but even with the water I've been sipping, my mouth is so dry that it takes longer than normal just to perform that simple task.

"Oh."

He laughs. Actually laughs. And it reminds me just how different today's Silas has been from the one I met the other night. I smile back at him. It feels really good to know that even for a few seconds I pulled him back from that. I spend most of my days trying to make a difference, and none of it has ever felt quite as satisfying as that laugh.

"How's Matt?" he asks.

"Telling everyone that he met you and Carson. He won't shut up about it, actually."

"Well, I'm glad someone left that party happy."

"I didn't exactly leave unhappy, you know. A little confused, yes. Overwhelmed. But not unhappy."

Then I wonder if he wasn't talking about me, but himself, and I'm not sure how I feel about that. I won't feel guilty for leaving on Friday. It was the right thing to do. And if he was so upset at how things *didn't* turn out, he could have gone downstairs and found another girl. I'm sure he would have had no issue there.

Maybe he did do that.

He gets up to refill his glass of milk, and I drag in a few gulps of water because I suddenly don't feel so well. I don't want to think about what he did after I left. He sits back down and I say, "Tell me what's wrong."

He shakes his head, and all traces of that earlier laugh and smile are gone.

"Still trying to fix me?"

"I wasn't trying to fix you that night, Silas. I just wanted to know more about you, wanted you to talk to me. Same as now."

He scowls. He opens his mouth, but then pauses and looks at me, really looks at me. His eyes narrow slightly, and he purses his lips, thinking. It's becoming even harder to swallow as I sit there wondering what it is he's seeing when he looks at me. When I've waited as long as I can to ask the questions burning inside of me, he leans across the table and beats me to it.

"What if I wanted you to fix me after all?"

Chapter 11

Silas

don't know why I said that except that she seems like the kind of girl that might actually be able to do it. I look at a girl like that, who's somehow wild and polished at the same time, and I feel like she has to have it all figured out. If anyone does, it's her.

So, I keep going.

"What if there's something wrong with me? And what if it's slowly destroying the only things I care about? How do I fix something like that?"

She stares at me, unblinking, and I wish I could pluck all the thoughts from behind those blue eyes. I lower my gaze first, and I notice her hands are clutched tightly around the edge of the table.

"It appears I now know two ways to make you stop asking questions."

That starts her up again.

"You don't really think that, do you? That you're broken?"

"It's a working theory."

"Silas, most broken people aren't self-aware enough to realize that they need help. Just the fact that you're asking means that you're fine. Whatever it is . . . you're dealing with it."

I laugh, and it probably sounds dark and mocking, but I can't help it. She's so damn naive. I've known people all my life that were straight-up busted, and they knew it. They knew how fucked they were, but that didn't make them any better at getting control of it.

"No, I'm not. I'm not dealing with it at all. I'm fucking disintegrating, but I'm not dealing."

"I think you're just frustrated, and maybe it feels right now like—"

The thing I like about her . . . that air of sunshine that radiates off her . . . it's the same damn thing that I can't stand. So I skip the pep talk and cut straight to the point.

"I've been suspended from the football team."

She stops, her mouth still open around the word she'd been about to say. Her eyes soften, and her head tilts to the side.

"H-How? What happened?"

"I got in a fight."

"Another one?"

I drop my head down into my hands and grip my hair just hard enough to hurt.

"Yes, another one. And Coach knew about the first one, too."

"Is fighting against the rules?"

"It's kind of an unspoken rule not to deck your own teammate."

She makes this humming noise behind her pursed lips, and I want to take the words back, reel them back in and lock them away. She somehow still has a decent opinion of me after the other night, even though she walked away, and if I don't stop I'll destroy that, too.

"Why?"

"Because he made me angry."

"*Why?*"

"Because he's a prick."

She huffs. "I mean why did you get angry?"

"Because . . ." I press my hands down flat against the table and stand. I can't sit here and talk about this with her like it's normal. "Because I just did."

"Nope. Not going to cut it. What made you mad?"

I push away from the table, walk to the fridge, turn, and walk back.

"He said I was going to end up like Levi."

"Levi is the first guy you got in a fight with, right?"

I nod, and she props one elbow on the table to rest her cheek in her palm.

"So what about Levi makes you mad?"

I can't. I couldn't explain it to Coach, and I won't explain it to her.

"I'm not talking about this, Dylan."

"You asked me how to fix it. How am I supposed to help if you won't let me?"

"I don't actually expect you to help—"

"Why not?"

"Because I'm not your charity case."

She stands and crosses toward me, and my kitchen feels too damn small with her this close. All I can see are all the surfaces I want to press her against to end this conversation.

She lays a soft hand on my forearm, and her touch burns.

"You're not a charity case."

I thought the night that we met that she was one of those "good girls" looking to take a bad boy and pretty him up to take home to Mom. I've had my fair share of those that I have gladly kicked to the curb. I'm not about to let someone else change and manipulate me to make me into something that makes them happy. Then I thought she was a nice girl looking to get a little wild, maybe freak her parents out.

But looking into her eyes, I don't think that's her anymore. She wants to help me for my sake, not for her own. I am her charity case, no matter what she says. But I'm not so sure I mind that.

"Maybe I want to be your charity case. Would you do that? If I asked?"

Her eyes widen. "Do what exactly?"

I drag my hands through my hair and pace away from her. "I don't fucking know. Fix me." She makes a noise almost like laughter, and I cross back to her and grip her shoulders. She swallows, and her eyes are serious on me now. "It sounds stupid, I know. But I'm so close to losing it all, Dylan. This life I have now . . . it's everything to me. And Coach is ready to cut me if I don't completely clean up my act. I've been doing it my way, and I'm failing. So I think I need to try something different."

Maybe it's not enough anymore to pretend that I belong here. I have to change.

"I'm just not sure what you're asking of me, Silas."

Goddamn it. Neither am I.

"You help people. That's what you do. That's what I'm asking for. I need to be better . . . be good. For the team. For me. I just need to get my shit together."

"Just the fighting? Is that what you're talking about?"

"All of it. The fighting. The partying. Booze. Pot."

"Bad-boy rehab?" She still looks skeptical.

"I'm supposed to be a leader, Dylan. I'm supposed to make this team stronger, but right now I'm its biggest weakness."

And God, I must look so fucking pitiful, because she bites her lip, her big eyes soft and sorry. "Okay."

"Okay?"

"I'll help."

I want to fucking kiss her. Pull that bottom lip between my teeth, instead of hers. But I settle for pulling her against me and squeezing tight.

She makes a little squeak, and it takes her several long seconds before she rests her hands lightly against my bare chest.

"You have to actually listen to me, though."

It's distracting, feeling her breath against my skin, but I nod and say, "I will."

"And you have to talk to me. Answer my questions. I can't get to the root of your actions unless I know what you're thinking, how you're feeling."

I stiffen. I know she's right, but that doesn't mean I relish the idea of talking about my shit . . . especially not with her.

When I don't reply, she tries to pull back, but I keep my arms locked around her waist. So with her stomach still tight against mine, she leans back her shoulders and looks at me.

"If you want my help, that's the price."

I ask, "What if we worked out a trade? Like the other night."

Pink floods her cheeks, and her tongue peeks out to wet her lips. "You want me to kiss you to get answers to my questions?"

"I was thinking more a question for a question, but I'm fine with your idea."

She shakes her head quickly. "No, question for a question sounds good to me."

I must be twisted because the more she tries to pull away, the more I want to kiss her. Maybe there's something to that whole hard-to-get thing after all.

"First question," I say. "What are you afraid of?"

"What do you mean? Like spiders? Heights?"

I smile. "No. I mean what are you afraid of with me?"

"I don't know what you're talking about."

I trail my fingers along the smooth skin of her jaw and cup her cheek. "You want me. I know you do. But every time you get too close, you run. So what about me scares you so bad?"

She exhales, and her breath fans over my mouth, teasing me.

"It's not you. Not really."

"It's not you, it's me? That's what you're going with?"

"I should have said it's not *completely* you. You're intimidating, definitely. But it's more that . . . I don't know what I want."

I use my other arm still around her waist to tug her body tighter against mine. "Liar. If the number of times you've looked at my mouth in the last minute is any indication, you know exactly what you want."

"I can't trust that. Myself. Have you ever woken up one day and realized that you're not who you thought you were? That you have no idea who you really are? Because I have. And it's awful. To not be able to trust your own mind. And I can't think about what I want because I'm too busy trying to find the rug that was pulled out from beneath my feet."

"Sounds to me like you're thinking too much."

"I *have to think*. Otherwise, how can I—"

"No, you don't, babe. I might not know much, but I know the things that matter, the things you love . . . you don't have to think about that. You just know." Like I know that I'd do whatever it takes to stay on the team. Because it's what I want . . . more than I want to party and have a good time, more than anything. "Fact is, knowing what you want and knowing who you are . . . those are two separate things. One is complicated. The other isn't. You're trying to take something simple and make it hard, and there are enough hard things in life without you adding more for yourself."

She closes her eyes on a sigh, and her lashes are so long against her pink cheeks. She says, "I don't actually think you need me to help you. You've got a better handle on things than I do."

"Not true. You might think too much, but I don't think enough."

Her gaze meets mine again, and this time she's smiling.

"Maybe we can both learn a thing or two from each other."

"Deal," I say.

"Deal?"

"You help me get my life back on track, help me turn things around, and I'll help you figure out what you want."

"And I suppose in your plan, us sleeping together is the first step to figuring out what I want?"

"It's an option."

"Silas . . ."

"When I look at you, I see a girl who has it all together, laced up tight like *mistake* isn't even a word you know. But I think you're starting to suffocate. I think that's *why* you got arrested Friday, why you came with me, because you needed to breathe." Her top knots by her neck in a silky bow, and I pull on one of the strings, undoing it. She doesn't stop me.

"Don't you think this will only complicate things?"

"Not if you let simple things stay simple. We don't have to sleep together, not to figure out what you want. I could just touch you. Because Jesus, Dylan, I've never cared less about my problems than when I had my fingers inside you. I think I could forget the whole world if I had my tongue there instead."

And if I were *really* inside her, inside that tight heat, Christ, I'm aching just thinking about it. She swallows, and when I run my hand down her neck, I can feel her pulse fluttering wildly beneath her skin.

"Silas . . ."

I wait for her to continue, but she doesn't, and I'm fine with that because I like the way she says my name. Breathy and sweet.

I run my thumb over her pulse again and again, and I know she feels the pull just as strong as I do.

"Don't think," I tell her. "Not this time. Go deeper. What do you want? Not what *should* you want. You want me gone, push me away. You want me here, pull me closer. Simple as that."

"Simple," she repeats.

Then she kisses me.

It's tentative at first, but she doesn't hesitate when I open my mouth against hers. She tastes just as sweet as I remember, and her tongue slides against mine, hot and needy. Her hands on my chest slip down to grip my waist, and that glide of skin against skin is so damn good. But not enough. Not even close.

I press her back against the counter, and these athletic shorts do nothing to disguise how much I want her. My hardening cock pushes against her belly, and she breaks the kiss to lean back onto the counter and look up at me. I imagine her that way on my bed, propped up on her elbows, waiting for me to crawl up her body.

Now that the bow on her top is undone, I can see that the line of buttons extends all the way up to her neck. She looks so prim and proper, and it drives me fucking crazy. I just want to rip those buttons off, but the shirt probably costs more than most of my belongings combined. Instead, I carefully slip the first button out of its hole. She doesn't move, only stares up at me, so I undo a second one.

"You look like you're thinking again, Pickle."

Her hands fly up to my chest again, and she pushes me back a few inches, enough that she can stand up straight instead of leaning back to look me in the eye.

"I swear to God if you call me that again, I'm walking right out the door."

A smile stretches across my face, and I don't know how she does it. How she pushes everything away until she's the only thing left in my head. Before she knocked on my door, my head was so fucking dark . . . I'm not sure what I would have done.

"That sounds a little like someone is catching their breath."

I grip the counter on either side of her and push forward. Her arms bend until they're trapped between our chests. I lean in until our mouths are inches apart, until I can taste her breath.

Quietly, I ask. "You want me, Dylan?"

She sucks her bottom lip between her teeth for a second, and when she lets go, it's wet and rosy, and I want to pull it between my teeth, too.

"You don't have to have everything figured out. God knows, I don't. I'm just asking about right now, in this moment. Do you want me?"

Instead of trying to push me away again, the hands on my

chest smooth upward. Then slowly, she slides her hands around my neck until my chest is flat against that smooth, silky shirt.

"Of course I want you. Have you *seen* you?"

"I see *you*."

She swallows, and her eyes bore into mine when she replies, "Yeah, I think you do."

I pull away enough to pop open another button, revealing the top of her cleavage. She shifts closer, and she's soft everywhere I'm hard, and the friction turns my spine into a live wire.

"For the record, I still think this might be a bad idea."

"For the record, I think it's the best idea I've ever had."

Her fingers trace lightly back and forth over the back of my neck, and I'm a ticking time bomb. Each stroke makes my fuse a little bit shorter, and I need to get those buttons undone before I forget about not destroying her shirt.

With an agility and speed that I was missing today in practice, I have the rest of her buttons undone and her shirt open in seconds. Her bra is this pale purple that cups her small breasts perfectly. Her narrow waist flares out into curvy hips covered by a snug skirt. I can't decide whether I want the skirt off or hiked up around her waist.

Deciding on the latter, I grip her hips and lift her up onto the kitchen counter. There's a certain appeal in seeing her still in those fancy clothes, but pulled and bunched and revealed however I can manage. I love to see her go from pristine to disheveled all because of me. Slowly, I push the edge of her skirt up her thighs. When I can't move it any farther, I say, "Lift up your hips."

She wets her bottom lip, and my cock twitches at the sight. Her nerves just kick up my adrenaline. I give her a few seconds to adjust, taking two steps back to look at her.

She snaps her legs closed and sits up straight. "What are you doing?"

"Trying to decide exactly what I want to do to you."

She hunches over, shaking her head and laughing under her breath. "It's like you're trying to give me a heart attack."

"I don't want to give you a heart attack. I want to make you come. The question is just how."

She tilts her head to the side and blinks at me. "How are you so comfortable with this?"

I don't think she wants the real answer to her question . . . that I've been doing this for a very long time, since before I was really even old enough to understand half of what I was doing.

"I just know what I want, what I like. And if you'll let me, I'll help you figure that out, too. You want that?"

Tentatively, she nods. I cross to her again and slide my hands up her thighs to where I left off with her skirt.

"So, tell me what you like, Dylan Brenner."

"I don't know."

I give a light pinch to her thigh, and she yelps.

"Tell me what you like. Don't think. Don't worry about what you *should* like."

"I liked what we did Friday."

I slip my hand underneath her skirt, all the way around to cup her ass.

"Which part?"

"Uh . . . all of it."

I dig my fingers into the fleshy curve of her butt.

"Be specific."

"You're, um, a pretty fantastic kisser."

Of all the things I want to do to her, kissing is the blandest option, but it's a place to start. I use the hand on her ass to pull her to the very edge of the counter. Her legs spread wider to accommodate my body, and her skirt stretches around her thighs. I cover her mouth with mine and press our hips together. The only thing between us is my shorts and her underwear, and I can feel the heat of her. Her mouth opens on a gasp, and I take my chance to taste her.

She makes these quiet little noises of pleasure that send my blood pumping faster. Her tongue pushes into my mouth, and her fingers tangle in my hair. I rock my hips into hers, and I'm lined up just right so that I could slide right into her if there weren't any fabric in the way. I thrust forward, wanting to be closer to that heat, and pull her legs up to wrap around my waist.

I lean my forehead against hers. "Tell me what else you like."

She breathes against my mouth, and with her eyes still closed, she says, "Your hands in my hair."

I grin. "I like that, too." I pick up the braid laid over her shoulder and pull off the band wrapped around the end. "I love your hair." It's golden and wild and hints at what I think is hiding beneath that laced-up exterior. "The night we met I couldn't decide which I liked more . . . the idea of pulling on this braid as

I fucked you or undoing it and watching it fall all around you as you rode me."

She moans quietly, and I give the braid a quick tug before I start separating it.

"What . . ." She pauses, swallows, and begins again. "What do you like?"

I bury my hands in her hair and drag her lips up to mine, grinding my hips into hers. "I like the way you blush when I talk about what I want to do to you. I like when you pull on my hair, too. I like when you dig your nails into my skin without even realizing you're doing it. I like having your legs wrapped around me."

She clears her throat. "I mean . . ." She slides one of her hands between us and down to cup me through my shorts. "What do *you* like?"

I drop my head to her shoulder and drag in a labored breath. I push forward into her hand because I just can't help it. She strokes her hand up the length, and I attack her neck with my mouth. Suddenly impatient, I kiss my way down to the valley between her breasts, and nip one curve when she squeezes my erection.

She slides down off the counter, and I step back to make room, but only just enough. She reaches beneath my waistband and wraps her small hand around my dick.

"Tell me," she says, and I fucking love that she's turned the tables on me. "Tell me what you want."

The last thing I want to do is stop her, but part of me thinks she's doing this on purpose. If she focuses on other people, on what they want, she never has to decide for herself.

"I don't know if you're ready for what I want, baby."

Her eyes are wide and even though she probably knows I'm right, she asks anyway. "What?"

"I want to bury my hands in your hair while you take me in your mouth. I want to see those perfect, rosy lips wrapped around my cock. I want to tell you every dirty thing I imagine doing to you, and then I want to do whatever you'll let me do."

She licks her lips and fuck.

Fuck.

I'm so hard it's painful, and her grip is too light, too still.

"Um," she mutters.

"Told you it was too much."

She's got this determined look in her eyes, even as she looks terrified. And I almost want to see how this plays out, see how far she's willing to go. But considering she's the only thing in my life right now that doesn't make me feel like shit, I don't want to scare her off too fast.

And I don't want this to just be about me.

I kiss her on the cheek, and then pull her hand out of my shorts.

My dick fucking hates me, but it will keep until I've got her comfortable.

"Wait, I—"

"Later," I answer. "I believe I promised you something else."

I gather her skirt up and drag it up to her waist, then I lift her up onto the counter again. I lean over and kiss her inner thigh as I curl my fingers around the waistband of her dark blue thong. I groan because I wish I'd gotten a look at her ass in it before I put her up on the counter.

Another time, I tell myself.

Impatient, I drag the scrappy piece of fabric down her legs and shove it in my pocket. Dylan's legs stiffen, but I place a hand on each thigh to hold her open for me.

"You asked me what I want. This is what I want. I've been fucking dying to taste you. I want to make you do more than breathe. I want you to scream for me."

It's more than that, though.

I want to make her come so hard that for the rest of her life, she remembers me anytime someone touches her. I'm going to leave my mark on her perfect body, beneath the skin where she'll never get me out.

I want to ruin her for anyone else.

And I'm pretty damn good at ruining things.

I drop to a knee to get a better angle to do just that, but before I even touch her, the front door bangs open, and I hear Torres and Brookes heading our way.

Chapter 12

Dylan

His mouth is so close to me, and I can feel his breath. Henry never did this, and even though I'm terrified and self-conscious, I feel greedy. Henry and I didn't exactly have an explosive sexual relationship. It was . . . normal. Regular.

Whatever else Silas Moore might be . . . regular, he is not.

Just the anticipation of his mouth down there puts most of the sex I had with Henry to shame. My eyes are squeezed shut, and I'm in danger of biting straight through my bottom lip when Silas jerks back and stands up.

I whimper, wondering if he's going to just keep playing these games with me until I'm so far gone that I let him do whatever he wants to me.

And there's a real danger I will let him do *whatever* he wants to me.

Then he pulls me down off the counter, and I stumble into

him, my legs too numb and unprepared to stand. My skirt is up around my waist, and he's just begun pulling it down over my rear when two guys walk in the kitchen.

For a few seconds, I don't do anything. My mind starts screaming at me to move long before my body actually manages the action. I dive behind Silas at the same time that he steps over to cover me.

"Oh my God," I mutter as I try to get my shaking hands to button up the shirt that had been wide open when they walked in.

One of the guys is the Hispanic guy who'd been walking around without a shirt at the party. The other is a super-tall black guy who's staring at Silas with an expression that makes me wither, and it's not even directed at me.

The first guy, Torres, I think, was his name, says, "Ah, man. What did we say about sex in the kitchen? Anywhere else but the kitchen, dude."

I nearly rip the button right off my blouse. I wouldn't have had sex with him in the kitchen. *Would* I? Oh God, what I was going to let him do was hardly any better.

Silas is right . . . I do feel a bit like I've been suffocating. I think that's part of why the breakup with Henry didn't upset me as much as it should have. We'd been together so long, and our families loved the idea of us together, and it started to feel like my future was already written in stone. He would propose, I'd say yes, we'd have kids, and get old, and that would just be it. The end.

Normal.

Thinking back on that now, I almost want to cry with relief that he ended things. Because I don't want to be normal.

But just because I was feeling trapped isn't a good enough reason to go jumping off the first cliff I see.

Silas's other roommate speaks next, and his voice is low and reproachful. "You really think that's the best way to deal with this?"

Silas shakes his head. "It's not what you think it is, Zay."

What does he think it is? And what *actually* is it? Because I'm not sure I know myself. We'd made some kind of weird bargain, and I knew what I was doing for him . . . sort of. But I was still a little unclear exactly what he was doing for me.

Other than turning me into a hormonal, lecherous mess.

"I told you. I fucking *told* you that you do this to yourself."

Silas drops his head, and instinctively I place my hand on his back in support. They might not see it, but I know how torn up he is over this. He was so different today. I could be imagining it, but I think Silas stands up a little straighter under my touch.

"Listen—"

"No. I watched you fuck yourself over this weekend. We all watched it today at practice. I don't know if you've just stopped caring or what, but you're bad for the team."

I peek around Silas's back just in time to see the way those words contort his expression. And I say something. Because that's who I am. I'm the girl who says something. Maybe not for myself, I don't always know how to speak up for me, but for others? That's what I *do*.

"This is the exact opposite of what he needs right now."

His roommate, Zay, glances at me, and if possible his expression turns even colder.

"No offense, but I don't think what you were giving him is what he needs, either."

My mouth drops open, and I see Silas stepping forward out of the corner of my eye and I throw out an arm to stop him.

Then I give my best diplomatic smile and say, "No offense, but you don't *know* me. And I don't think you know your friend all that well, or you'd know that he cares a lot. And he's already on his knees and doesn't need you pushing him down farther."

Torres snorts and says, "On his knees, was he?"

I skip straight over embarrassed to furious.

"No wonder he's spiraling out of control. Clearly he doesn't have any support from his so-called friends. One of you just wants to make jokes and the other wants to yell at him. Both of which are only going to make things worse!"

"Listen," Zay says. "I'm sure you're a nice girl. And you obviously mean well, but I think you're overestimating why he brought you here. You might think you're here to support him while he's upset, but trust me, if we hadn't walked in, you would have been gone the minute he was done with you."

"Brookes." Silas's voice is hard, and when he lays a hand on my shoulder, I realize I'm trembling. "Lay off. This has nothing to do with you."

"You want me to go in the other room so you can finish dragging this girl down with you?"

"Brookes. I mean it. *Lay. Off.*"

I know as soon as the other guy opens his mouth where this is heading. Right as Brookes says, "Fuck you," I slide in front of Silas and place a hand on his still bare chest to stop him from barreling over there and starting his third fight in less than a week.

"Hey," I say. His chest is pushing forward against my hand, but not enough to move me like I know he could. "Hey. Look at me. Getting angry at him won't change the fact that you're angry at yourself."

He glares over my shoulder. "Maybe not. But it will take my mind off it."

I grab his jaw and make him look at me. "We made a deal. You have to listen to me or none of this works. Getting angry at him doesn't fix anything, so let it go."

He lets out a harsh breath, and under my hand, he grinds his teeth together.

"Fine." His eyes shift from me to his two roommates, and I let my hand drop away from his face. I go to move, but he rests a hand at my waist, keeping me close. Then he says to his friends, "I fucked up today. I know that. I knew it even as it was happening. And I'm gonna figure my shit out. I promise."

That was actually a pretty mature almost-apology.

My heart clenches for a moment because I can feel the desperation buzzing around him. He does have issues. And I don't love that his first inclination is always to get angry, but there's something there. I can't quite put my finger on it, but even with the violence and the issues and the dangerous sex appeal . . . there's something about him.

I believe in him.

His friends don't say anything, and when I turn to look at them over my shoulder, they're leaving the kitchen. But Silas apparently isn't done.

"Isaiah." His friend turns. "I *am* sorry, but I will kick your ass if you can't mind your own business."

I sigh, and think, *baby steps.* His friend nods his head thoughtfully and exits the kitchen without a word. I relax and breathe easy for the first time since his roommates walked through the door.

Silas pushes some of my hair behind my ear, and I glance up.

The look in his eye flattens me, twists me up, and wrings me out. A girl could read all kinds of things into the look he's giving me.

"Thank you," he says. "You were right. That would have made things ten times worse."

"That's what friends do."

That look disappears. And I'm both incredibly relieved and a little sorry to see it go.

"So . . . what's the plan?" he asks me.

For possibly the first time in my life, I am completely without a plan. I've got no backup, no safety net below me in case I screw things up. And I can't decide if it's more exhilarating or terrifying.

He must get where my head is at because he clarifies: "Our deal. What do we do first?"

It's hard to think with him this close to me, and I'm still a little too caught up in what we almost did as part of that *deal.*

"I answered your question. So now it's my turn."

He doesn't look happy, but he shrugs, and I figure that's as close as I'm going to get to a go-ahead.

"You asked me what I'm afraid of . . . now I want to hear your answer." He opens his mouth, and I cut him off. "And I don't mean getting kicked off the team. I want to know what's behind that . . . what happens if you do get kicked off the team? Why is that the worst thing that could happen?"

The stare he pins me with is dark and clouded, and his jaw is clenched so tight it might as well be wired shut. And I take pity on him.

"You don't have to tell me right now. But that's part of this, Silas. If you're not willing to eventually let me in, there's no point in me sticking around. Think about it."

"I don't need to think about it. I'll do what I have to, but . . ."

"But you need a little time. I get that. We'll start small."

"With what?"

I think for a moment and then ask, "What are you doing tomorrow?

The expression that pulls at his face is excruciating.

"Nothing. I'm suspended from practice for a week."

"Good. Then I've got an idea. I'll pick you up at eight forty-five in the morning. Wear something that you don't mind getting messed up."

I turn to leave, but I get precisely two steps away before he catches my hand and pulls me to a stop. His thumb rubs over my knuckles once, and then he lets me go.

"He's right, you know. I will pull you down with me."

I lift my chin and reply, "If I go down, it will be because I jumped, not because you made me fall."

He shakes his head and laughs once under his breath.

"I don't even know what that means."

I want to tell him that that's exactly what he's been doing. Whatever it is that he's worried about has him so messed up, so afraid that he's going to fail that he's sabotaging himself. Self-fulfilling prophecy. But I think he's been preached at enough for the day, so I just smile and say, "See you tomorrow."

Hopefully. Provided my father doesn't lock me in my old bedroom and never let me out. I'm almost out of the kitchen when Silas calls out again.

"Dylan?"

I turn.

"He was wrong about the other thing, though."

"What other thing?"

"If they hadn't walked in . . . I wouldn't have been done with you. Once never would have been enough."

I leave.

I leave before I give in to the need to touch him again, to coax *that look* back to life. I leave before I fulfill my own prophecy and dive headfirst into something that could ruin me. Ruin us both.

It's not until I'm climbing back into my car that I realize that I didn't get my underwear back.

I drop my head against the steering wheel and groan. So much for keeping things simple. "You are in so much trouble, Dylan Brenner."

And trouble's name is Silas Moore.

"YOUR FATHER ISN'T here."

That's the first thing Mom says upon opening the door when I arrive for dinner that night. I let out a breath and allow my rigid posture to relax. I changed clothes before coming over because I couldn't touch my shirt or skirt without remembering the way Silas had pushed my clothes aside. I'm at my most comfortable in flowy skirts, oversized shirts, and sandals. But in my parents' world (and Henry's world), I got used to slacks, pencil skirts, and fancy blouses. Mom sweeps her eyes down my form, and she doesn't say anything, so I assume my black pants and cap sleeve top meet her expectations.

She doesn't work, unless you count serving on various boards and charities, but even at home, she's always dressed in business attire. I step inside the house. My heels click against the familiar shiny hardwood floor. Even after all these years, being in this house still feels a little like being in a hotel. Everything is a little too polished, a little too decorated, a little too clean to feel like home. Or at least the kind of home that I see in movies and read in books, a place where you're at ease and feel comfortable and safe. I've never really had that kind of home, not even now that I live on my own.

My roommate, Antonella, is even more of a perfectionist than I am. I organize everything into boxes and shelves and drawers. She's the same, only armed with a label maker and a tendency to color-code . . . well, everything. I was really lucky to meet her in my history class the year before last. We sort of gravitated toward each other because we were both quiet, serious, and studious. I've branched out a little from that . . . found things I like doing outside of school, but Nell is still all about class, class, and more class. She takes an ungodly number of them, and our roommate bonding only consists of doing homework in the same room.

I follow Mom into the kitchen with its sleek, modern lines, stainless steel, and professional equipment.

"Where is Dad?" I ask as she checks on the food she's keeping warm in the oven.

"His flight had a slight delay, but he should be here soon."

I nod, grateful for the tiny reprieve to continue thinking about how best to approach the conversation of my arrest with him.

"Is the table already set?" I ask. It would be good to have something to do.

"It is. I'll admit, I've been a little bored with your father gone. I actually set the table nearly an hour ago just to pass the time."

I laugh because even though she's not my birth mom, she might as well be. We're alike in so many ways.

"Do you want to practice your speech on me?" she asks.

I pull my lips up into a smile that feels too frail. "No thanks. I've thought through it so many times that it's kind of playing on a constant loop in my head."

"Then we'll talk about something else." I love her. So much. Sure, she's not the homey, coddling mom that I dreamed of having as a kid. She never snuggled beside me in bed or played board games with me or let me eat cookies before dinner. But she's kind. And I've never met a more levelheaded, understanding person in all my life. All I ever wanted was to be like her, but if this week is any indication, levelheaded is going to take some work.

"How's Henry?"

She is stubborn, though. Something I could live without.

"We haven't spoken."

"Oh, honey. You realize this is just a phase, don't you? It happens in every relationship, especially ones that begin as young as yours did. He's a man and he's young and stupid, and he thinks he needs to see what's out in the world in case he's missing something. But he'll see soon that there's no one out there better for him than you."

I don't answer. He might decide I'm what's best for him, but one of the few things I do know right now is that Henry breaking up with me was the best thing that could have happened. It's not that Henry was bad. He's a really nice guy, and I could certainly do far worse, but . . . he's just Henry. And I don't want to live the rest of my life with someone who is *just* anything.

"You're handling it really well, darling. I'm proud of you. It shows how mature you really are."

She's not referring to the arrest, of course. Because that's the opposite of handling anything really well. She means emotionally . . . or the lack of emotion anyway.

I was here when Henry broke up with me. He'd asked to come over and we'd sat on the wooden porch swing outside while he explained that he didn't feel the same way about me as he used to. When it was over, I went inside and told Mom, and I think she expected me to lose it. To break down and sob right there in the foyer. Instead, I'd gone into the dining room to set the table like I always did when I stopped by for dinner.

"Thanks, Mom."

"I know you said you didn't want to talk about it, but you can tell me if this protest business was about Henry. You've always been so mature for your age, and your father and I both understand that emotions can make people behave erratically."

"It's not about Henry," I tell her.

He was just the catalyst, the first string to snap before all the rest followed. I wasn't lying when I told her that my explanation was running on a loop in my head, but what I didn't tell her is that there are other words I can't get out of my head, words that keep drowning out that practiced speech.

I think you're starting to suffocate.

I hear the front door open then, and the thump of my father's briefcase being dropped by the door. Mom places a cool hand on my cheek and leans in to press a kiss against my forehead.

"You'll be fine. You know your father loves you."

As he enters the kitchen, he's loosening a maroon tie. He's old enough that his hair is silvering on the sides, but his face still looks young and healthy. I don't know how he does it with all the stress from work. Nor do I really even have a great grasp on what "work" is. All I know is that he inherited money from his father, and then invested it in a number of places that paid off. I know he owns significant shares in a number of different companies, still invests in the occasional start-up, and serves on multiple boards, including the board of regents at Rusk.

He kisses Mom on the cheek and then says, "Dylan," in a quiet greeting before kissing me on the forehead.

"How was New York?" Mom asks.

"Hot," he answers. "Miserable, actually."

She clucks her tongue and helps him remove his suit coat.

"You go get settled at the table. Dylan and I will bring in the food."

She goes off to hang up his coat, and I grab a potholder to start removing the food from the oven. Mom is one of those women who won't serve the food in the same container they make it in. Instead she lays it all out on nice plates and platters like every night is a dinner party.

Another thing I'll never get used to. That's just something else to wash when dinner is over, and for what? To look pretty for the two minutes before people start digging in? It's not until after we do just that, ruining the presentation of Mom's food, that Dad speaks up.

"Well, then, Dylan. Let's hear your case."

I take a deep breath and start in.

"I know you're disappointed. I behaved in a way that didn't reflect well on myself, this family, or the cause for which I was advocating. I'm not giving you excuses because I don't have one. I made a mistake, a rash decision, and though I regret it, I've learned from it. I let frustration and impatience rule me rather than acting reasonably and intelligently. And I'm sorry."

It comes out how I rehearsed it, to a T.

"That's all well and good, sweetheart, but it doesn't tell me why."

My brows furrow, and I try not to frown. "I let frustration—"

"You've said your speech, Dylan. It was well thought out and respectful. Thank you for that. Now let go of the pretense and give me a real explanation."

My lungs are filled with dust, I can't seem to inhale or exhale. Having an incredibly intelligent and resolute businessman for a father really sucks sometimes.

"I don't have one." Or rather . . . I don't have one that won't make me sound like an ungrateful, spoiled brat. So what if being part of this family is a little suffocating? It's still a family. It's still something that wasn't supposed to be in the cards for me, but somehow these two people who literally have enough money to have anything they want . . . somehow they wanted me. And I'm not going to drag that through the mud. Not after all they've done for me, the things they've given me that I could never have dreamed of having.

I *want* to be perfect for them. That's all I've ever wanted . . . to make sure they never for one second regret taking me in.

"Sweetheart," Mom says, laying a hand on Dad's arm. "You know she has a lot on her plate right now." Henry. She's blaming it on Henry. "Perhaps she was feeling frustrated about other things and misplaced those feelings."

I shouldn't let her talk for me, I should say what I'm feeling. That's what Silas would tell me to do.

I close my eyes. Now is not the time to think about him. He is so far away from this world, this life I have here . . . it's not even funny. If I bring him into this place, even in my thoughts, one of two things will happen.

This place will win, and I'll drown in guilt over the things I've done with Silas.

Or Silas will win. The new, unstable me will win, and it will shatter this last remaining façade I have. My parents will know just how far I am from living up to their expectations.

And neither of those is something that I want. So, as of this moment, I put up a wall, and refuse to let either world cross into the other.

Besides . . . Dad is still going, so I'm not out of the woods here yet. He says, "Be that as it may, she has to think about the repercussions of her actions." He turns to me. "We've raised you to think for yourself, to be smart. And while I understand and respect your feelings about the shelter, you have to remember that I work with the city council on a regular basis. Your mother went to college with the mayor's wife. It's one thing to participate in a group protest, I won't deny you that, but to single yourself out in such a way as you did, puts this entire family in a difficult position."

I hadn't even thought about that. It's a small world in the elite circle my parents run in. Of course they would know all the big players in town, the ones who control where the money goes.

"You're right. I didn't think about the ramifications of what I was doing. I just . . . I wanted to make a difference. And this is something happening in our backyard, not some big political movement in another state or another country. It's so close, and I let passion cloud my judgment." And even though I make a habit of not talking about my childhood, of pretending like it was another life, another world, I mention it then. "And I know what it's like not to have the basic things, not to have a home. That's hard enough; it shouldn't have to get harder for those people."

I try and fail at keeping the emotion out of my voice. My parents respect logic, not feelings. And one has no place with the other.

"You can't fault her for being compassionate and for acting instinctively, Richard. That's how you do business, and she's just emulating her father. And really, as far as mistakes go, it's a small one in comparison to what other children her age get up to. And people talk, I happen to know for a fact that several of the councilors' kids have been in trouble for far worse. They'll understand."

"Yes, but I hold Dylan to a higher standard. She's better than other kids her age, more aware."

I'm not. I'm just better at pretending.

"And she's met that standard for years without any issues. She's not an employee, Richard. She's your daughter."

Dad lays down his knife, and it clangs against his plate. He frowns down at the food that he's only really been pushing around since the conversation began.

"So what do you propose I do? Let her off without any form of reprimand?"

I speak up then. "I decided to sign up for the Renew Project that the university is sponsoring, the one where students are repairing homes for the underprivileged and elderly in town. It's three days a week until school starts, and then every Saturday through the end of September. I thought it might be a good way to channel my frustrations into something positive. To give back."

"There," Mom says. "That sounds like a perfectly respectable way to redeem her actions."

Dad frowns, but says, "Fine. I suppose that works."

Under the table, I unclench my fists, the indents of my fingernails smarting on my palms. With that settled, Mom picks up the conversation for the rest of dinner, asking Dad questions about his trip, telling him about the few days she spent without him and how miserable she was.

And for the first time, I look at the two of them and wonder if they love each other. Or if they're just like Henry and I were . . . a good fit.

I think then about my birth mother. I never think about her. There's not much point since she died before I was put in foster care. But I can't help but wonder now how different my life would have been with her. Would I know myself better? Would I even *be* myself?

It's too much to think about. And it can't change anything anyway. That part of my life is long gone.

When I'm getting ready to leave and head back to my apartment an hour later, Dad wraps an arm around my shoulders and pulls me in close. "I don't like being disappointed in you."

Something pinches in my chest, and somehow, even though he's hugging me tight, that one sentence is the worst moment of the whole night.

"I don't, either."

Even after he lets me go, it still feels like his arms are constricting around me, like there are these bands that are always there, but now they've gotten just a little bit tighter, a little bit more noticeable.

I try to forget about them all the way home, try not to feel them as I crawl into bed. But there are too many things I'm trying to forget, and I can't seem to block any of them out effectively.

And Silas was right.

I so badly need to breathe.

Chapter 13

Silas

Brookes is in the kitchen when I head downstairs in the morning. There are few things that can make me get up this early in the morning. Football is one of them. Dylan is apparently another.

I walk past him for the pantry, where I dig out a couple of protein bars for breakfast. Dylan should be here any minute, so I don't have time for anything more.

"So, I guess you're not coming to practice," Zay says.

I look down at the old jeans I'd pulled on instead of athletic clothes.

"Coach told me not to." I peel open the wrapper on one of the bars and take a bite.

"For how long?"

I shrug. "A week."

He whistles. "And two games?"

"At least. He threatened worse if I don't get my shit together."

"I'm sorry, man. I should have said it yesterday. I can't imagine how you're feeling."

"Not good."

He stands and takes his dishes to the sink.

"What *are* you doing today, if you're not allowed at practice?"

"Something with Dylan. I don't really know."

"Dylan?"

"The girl who handed you your ass yesterday."

He crosses his long arms over his chest and surveys me.

"You're seeing her again? You guys a together or something?"

"Nah. Not really. She's, I don't know, a preppy rich kid sowing some wild oats. I doubt she sticks around long."

The words feel wrong in my mouth even before I say them. But just because I have to open up to her, doesn't mean I want to spill my guts to everyone. It's better if everyone thinks she is just another girl.

But as usual, Isaiah Brookes is a hard man to fool.

"Normally it's you that doesn't stick around long."

I throw away the empty wrapper for one bar and tear open another. I don't reply because lie or not . . . he's right, and I don't know why this time is different. My deal with Dylan isn't a relationship . . . I don't want or know how to have one of those, but I also hope this deal sticks. I have to make it work not just for football, but to keep her around. I can't think about why that's important right now, but it is.

"Is she part of this? Whatever mess you've got going on?"

"No. God no. She's just about the only damn thing that's *not* part of it."

The doorbell rings, and I finish scarfing down the last of my breakfast.

"That's her. Do me a favor? Tell Coach I'm working shit out."

I'm almost out of the kitchen when he calls out my name.

"Yeah?"

He says, "Be careful."

"I plan on staying far away from all kinds of trouble."

"I meant with this girl. I don't want it to fuck your head up more if it goes south."

I don't have a reply to that, so I just nod instead. I stride the last few feet to the front door and pull it open. Dylan pulls off her sunglasses and gives me a small smile. She's wearing a blue tank top that's almost the color of her eyes, and her thick hair is pulled back and away from her face. I can see the straps of a sports bra over her shoulders, and it has her tits pushed up and together. A pair of worn, perfectly fit jeans hug her hips just right.

She looks comfortable, and she's not trying to impress me. But I'm impressed anyway. Her eyes scan my own attire, and she asks, "You won't mind if those clothes get ruined, right?"

"What exactly do you have planned for us today, Pickle?"

Her eyes narrow. "I'm going to get you back for that. Just wait."

I step out onto the porch and pull the door shut behind me. "I look forward to seeing you try."

The car she's parked on the street out by my mailbox is a sleek steel gray number with smooth curves and money written all over it. I glance at my busted old truck in the driveway and decide that our vehicles pretty accurately represent the differences between us.

I can't help but run a hand along the car in admiration as I round the front to get in the passenger seat. I wouldn't mind running an appreciative hand over the car's owner, either, but she's been careful to keep a few feet between us from the moment we exited the house. When I climb into the car, though, it's small enough that my elbow touches hers on the middle console.

"So what has Dr. Dylan prescribed for the day?"

She pulls out onto the road and heads away from the university.

"You can't be mad."

Not what I want to hear this early in the morning.

"Shit. You're not taking me to some kind of crappy self-help thing, are you?"

"Not self-help, no. But there is helping involved."

The mysterious smile she gives me is fucking sexy, and I reach over and trail my finger over her bare shoulder. She shivers, and I shift my hand up to brush across her neck, too.

"You're going to make me have a wreck."

I glance out the windshield. "You're coming up on a red light."

When she slows to a stop, I lean across the console and kiss the place where her neck meets her shoulder. She shifts away as soon as my lips touch her skin.

"Silas." Damn. I've heard that tone before. I look up, but I don't move away. If there's anything I am, it's stubborn, and I've not had nearly enough of her to be done yet. She says, "I've not exactly handled this in the best way."

"Then go back to my place, and we can handle things right. Or pull over, I'm not picky."

She rolls her eyes, and puts a hand on my shoulder to push me away. I go, but not happily.

"That's not what I mean, and you know it. Clearly, I'm attracted to you." Well, at least she's admitting it out loud. "But the thing is . . . we're not dating. And we're not going to date. So I think it's better if we keep things between us as platonic as possible."

"What if 'platonic as possible' is not at all platonic?"

"It has to be."

"I think you're confusing dating with being in a relationship. Dating can be casual. Dating is low pressure. *Dating* isn't off the table."

Fuck. I have to be addicted to this girl or something because I have never *ever* actually brought up the idea of dating a chick. Usually, it's them who brings it up. Or they just assume we're dating after one hookup. I haven't even slept with this girl, and I'm already falling all over myself to do something I never do.

"And what happens then? We go on one *date*. We sleep together. And then you're done dating me?"

"I told you, Pickle. Once is never going to be enough where you're concerned."

"Great. So maybe we see each other a handful of times. That might sound appealing to you, but not to me." She stumbles over the last words, barely gets them out.

"Why do you always insist on lying to me? It *is* appealing to you. You just don't want to admit it." She looks at me like an animal who has been cornered, like she knows she's caught.

Then a horn sounds behind us. The stoplight is green, and Dylan rushes to push the gas and direct the wheel.

I don't give her the opportunity to backtrack or change the subject.

"I think I understand you, Dylan. You don't want a casual relationship with me because you've probably been taught all your life that that kind of relationship is wrong. Or you've been told it always ends up leaving you heartbroken after you get too invested. And maybe that is who you are. Maybe you're the kind of girl that can only be in serious relationships. Or maybe that's just the kind of girl you've told yourself you are. I bet you've never been in anything but long-term relationships."

She swallows and tightens her grip on the steering wheel, hiding her face from me as she turns the car onto another street.

"I'm right, aren't I? Come on. Tell me. How many relationships?"

She clears her throat and then with her chin up answers, "Two."

"And how long did they last?"

"A year and a half on the first, and . . ." She trails off.

"And?"

"Four years. And some change."

"*Damn.* Four years? You just turned twenty-one, and you're telling me you've spent over five years of that in serious relationships? You've probably been in a relationship since the moment you were allowed to date."

She shrugs, and I know I'm right.

"You might think you need to stay away from me because I'm not your usual relationship material, but I think that's exactly *why* you need me. You need to just have some fun. Be young for a little while before it's too late."

She sighs, flipping on her blinker with a little too much aggression, and turning onto another residential street.

"Okay."

For a moment I think I'm just hearing what I want to hear.

"Okay what?"

"Okay, I'll stop thinking so much."

I wait for her to pause at a stop sign, and then I lean over and kiss her. She makes a surprised sound in my mouth, but then she hums when I drag my lips over her once, then again.

Someone honks behind us, but this time they can fucking wait. I throw my middle finger up to the douche behind us and press her back against her seat just long enough to make sure she knows she's made a good decision.

I hear the car peel out around us, still honking, but I'm not about to let her run on me again.

When she's making those little breathy noises again, and her hands have left the steering wheel to clutch at my hair, I slowly pull back.

"I think we're already making tremendous advances in your therapy, Pickle."

The dazed look on her face lasts only a few seconds before she pushes me back over into my seat and says, "God, you're so arrogant."

I laugh and don't deny it.

She smooths her hair down and pulls away from the stop sign. She glances at me out of the corner of her eye every few seconds for the rest of the drive. Each look is like a shot of adrenaline and by the time she says, "We're here," it's all I can do not to pin her to the seat again.

She slows to a stop behind a truck parked on the side of the road. The street is lined with cars for several hundred yards ahead of us, and a group of people is gathered in a yard a couple of houses down.

"We're doing something with other people?" I sound like a whining kid because I'd thought I would have her to myself, that I could continue whittling down those walls of hers.

"Come on. We're running a little late, and we still have to check in."

I sigh and push open the door. As we get closer, I see tools and paint and hardware, and the picture begins to come together.

I loop an arm around her neck, and though she tenses, she doesn't push me away. I lower my mouth to her ear and say, "You're putting me to work."

"You want to be a better leader for your team. First step to being a leader is learning to put others before yourself. Besides . . . sometimes a little work is good for you."

"I can think of another way you could have put me to work that's much more enjoyable."

She does push me off then, but she's smiling.

"I'm not talking about you and your . . . You know. This kind of work is positive. We're helping people."

"My way is just another kind of helping. And I promise it would be a very positive experience for all involved."

"Just when I think I've got a handle on your ego, it gets even bigger."

I grin. "I thought we weren't talking about me and my you-know."

She shoves at my arm, barely moving me an inch. "Oh my God. You're terrible."

"Dylan?" She stops, and the smile drops from her face as she swivels her head to look at the guy who's stepped out of the group to stand before us on the sidewalk. Her easy demeanor disappears, and I can almost see her lacing herself up again, reining in her smile, her laugh, her posture. I even watch her pull her hands through her hair, as if she's trying to tame it into something more presentable.

"Uh, Henry. Hi."

Henry. The name sounds familiar, but I don't know the guy. His hair is all gelled, and I'm pretty sure he spent more time fixing it than every girl in the crowd. He looks like he's dressed for a tennis match, rather than construction, and he's wearing this pretentious smile that already annoys me.

"What are you doing here?" he asks.

Dylan is calm as she answers, but I can see tension in her face that wasn't there a few moments ago. "I called Kim this weekend, and asked if she still needed help. I thought you were too busy and decided not to do it."

He sinks his hands into the pockets of his shorts and jangles what I'm guessing are keys inside. "My schedule freed up unexpectedly."

It hits me then who this is. The ex. And damn it, I knew this would be the kind of guy she dated.

The kind of guys that are like a fucking magnet for my fists.

"Who's this?"

"Silas." I hold out my hand and when we shake, I might squeeze a little harder than necessary. He gives a satisfying flinch, and Dylan hooks her arm around my elbow and starts pulling me away.

"Come on. We need to check in."

"Nice to meet you, Henry." I throw him a grim smile and let her pull me away.

When we're halfway across the yard, she whispers, "You can be such an ass, you know that?"

"Me? I spoke to that guy for ten seconds, and I already know he's a giant douche. You dated that for four years?"

"He's nice."

I scoff. "First, I doubt that. Dude has spoiled dickwad practically written across his forehead."

"Silas, we're not talking about this now."

She steps away from me and up to a folding table where a teenager sits with a clipboard.

"Dylan Brenner," she says. "And a guest."

The kid pops her gum and looks over at me. "He'll need to fill out a release form."

She taps a stack of papers and holds out a pen. Dylan gives me an expectant look, and I hold back my groan. I fill out the damn form and pass it to the girl.

She blows a bubble, pops it, and then says, "Join the group. Greg will assign you your tasks."

That out of the way, I start in again, "So . . . he's *nice*. That's really the best you've got? You give him four years of your life because he says 'please' and 'thank you,' and you're scared just to date me?"

"Silas . . ."

"Seriously. Help me understand. Is it because he's rich?"

"Excuse me?" There's a vague warning ring in the back of my mind that I should shut my trap, but I can't let this go. I need someone to explain to me why guys like her ex get anything and everything they want just because they're labeled "good." What the fuck does that even mean?

"It's a valid question," I say.

"No, it's not because he's rich," she snaps. "It's because he doesn't punch people who make him angry. He doesn't drink or do drugs to deal with his problems. He cared about me. He didn't just want to have sex with me for a little while."

There are razor blades in my lungs, and when I suck in a breath, it tastes like fire. And I want it out, want to spit it back at her.

"If that's all I am, why bring me here? Why do you give a fuck at all?"

Her perfect lips hang open like she's shocked herself, and I can see something like regret blooming over her cheeks. I want to hate her. I want to storm off and walk the fuck home. I want to pull her to me, pry her lips open with mine, and take whatever that mouth will offer even if it's only insults and sour words.

The thing is . . . she's right. I know that's who I am. She's just the first person besides me to say it out loud. She starts to reply, but a voice from the front of the crowd calls everyone to attention. A middle-aged guy stands on a chair with a megaphone to amplify his voice.

"Hello. My name is Greg, and I want to thank you all for being here. Today we're working on the house of this young lady here." He gestures toward a tiny old woman standing on the ground next to him. Her skin is weathered and cracked like old leather, and when she waves, her flesh moves like it's not attached to her body. "Mrs. Baker has lived in this house for forty-nine years, and this morning we're going to be helping her make some repairs and renovations. She worked as a nurse at the local hospital until she retired ten years ago. She spent a lifetime giving to this community, and Mrs. Baker, we're delighted to be able to give a little back to you today."

"Silas," Dylan whispers next to me. I ignore her and focus on the guy in charge. I don't know why what she said makes me feel so shitty.

I am all of those things she mentioned. But I'm trying. Why else would I be here? But if that's the kind of guy she wants, fuck it.

I think what bothers me most is the idea that those things are all I am to her. I've always thought football was the great balancer in my life. It makes up for all the other things I'm not. But Dylan doesn't give a shit about football, and unless I get my act together, I won't even have that.

And what am I then? *Who* am I then?

Greg moves through the gathered crowd, splitting people into groups for different tasks, appointing leaders. I get put in a group with Henry, which is fucking perfect.

I hope he steps on a nail and gets tetanus.

Dylan is put in another, smaller group, and I'm beginning to think this little experiment is going to end with me being even more irrationally angry than I already am.

At least I'm given a cool job. Me and a few other guys are tearing down some rotting and warped siding from the front porch and replacing it with new wood. I'm given a crowbar and a hammer and told to go to town. And I do exactly that.

There's satisfaction in the creaking sound of the wood giving way. The nails groan as I use the crowbar to lever off the old siding. And when I encounter a few particularly stubborn boards I use the hammer to add some extra force.

I lose myself in the task, sweat beginning to trail down my back as I work. The sun glides higher into the sky, and pours light and heat down in smothering quantities. I strip away the bad wood piece by piece. Sometimes it crumbles in my hand, snaps or bends where it shouldn't. Then I'm left using my hands, my hammer, my foot—whatever I can to tear the stuff away until finally, I can see the framework beneath. All that's left are the studs to which we'll attach the new siding. When I'm done with my section, I move over to the next, where Henry has barely done half of what I've managed.

For a while we work in silence, and I forget he's even there. Then he asks, "So how do you know Dylan?"

I want so badly to say something to piss him off, some innuendo, but I know she wouldn't like that. And what I say could make her look bad, and I get the feeling she's one of those girls who are incredibly concerned with how other people see them.

Maybe that's why the idea of dating me seems so ludicrous to her.

As satisfying as it would be to piss the guy off, it's not worth pissing her off, too.

I shrug. "We ran into each other last week. Got to talking. Hit it off."

Okay. So maybe I'm not completely above implying that there's something between us. But it's less to piss him off, and more to make very clear that he has no hold on her anymore. If he thought he could do better than a girl like Dylan, the guy is a fucking moron, and he deserves to have that rubbed in his face a little.

"Hit it off?"

"Yeah. She's pretty spectacular. You don't meet girls like her every day."

Henry nods, pausing in his attempt to remove a stubborn board, and says, "Right."

I look at this guy, and it makes my blood burn hot that he had four years of her life. That he's *had* her, and I haven't. And I let my mouth get away from me. "And just between us, that girl is smoking hot. At first, she seemed a little, I don't know. Shy. Restrained. But when she loosens up . . . damn."

Henry tugs hard on the board, and his hands slip, sending his crowbar tumbling to the ground.

"Here. Let me."

I step in front of him and pry it off with one hard pull.

His expression looks like he's been run over a few times, and I figure I've made my point and can get started on replacing the siding in my section.

He may have had her for years, but I've got her now.

Or I'm going to. I'll prove to her that I'm worth her time. If I don't, I'm just as big a dumbass as he is.

Chapter 14

Dylan

finish the first task I'm on, helping to repair the handrail on the stairs at the back of the house. Greg assigns me to start removing some kind of creeping vine that's taken over one side of the house, and tells me to look around for a partner who's not busy. I find Silas at the water cooler, in the middle of pulling up his shirt to wipe at the sweat on his forehead.

I forget how to walk at the sight of his stomach. I just stop halfway across the yard and stare. It's not like I haven't seen it before. Totally got up close and personal with it (with a lot of him) yesterday. But there's something about seeing just a peek of it that unravels my brain. His jeans also hang perfectly on his hipbones, and I swear if I snapped a picture I could sell it to some magazine or clothing designer. He looks that good without even trying.

I watch him take a drink of water and I think for the hundredth time that I'm a jerk. I feel awful for what I said to him earlier. It's all I thought about while I worked. The way his expression locked up and he wouldn't look at me—I'm drowning in guilt. Here I am wanting to help this guy because I see something in him, something worth protecting and cultivating, and instead I stomp all over it.

And why? For *Henry*? To keep the walls up between my two worlds? Or maybe it's because where my jail buddy is concerned, my control is a frayed thread that could snap at the slightest provocation.

Maybe I want it to snap, and that terrifies me.

I take a deep breath and with my head down, march over to the water cooler. I spend a few moments filling up a cup to let myself adjust to his nearness, to the fact that he didn't move back even an inch when I stepped up beside him.

"How's it going?" I ask, my head still down.

"Fine. Though your ex has the upper-body strength of a *T. rex*."

I bark out a laugh and nearly drop my water. And I keep laughing because it's so true. When I moved into my apartment, Henry was completely useless. I cover my mouth while I struggle to get myself under control, and Silas's smile is so warm and gentle, it feels almost like our last conversation didn't happen.

With the sun beating down on his back, his hair seems more golden than normal, and he really is unfairly gorgeous.

"You still busy? I've got a new project that I need some help with."

My eyes are drawn to his Adam's apple again as he takes another drink. That freaking thing is going to be my downfall.

"No, I'm done. With my part anyway. Henry might be here until nightfall."

I close my eyes and bite back a smile. Feeling a little vindictive over an ex is normal, right? Totally valid.

"Come on, then."

I lead him back to the section of the house we're supposed to clear from vines. They've crept their way from a nearby tree, all the way up to the gutters. Silas whistles. "I think we're gonna need a ladder."

I nod. "I'll go see if I can find one."

He touches my shoulder to stop me. "I got it." Then just for a moment, he tucks a stray hair behind my ear, and his fingers linger on my neck. As he leaves, I can't help but wonder if this is what dating Silas would be like. Little touches. Warm smiles. Uninhibited laughter.

Could it be *good*? Could it be more than just mind-blowing kisses and miraculously talented hands? Am I crazy for even thinking that's a possibility?

I have to remember that Silas and I live by very different definitions, and *dating* would no doubt fall into those disparities.

I pull on one of the pair of gloves that Greg gave me and start clearing away the brush at the bottom of the house. I give an experimental tug on a grouping of vines. The thickest one holds fast, but I manage to grip a smaller one and pull a couple feet of it away from the house before it snaps, just leaving a piece of it in my hands.

I'm bent over at the waist tugging at the larger vine again when Silas returns.

"Bad news."

I glance up and he's staring at my butt. I straighten, but his eyes stay glued to a backside that I know is on the larger side because I don't really have the time or inclination to spend much time working out. And by much, I mean any.

"Bad news?" I prompt.

He looks up at me with a lopsided grin, completely unapologetic, and says, "All the ladders are being used, so we'll have to improvise."

"We can work on the stuff we can reach until one opens up."

"It might be a while," he says. "But I've thought of an alternative."

I raise my eyebrows in question.

"If you sit on my shoulders we should be able to reach pretty close to the top, enough that you could probably pull at the highest stuff."

"Is that why you were staring at me?" I don't say at my butt, because we both know what I'm talking about.

"I'm not sure that's a question you want me to answer in public."

Well, clearly my earlier outburst didn't faze him at all. Or if it did, he's not letting me see.

"Are you sure it's not better to wait for a ladder?"

"That doesn't sound better to me at all."

I try to ignore the flirting, not to take it too seriously, but he's gorgeous so it's more than a little difficult to keep a clear head.

"You're not going to drop me?"

"I'm not Henry. I think I can handle you, Pickle."

"You're never letting go of that, are you?"

"I could be persuaded."

Yeah. Not even touching that one.

"Let's just do this."

I grab his forearm and lead him around the back of the house to the steps and climb up two of those to give me a little extra height. He bends until he's practically resting on his heels, and then using our newly repaired handrail for a brace, I put one leg over his shoulder and then the other.

"Ready?" he asks. I keep a hold on the handrail and then tell him yes.

He stands like he's got twenty pounds on his shoulders instead of a whole person, and I lock my legs tightly around him, hooking my feet around his sides, and sinking my hands into his hair while I try to find my balance.

"Not how I pictured having my head between your legs for the first time."

I slap his shoulder hard, and he laughs. "Just being honest."

"Honesty is not one of your issues." I mean it to be a joke, but he stills beneath me, and I know I've brought up the memory of our earlier argument, and it must bother him, no matter how much flirtation he hides behind.

His arms lay against my calves and his hands hook over the top of my thighs to hold on, and he starts walking back to our work area. He lets me direct him to stand where I want him, and then with my legs squeezing tightly to hold myself in place, I reach up and begin to pull.

My first lump of freed vines falls all over Silas's head below me, and I make an idiot of myself apologizing again and again, like somehow he might know I'm really apologizing for everything.

"Just be glad it isn't poison ivy," he says.

I gasp because I didn't even think of that, nor do I know for sure it's not. Maybe that's why Greg gave me the gloves.

"Oh my God. What if it is?"

I lean over to look at his face, checking for reddening skin, and he has to reach out one of his bare hands to balance himself against the house in response to my movement. And now his naked hand is on the vine, and he's going to hate me by the time this day is over if I keep this up.

"It's not," he says.

"You're sure?"

"I'm sure. The stuff was all over the house and yard I lived in during high school."

I pause, going over his odd choice of words. *The house he lived in during high school.* Not a home. Not his childhood. He talks about it like I talk about growing up in foster care. And I wonder, maybe, if we have that in common. If maybe he wasn't quite as lucky as I was.

"Ask me a question," I say.

"Why?"

"Because I want to ask *you* one, but it's not my turn."

"Even though I didn't answer your last question?"

"Oh that one's still on the books. I'm just kind and generous and am willing to give you some time before I cash in."

He laughs and shakes his head, and his cheek rubs against the inside of my thighs. The movement makes something warm curl low between my hips, but it's doused seconds later when he asks his question.

"Fine. Why did you and Henry break up?"

I stiffen, but fair is fair. So I answer, "You'd have to ask him to know for sure, but he told me he just didn't feel the same way about me anymore."

"He broke up with *you*? Are you fucking kidding me?"

I shrug and pull on another vine.

"Well, I say good goddamn riddance."

I can't help my smile. "Bad Boy Rehab task number two—maybe try to cut back just *a bit* on the cussing."

He draws a thumb down the side of my thigh into the sensitive hollow at the back of my knee.

"I've got a dirty mouth, babe. No changing that. You'll just have to count it as part of my charm."

Charm. I resist the urge to snort. Charm is smooth and subtle. Silas Moore is a force of nature. A freaking avalanche. He doesn't have a subtle bone in his body.

I let the cussing go for now, and take my turn.

"Where are you from?"

"Nowhere that matters. Out in the middle of nowhere in West Texas."

"Where?" I try again.

"You wouldn't know it even if I told you. Between Odessa and Lubbock. The whole place is an ever-expanding pit of nothingness. Just dust and mesquite trees and deadbeats who always talk about leaving, but never do."

I swear to God, even with this question quid pro quo, getting information out of this man is harder than finding the perfect pair of jeans.

"What's the harm in just telling me where it is if I won't know?"

"Because I got out, Dylan. I'm one of the few, and I'm not going to spend my time talking about it like I never left. I'd rather pretend it never existed."

I swallow all the questions I still have and postpone them for another time. Asking questions doesn't work with him . . . at least not yet. The more I ask, the more he fights back. I guess we're kind of similar in that way. I don't like answering questions, either.

I need him to trust me first.

I concentrate on the vines again, and I develop a system where I pull out and to the right, so if anything falls it doesn't fall into his face. As I pull the vines away, they take the paint with them, leaving these patterns on the wood where the vines used to be. It looks almost like the vines are still there because every little leaf has left an imprint.

Silas might want to forget where he came from, but he's just like this house. He can strip away the town, his past, his upbringing, but they all leave marks behind. And like we'll do to this house when we're done, Silas has painted over those marks, and he doesn't want anyone else to know they're there.

Another thing we have in common.

Though I've never exactly fit comfortably in my new life, I try not to acknowledge my old life, either. I was in foster care from three years old on, and I don't remember anything before that. I suppose most people like me hit that stage in their teens or twenties when they're filled with a desire to know where they came from, why they were dealt the hand they have. They go looking up their birth parents or other family.

There's no point in that for me. Richard and Emily told me when they adopted me at nine years old. Even then, they'd treated me with a rational practicality, like I was an adult who just happened to be two feet shorter than them. They didn't give me all the specifics of my birth mom's death, but I think it was something messy. Drugs, maybe. Or suicide. If it were something like a medical issue or a car accident, they would have told me. I could ask now, and they would give me whatever information I want. But do I really want to know if it's that bad? I don't remember her. And it's easier that way.

I work in silence for a while, and eventually I notice that Silas has started working below me, too. He still has one arm wrapped around my shins in case I were to lose my balance, but with his right hand, he's pulling away vines and adding to my pile.

"There's an extra pair of gloves, you know."

He shrugs. *With me on his shoulders.* It's like he doesn't even feel me. "It will keep my calluses up until I get back to practice and back in the weight room."

I don't ask why he would *want* calluses. I just write it off as some sports thing that will never make sense to me.

"When do you go back?"

He blows out a breath. "Next week. As long as I'm certain I won't lose my head and fuck things up even worse for myself."

"How will you know you're ready?"

"I was going to have you tell me."

"Silas . . . I can't do that. How could I possibly know what's going on inside your head?" I leave off the implied *unless you tell me*.

"You're the authority on having your shit together. I figured you'd be able to recognize when I got there, or when I was on my way or something."

If only.

"Apparently I don't have things as together as I thought."

I'm working on a particularly strong vine. I tug hard, and my hand slips right out of the oversized glove I'm wearing. I swirl my arms, trying to right my balance, but it only makes it worse. I'm falling backward. We both are. I might scream something. Silas's hands clamp down on my thighs like bands of iron, but I'm still teetering.

It occurs to me to protect my head, just as Silas pitches himself forward onto his knees. He hits hard, and the jolt unseats me from his shoulders, but thanks to him I'm closer to the ground. And with reflexes practically in superhero range, he even manages to snag my hand as I'm falling. His hold keeps me up just enough that my bottom hits first, followed by my lower back, but my head never goes down.

Even with Silas's efforts, my tailbone hurts like a mother, and my lower back spasms painfully, so I let go of his hand and lay back against the grass. His knees have got to be hurting just as badly, but he still shifts to lean over me.

He blocks out the sun, and maybe it's the pain or maybe it's just him, but it feels like one of those rare total eclipses where you know you're not supposed to look because it can destroy your eyes or something, but it's so incredible that you can't help it.

"Dylan, are you okay?" He says the words slowly, and I get the feeling that he's already said them once, and I just tuned them out.

I blame the pain, but when the impulse rises, I let my hand stretch out and touch his face. Just a skim of my fingers across his jaw, but the jolt of energy I get from that small touch is nearly as debilitating as the jolt from my landing.

He closes his eyes, and without his gaze on me, I come back to my senses. I draw my hand away just as a few people round the edge of the house, drawn no doubt by the screaming that I probably (almost certainly) did a lot of. A few others lean over the roof to check out the situation, but my eyes automatically search out Henry to see the look of complete horror on his face at the sight of Silas hovering over me, one of his legs between mine.

I realize I still haven't answered Silas, so I say, "I'm okay," and use the same hand that had touched his face to push him back enough that I can sit up. My tailbone protests, but I grimace until it passes and ask, "Are your knees okay? That was crazy, but I'm pretty sure I would have cracked my head open if you hadn't done it."

He shifts back to sit beside me and closes his eyes as he slowly straightens out his legs. That's the only outward sign of feeling he shows, but I know it had to hurt badly to hit with the force of his own body, plus my extra weight.

I have a sudden horrible realization that something like that could *really* hurt him. Aren't knee injuries really common for football players? What if I've just ruined his career, ruined *his life?*

"Oh my God. Oh my God." I don't even feel any pain as I lurch up to my knees and grab his face. His eyes open to look at me, and they look dark, too dark, almost clouded by something. "Tell me you're okay. Is it your knee? *Knees?*" Oh God, what if I've done something to both his knees? He doesn't say anything and there are fireworks of panic exploding one after another in my chest. "I'll go get my car. We'll get you to the hospital. Ice! I'll also get ice from Mrs. Baker before we leave. And pillows. To prop up your legs in the car. I'm so, *so* sorry. Just . . . I'll be right back. Don't move. I'm so sorry."

I start to stand, and my legs wobble like a newborn colt. Just as I get them steady, Silas tosses his head back and laughs.

It's only then that I notice the full audience we've gained, and at Silas's reaction, they all begin to laugh quietly, too.

"This better mean you're okay." I point a threatening finger at him. "Because you're not allowed to laugh if you're actually hurt."

He holds a hand to his abdomen and laughs even harder.

God, he's such a jerk.

A really handsome jerk, who kind of, sort of sacrificed himself for me, and looks even more gorgeous when he laughs. A laugh, by the way, that's low and throaty and pretty much makes my ovaries melt.

I know when I'm fighting a losing battle. It's a sensation I've felt at many a meeting or protest. And this battle with Silas, he's winning by a landslide.

Chapter 15

Silas

I don't mean to laugh, especially because my knees do hurt like a bitch, but her panicked determination to wheel me away to a hospital after a measly fall is just so damn cute.

If the same thing had happened to me on the football field, I would have been called a pansy already and told to get up and walk it off. I decide to do just that, and when I bend my knees to stand, pain spears through the joints. My legs are stiff, too, like I'm caked in drying cement. I must wince because Dylan is kneeling by me in seconds, her blue eyes intense on me.

"You *are* hurt. Damn it, Silas!"

I can't remember if I've ever heard her cuss or not. Those words sound better from her lips than I think they ever have.

"I'm fine. Just a little stiff. It will go away."

"How do you know?"

I give her a look. "I have some experience hitting the ground with considerable force."

"Smartass." I *really* like it when bad words come out of that good girl mouth. "What can I do?"

"Just help me up."

She crawls underneath my arm, but she's not strong enough to help me up, and it's taking most of my willpower just to bend my knees. Putting pressure on them to lift myself up isn't happening. It's the project leader, Greg, who takes hold of my other arm, and together they help me up.

I shut my eyes against a pain so sharp, it feels like my nerves are rubbing raw against my bones. Dylan is right up against my side, and if her arms wrap any tighter around me, I'll have difficulty breathing in addition to difficulty standing.

"Walk," I mutter. One word is all I'm going to manage right now.

"Are you sure?" Greg asks me.

I nod.

Dylan says my name, and I make myself look at her. Her teeth are clamped down on her bottom lip, and her eyes are flickering around my face at lightning speed. "Nothing's broken," I tell her.

If something were broken, I'd be screaming where I stood. Ditto for torn ligaments or tendons.

Greg takes a step forward, and I follow. There's no good way to do this. I can't hobble or hop because both knees are smarting.

"Maybe you *should* take him to the hospital," Greg tells Dylan.

"No."

"Silas, please. What if something is wrong?"

I take another step, and the pain continues, but I'm getting used to it. It'll fade soon, and I'll just be sore. That's all.

"Keep walking," I say.

The stiffness is still there. I'm keeping my legs as straight as I can with each step, and after a few more strides, I can bear enough of my own weight that I let go of Greg, and just use Dylan to keep me steady.

"See?" I grunt at her. "Better already."

"You are such a liar."

"She's right, man. Your expression looks like you just took a knee to the balls."

I look up and Dylan's redheaded friend Matt is ahead of us. I didn't even know he was here, but it's kind of nice to see another familiar face.

"I've survived that before, too."

Dylan mumbles, "Probably multiple times."

It shocks a laugh out of me even through the ache. "Hit me while I'm down why don't you."

"Yeah, well, you're a cocky bastard, and I'm mad that you laughed. And that you won't let me take you to the hospital."

Dylan Brenner might have plenty of practice telling other people no, but I'm not sure she's heard it very often herself.

"At least let me take you home, so you can rest."

"That sounds like a deal."

She scoffs. "You and your deals."

"You like my deals."

It's Matt who cuts in: "You guys even have inside jokes now. This is so freaking weird."

She says, "Matt, can you get some ice from Mrs. Baker?"

"Don't bother," I tell him. "We're five minutes from my place."

"It's going to start swelling soon."

I bend my face down to hers and rest my forehead against her temple. "Thank you for worrying about me," I murmur into her ear. "But really I'm fine. And I'd just like to go home and handle this without an audience."

She swallows, and with my head still touching hers, she nods.

I look back up at Matt, and notice Henry watching from a few feet behind him. Matt says, "I'll help you get him in the car."

Dylan apologizes to Greg, but says she won't be coming back to work in the afternoon. He tells her to take care of me, and something inflates in my chest at those words. He asks her to call him after she gets me settled so he can get all the information about the accident down in a report.

By all logic, the thought of *being taken care of* should annoy me. But because it's her, it's different. Everything is a little bit different where Dylan is concerned.

Even when I get to the point that I could probably handle walking on my own, I don't say anything, and continue letting her walk along with me.

Our pace is slow as we cross the yard, and I'm thankful when Matt volunteers to go get Dylan's car where it's parked a few houses down.

"This is all my fault. I'm so sorry, Silas."

"It was my idea not to wait for the ladder."

"I pulled too hard on the vine."

"I decided to drop to my knees."

"Because of me."

"Damn right, it was because of you. I promise you, this is nothing. A few days of rest, and I'll be fine. Better my knees than your head. That wouldn't have been fixed with a few days rest."

"I had my head covered. I would have been fine."

"I don't care. If I had it to do again, I'd do the same thing."

We stop and wait for Matt on the sidewalk in front of the house, and she squints against the sun as she looks up at me. I can see her cataloging me, examining my words and my actions, and filing them all into the appropriate boxes in that too-ordered head of hers. She thinks and rethinks through everything she does and says. And if everything in her head is perfectly organized, mine is more akin to a trailer park after a tornado, something I experienced a number of times as a kid. I know the way those funnels hop, destroying one house and sparing another. I think that's what's happening to me. My past is creeping up on me, dropping down from the sky when I least expect it, demolishing some parts of me, and leaving others for another day.

And what my history hasn't bulldozed, Dylan is flattening, sweeping through my life like a flood that I'm welcoming just so I can drown in her. I'm doing just that, caught up in her gaze, when her car glides to a stop in front of us.

It takes some maneuvering, getting me into her sporty car and keeping my legs stretched out as much as possible. I end up in the backseat, knees slightly bent so the door can close. It hurts, but it's worth it to get out of there and on the road.

By the time we get back to my place, though, my knees have gone stiff, and I know they're swelling.

It's just a sprain. It happens. I've had them before from the occasional rough tackle. It will hurt for a couple of days, but that's it. That *has* to be it.

I refuse to let it be anything else.

There *cannot* be another thing keeping me away from football, because I won't survive it. I'll self-destruct so quickly and efficiently that it will make the current damage in my head look like a fucking walk in the park.

The front porch steps are a bitch, but I manage to get up them with nothing worse than a grimace.

I don't have the energy or the willpower to climb upstairs to my bedroom, so instead, I shuffle to the couch in the living room. There's a bag of chips, a fast-food wrapper, some shoes, and a balled up T-shirt on it that Dylan removes without a blink.

Then she immediately heads for the kitchen. "Let me go get you some ice."

I call after her, "There should be some cold packs in the freezer already. We tend to get injured a lot in this house. And medicine in the cabinet next to the microwave, but if you can't find any kind of anti-inflammatory, there's some in the medicine cabinet in the upstairs bathroom."

With her gone, I reach for the button on my jeans and flick

it open. I kick off my shoes, and slide my pants off with as little bending of my knees as possible.

When I see my knees, I curse. They're already swollen, as I suspected.

I hear a high-pitched noise behind me and turn to find Dylan looking at the ceiling, holding out two ice packs, a glass of water, and some pills.

"Sorry. I didn't realize you'd be . . ."

"I'm not naked, Dylan. You'll know when I am."

"Yeah, but—"

"I can't exactly ice my knees with jeans on."

Her eyes leave the ceiling and go to my legs, and she sucks in a breath. Then her eyes lift a little higher, to the growing bulge I can't hide, and she exhales in a rush.

She's embarrassed and shy for a moment, but then a change comes over her, determination in her expression, and she crosses to me.

"Sit," she commands.

I do as she says, wincing at the twinge of pain in my knees.

She wraps the cold packs in kitchen towels that I hadn't noticed draped over her arm, and then she makes me sit back against the armrest and situates the ice on my knees.

"I like Nurse Dylan," I say. "She's hot. And bossy."

She shoves the bottle of pills in my face and says, "Shut up and take these."

"You still mad at me for laughing?"

I shake out a few pills into my palm and grab the water.

"No, I'm mad at myself."

I swallow quickly and ask, "Why?"

"Because I got you hurt. I'm supposed to be helping you, and instead I'm making things worse."

I put the water aside, and with one well-placed pull, I've got her tumbling into my lap. The impact jostles my knees a little bit, but her flustered look is worth it.

"You've got a thing for pulling me into your lap, don't you?"

"Hell yeah, I do."

I slip a hand up her back and curl it around the nape of her neck, pulling her closer into my chest.

"What are you doing?"

"This morning I had my lesson; now it's time for yours."

Her cheeks flush. "A lesson in what exactly?"

Her wide-eyed, innocent look goes straight to my dick, and she can no doubt feel it vying for her attention at her hip.

"Get your mind out of the gutter, Brenner. I'm not teaching you anything like that."

I could be imagining it, but I think for a brief moment she looks disappointed. And *fuck* . . . I might be making a liar out of myself very soon.

"Lesson number one. Everything wrong in the world is not your fault."

Her brows furrow.

"I know that."

"No you don't. You take everything on yourself. That protest at the shelter. When people weren't listening, you thought it was *your* responsibility to make them. Matt getting arrested. I was there . . . I heard you apologizing again and again to him."

"But he's my friend, and he—"

"Is an adult who makes his own decisions."

"But—"

"When I asked you about your breakup with Henry, you shared the blame. Like it was somehow your fault that he's a fucking idiot. And now you're apologizing to me, again for something *I* did. Not you."

"But—"

"New rule. Every time you apologize, I get to shut you up."

Her eyes widen. "And how are you going to do that?"

"I've got a few ideas."

She presses her lips together tightly, like she's worried she might just spontaneously apologize. I grin, enjoying the emotions playing across her face. Nerves. Curiosity. Indignation. Embarrassment.

For the first time in my life, I want to ask her questions, want to dig until I find the thoughts responsible for each of those expressions. Normally, I steer clear of questions. Getting to know a girl just complicates the whole exchange.

I promised Dylan simple. I convinced her that was what she needed, and now I'm starting to think it's not at all what I want.

Chapter 16

Dylan

Needing a break from the intensity of being this close to him, I awkwardly climb off his lap and say, "I'm going to grab some pillows for you. Is it okay if I go in your room?"

"Go ahead," he calls back.

I take in a calming breath and scale the stairs. My eyes flick to the restroom door where we kissed for the first time, and the back of my neck flashes with heat. I remember the way his hand had curled there, holding me against him, even though nothing could have made me move away in that moment. He'd done the same thing on the couch downstairs, and part of me had *really* hoped that was where he was going with that lesson. I blink and shake off the memory. But I can't get the nerves to flee as I open his bedroom door. I don't know what I expected to find . . . drug paraphernalia, condom wrappers, dirty clothes.

There's none of that. The room is clean and neat. Even his bed is made. It's simple, sparsely furnished with no real decorations, unless you count sports equipment, and a few Rusk mementos. He's got four pillows on his bed, two on each side, and I grab them all. With them held tight to my chest, I breathe in the scent they carry, clean and masculine with just a little spice.

I take one last look around his room, and imagine how things might have gone differently if I'd followed him in here during the party. Would I ever have seen him again? Would that have been it? Or would that have just been the first of several times, like he's implied?

I shake my head because I'm being stupid. While I'm up here imagining things that can't be changed, he's down there in pain and uncomfortable. I rush down the stairs and back into the living room to find him with his eyes closed. He's removed the Rusk T-shirt he was wearing earlier, leaving him in just a white, fitted undershirt and his black boxer briefs. I swallow, square my shoulders, and walk up beside him. I drop all of the pillows on the ground but one, and then touch my fingers to his shoulders.

He looks exhausted and I say quietly, "Lean up."

He plants his hands beside him on the couch and pulls himself a few inches forward. I settle the pillow behind him. I'm still adjusting it when he leans back onto it, so I end up leaning over him, one arm on either side of his head, trying to straighten it so he's comfortable. I try not to think about how his head is even with my chest, but who am I kidding? It's all I'm thinking about.

"Now for your legs," I say. I remove the ice packs and place them on the coffee table. He lifts his feet for me, but only a couple of inches. I hook an arm under his calves to lift them higher so I can fit all three pillows under his knees. I hear him wince, and I pause for a second to look at the swelling before I replace the ice. His thighs are thick and muscled, and his knees are so inflamed that they're only a little narrower than the rest of his leg. I make sure the hand towels are wrapped neatly around the cold packs, and then place them back where they were.

I look for something, anything else to do. "Blanket?" I ask. I glance around the room and see one tossed on the floor beside a recliner. I pick it up and shake it out as he says, "I'm fine."

I bring the blanket back over with me, but he turns it down. I hug it closer to me and sink down onto the floor beside him. I lean back against the couch and stare straight ahead.

"I really am sorry. I promise I won't make you—"

I don't get the rest of my thought out because he sits up on one elbow, grips the back of my neck, and bends over to cover my mouth with his. His lips are warm, and when I don't immediately open my mouth, he nips my bottom lip. I suck in a breath, and his tongue sweeps past my lips. My whole body braces for the onslaught that is kissing Silas Moore, but this time, he's soft and sweet and patient, like we have all the time in the world. When I follow his tongue back into his mouth, he groans. The sound vibrates against me, and the sensation echoes out over the rest of my body. I shiver, and he pulls back until I feel only his breath against me.

"I told you I would shut you up the next time you apologized."

He slides his hand around to cup my jaw and kisses me again.

Once. Twice. And a third time. Hard. Then soft. Just my bottom lip. The corner of my mouth. His lips play over mine like he's trying to uncover every possible way to kiss me and check them off the list one by one. I open my mouth immediately when his tongue flicks out, but I taste him for only a second before he pulls away, wincing. He falls back against his pillow, and I notice for the first time that one of his cold packs has fallen on the floor, and the other is lost somewhere in the couch.

"Why didn't you tell me you were hurting?"

"Because then I would have had to stop."

My heart is a spinning top in my chest, and now that he's not kissing me and things are slowing down, I can feel myself about to topple out of control. I shake my head and get the ice packs back where they belong.

Now I just need to get everything else back where it belongs, too.

Except I'm starting to think that the idea of "belonging" anywhere is false. We go through our whole lives thinking that we belong in one place and not in another. We think certain ideas and actions have to be relegated to the tiny little boxes we place them in. What if we just react instead? What if we take whatever the world gives us and instead of focusing on what it isn't, we enjoy what it *is?*

I lean back against the couch and don't think as I begin to talk. I tell him about my journalism major, and how social media is changing the way news happens, changing the way the world interacts and reacts. He tells me about football, and how it's been the only thing he's wanted since a coach plucked him out of a standard PE class his freshman year. He pulls the rubber band from my hair, and I lay my head back as he spreads the long strands out over his chest. He combs his fingers through the waves carefully while he tells me about going to the state championship with his high school team and then losing.

"Before that . . . the world felt so damn small. Like a pair of shoes that didn't fit right. We lost and there were all these guys on my team, some I liked and some I didn't, and they were all crying and falling to their knees, and I was just standing there staring at the stadium around us, and all the people that came out to see these two tiny schools duke it out. And it didn't feel like I lost. Instead it was like I kicked open some door, and crawled out of my cage, and could stand up straight for the first time in my life."

"So that's how you knew I was suffocating. That had been you, too."

He picks up a lock of hair and twists it, and I shiver again.

"I think we were suffocating in different ways, but yeah. I guess that was it."

His hand in my hair has me so relaxed that I could fall asleep right there beside him on the floor. I close my eyes and turn my head to the side to rest against the cushion. Quietly, I ask, "You don't feel that way anymore?"

"I didn't. But lately the world is starting to feel pretty fucking small again."

"So kick open another door."

He continues playing with my hair with his left hand, but his right slips down to drag a knuckle over my cheek.

"I'm trying."

I WAKE UP when his roommates come home, but Silas sleeps right through it. I take them both in the kitchen to explain what happened.

"Hold up," Torres says. "Silas is doing community service? Is this because of the whole arrest thing? Or the fight with Keyon? Is Coach making him do it?"

"No. He's doing it because he's trying to get better."

The other roommate, Isaiah, is more serious, more intimidating. "Better from what?"

"I don't know. Something has him all stressed-out, though. And now he's hurt on top of that, so I'd appreciate it if you didn't add to that."

Torres cracks the knuckles of one hand against his other palm. "We got this. Silas is our boy. You don't need to worry about us, Captain Planet."

I roll my eyes, and go back out to find my keys where I left them on the coffee table. Silas looks younger when he's asleep. I mean, he's still beautiful and powerful, but that dangerous quality that had both repelled and attracted me from the very beginning is missing.

Or maybe it's just because I'm beginning to understand him. When I look at him now I don't see the sexy stranger with bloodied knuckles. I just see Silas.

I remove the cold packs from his knees that have melted and gone soft. I take them back into the kitchen and return them to the freezer. Torres is gone, but Isaiah is there watching me.

"Why are you doing this?" he asks.

"Because he's my friend."

That's what I say. I'm nowhere naive enough to believe things are as simple as that.

"Silas doesn't know how to be friends with girls. Either he'll break your heart or you'll break his."

I don't have an answer to that because it's the fear in the back of my mind that I haven't allowed myself to voice. But I'm not sure that's a good enough reason to stay away anymore. If I let all my fears become locked doors, then it will be exactly as Silas said. My life will get smaller and smaller until nothing else fits except me and the empty space from all the things I've let pass me by.

I'm figuring out what I want by trial and error, and maybe that's not the best way, but it's all I've got. All I know is that I *need* to be my own person, someone shaped by *my* desire, not fear of disappointing the people who are supposed to love me.

I just have to stay realistic, and I won't get hurt. From the very beginning, Silas has told me to keep things simple. That's the only reason I can do any of this. Because as long as we're just having fun, I've not made any irreversible decisions.

I'm just . . . exploring. Whatever is happening between Silas and me is a stepping-stone between the old me and the new me I'm working to find. It's meant to be temporary. As long as I remember that, we'll be fine.

I'll be fine.

I say goodbye to Torres and Brookes, and then make my way home still thinking about the things that Silas and I talked about. He's different than I expected him to be. So different. His tidy room. The gentle way he touched my hair. The hurt and the hope in his voice as he talked about football.

Silas might be less refined than Henry. Less traditional. Less open.

But even so . . . he feels like *more*.

And that's how I know I'm on the right path. It's not what's on the surface that matters—not in other people or myself.

Chapter 17

Dylan

M aybe we could do a letter-writing campaign?" I ask.

Javier steeples his fingers down at the head of the table and looks at me. His accented voice is soft when he replies, "They didn't listen to the petition, so I doubt they'll listen to letters."

"So we just do nothing?" I look around at the rest of our student activism group, and I can tell I'm the only one who wants to keep pushing the subject, and it makes me angry. "These are people's lives at stake. If this shelter closes, the one at St. Mary's only has thirty beds a night available. What about all the other people who don't fit? What about them?"

"Dylan." I can see Javier is trying to be kind, but he's done with this conversation. Matt places a hand on my knee beneath the table, but I keep going.

"There are whole families that need help. Children who do

poorly in school because they didn't get a good night's sleep or any food the night before."

"You're preaching to the choir, kid," Matt murmurs to me.

"No, I'm preaching to a group that's given up."

"We do not give up," Javier answers sharply. I forget sometimes that he's been doing this a lot longer than any of the rest of us. He and his parents immigrated to the United States from Argentina when he was twelve after his brother was killed during a political riot. He's a quiet, thoughtful kind of guy, but he can be pretty damn serious when he wants to. "We stop, rethink, reevaluate. And we face facts. Nothing will change if we are the only ones fighting. So we find support from more prominent members of the community. We wait for classes to start back in two weeks and come back at it then."

"But the shelter is closed now. What do those people do in the meantime? While we're waiting?"

"I don't have that answer. But we must be smart about this. We cannot effect change with sheer force of will."

He's right. I know he is, but that doesn't make it any easier to hear. We could spend every day protesting outside that shelter or City Hall or wherever, and it wouldn't change a thing.

Because the world isn't fair. It just fucking isn't.

So I stay silent when Javier asks, "Any other business before we adjourn?"

A senior named Alana passes out stacks of flyers for a lecture at one of the local libraries about religious awareness and tolerance. I take a handful and promise to drop them off at a few businesses around my apartment and my parents' house. Javier lets us know that at the next meeting, we'll begin talking about state legislature elections, and what kind of stuff we can do on campus to get more students to vote. Then he calls the meeting to a close.

While the others say their goodbyes, I take off. Matt is hot on my heels.

"Hold up there, spicy pickle."

"Don't start, Matt, not if you want your organs to remain in their correct locations."

"Jeez. I think hanging out with a certain sexy football player has made you more violent."

I really wish I were the kind of person who could follow through on my violent threats.

"I'm not more violent. I'm just tired of staying quiet."

"Riiight. Where are you off to?"

"Home."

"You mind if I come with you? I wanted to ask Nell a question about one of the classes I'm taking. The professor I signed up for is out on maternity leave, and now I'm stuck with some dude that is apparently the biggest jackass this side of wherever Shia LaBeouf is currently standing. Someone said they thought Nell had him last year."

I shrug. "Sure. I'm not sticking around, though, and you know you'll annoy Nell if you distract her too much."

"That girl needs some distraction like whoa. If she doesn't

spend some time out in the sunlight soon, she'll end up all pasty white like me. You won't even be able to tell she's Italian anymore."

"Please tell her that. I'd like to see her hand you your ass in the argument that follows."

He laughs and shakes his head. "I don't care what you say, Silas is rubbing off on you."

"Yes, well, you've rubbed off on me, too. Ooo! That's it! I've finally thought of an appropriately awful nickname for you. *Rash.* What with your red hair and persistent personality, I think it's a good fit."

"If you call me Rash, I will call you Pickle every chance I get."

"You *already* call me Pickle every chance you get."

"Hmm. Good point. But have some pity . . . how am I ever going to land a hot guy or girl of my own with the nickname *Rash?*"

"Think of it this way, *Rash* . . . when you do land that lucky person, you'll know it's for real if they stick around."

"You, my dear, are one coldhearted preserved cucumber."

He climbs into my car, and I'm treated to two more pickle puns in the eight minutes it takes to get to my apartment. Antonella is seated on the couch with her computer when we enter, her long dark hair pulled into a knot on the top of her head. I drop my purse by the door and head back to my bedroom to change clothes. As I pass, Matt asks, "Whatcha looking at, Nell?"

She keeps her eyes on the screen and answers, "Summer internships."

"You do realize that summer is pretty much over, right?"

"*Next* summer."

Matt whistles, and I leave him to pry whatever professor advice he needs from Nell, and close myself in my bedroom at the end of the hall. There are still a few outfits laid out on my bed from my attempts to decide what to wear before the Voice for Tomorrow bimonthly dinner meeting.

It's been a week since Silas was suspended from the team, and he gets to go back to practice tomorrow. His roommates are having a get-together at their place to watch some baseball game, and I'm going. Mostly I'll be there to keep an eye on Silas and make sure he doesn't do anything stupid the night before his big day back. But it's also the first time we're officially hanging out with no ulterior motive. He went back to work at Renew with me twice this week. When he showed up the second day all on his own, I might have pulled a muscle, my jaw dropped so fast.

I hadn't even bothered asking him to come because I figured he needed to rest more. And I was still feeling guilty about getting him hurt in the first place.

Lo and behold, the next morning I was standing toward the back of the group, far away from Henry, when he drove up in his rusty old pickup.

It didn't make me feel like the butterflies in my stomach took acid. I swear it didn't.

But something I've learned about Silas . . . when he sets his mind to something, he goes all out.

And oh God, I throw myself on my bed and cover my face with my hands because I can't help but make that dirty in my head.

He's ruined me.

Doesn't help that I'm a huge, hormonal mess because despite turning me on every eight seconds or so . . . we've not done anything but kiss this week. And I'm just about ready to beg for more.

And now I have to decide what to wear for this party with his friends, and *nothing* I own looks good enough.

I groan and lay back on the bed, probably wrinkling several of my wardrobe possibilities in the process. I take a deep breath and stare at my ceiling.

I should put something on my ceiling. Glow-in-the-dark stars or posters or paper cranes. That's something teenagers do, right? To make their rooms their own? I never did that, but it could be cool. Especially the paper cranes.

I'll do that. Just as soon as I learn origami.

I sit up and look at myself in the mirror. My hair is loose and wavy, and I'm just wearing a plain V-neck tee and some jeans.

"You're being silly, Dylan. It's a baseball game on television at his apartment. It's not a date. Not dinner or a movie or anything that requires this much thought. Just pick something."

God, I've resorted to actually talking to myself. In a mirror.

Who's the craziest of them all?

On a whim, I pick up a pair of shorts that are a little similar to the ones I wore the night Silas and I met. They come up high on my waist and show a good amount of leg. This pair is a bright kelly green. I pick a cute but comfy sheer top and pull it on over a white camisole. I look in the mirror and decide it's just sexy enough with the sheer fabric, but not trying too hard since it's loose and covers a decent amount of skin. That decided, I check the time on my phone. It's half past seven, and I think the game starts at eight.

I debate trying to kill half an hour so I can show up fashionably late, but I've never really been a fashionably late kind of person, and if I don't get out of this room now I might start freaking out about my wardrobe again.

I flip off my light as I head back down the hall.

Nell's head is still down when I enter the living room, but she looks up when I pass. She's exasperated, probably with Matt, but when she sees me, she puts a hold on whatever she'd been planning to say and mimes holding a gun to her head.

I swallow a laugh and head for the door.

She says, "Where are you going? You've barely been home at all this week."

Matt cocks one eyebrow. "Barely been home all week, you don't say?"

Then he makes an obscene gesture with his tongue and his cheek, and it's me pretending to shoot him with my fingers this time.

"For your information, I've been doing that stuff with Renew. And I went to my parents' place a few times."

"And . . . ?"

"And I hung out with Silas once or twice."

Matt jumps up from the couch. "Dingdingding! We have a winner, ladies and . . . ladies."

I ignore him and focus on my roommate. "Okay, then. Nell, I'll be back later tonight. Sorry to leave you with this guy. Feel free to kick him out whenever he starts annoying you."

I pick up my purse by the door and Matt says, "You know, a true friend would give me details. Let me live vicariously through you."

"Goodbye, Rash."

"Cruel and heartless, Pickle! Cruel and heartless!"

I'm smiling despite my aggravation with Matt's obsession. He's a good friend, and I vow to fill him in on everything just as soon as I wrap my own head around it.

A number of cars are already parked around Silas's place when I arrive. I pull mine up across the street and one house down. I'm relieved to know it won't be weird that I'm here before the game starts. Little pebbles get stuck between my foot and the sole of my sandal on my way up his driveway. I ring the doorbell, and am trying to shake one of the pebbles out when the door opens.

It's Brookes. And behind him is the pretty girl, Stella, that I met my first night here. The girl Silas hooked up with last year.

It shouldn't bother me. It really shouldn't.

But between her surprised expression and her quiet "Oh," I can't help it. It *does* bother me.

"Silas is in his room," Isaiah says. "You can go up if you want."

Torres passes by, carrying two bowls of chips from the kitchen. "Yeah, tell him to quit being antisocial and get his ass down here."

I feel weird going up the stairs, especially because Stella and Brookes are watching me and whispering. I put them out of my mind and jog the final distance to Silas's door and knock. No one answers, but there's music playing inside, so I figure maybe he didn't hear me. I knock one more time, and when nothing changes, I turn the knob and push the door open a few inches.

For one sinking moment, I cast my eyes toward his bed, afraid I'll see something there that I don't want to, but his bed is neatly made just like the last time I saw it. I push the door a little farther, music spilling out into the hall, and then I see him. He's by the foot of his bed, shirtless and doing push-up after push-up. There's a faint sheen of sweat across his muscled back, and I swear watching the way his muscles move could give reality TV a run for its money as far as entertainment goes.

Why *isn't* there a reality TV show filled with hot guys doing sweaty, mouthwatering tasks?

Oh, right. That's called sports.

I step over to the dock where he has his phone plugged in to play music. I turn down the volume, and he plants a knee on the floor to turn and look at me.

I suddenly feel weird about intruding on him here in his bedroom. I've only been in here the once, and that was really out of necessity. And he wasn't in here with me.

"Hey."

"Hey," he replies. He grabs his discarded T-shirt off the foot of the bed, but instead of slipping it on, he uses it to wipe at his face. "I didn't expect you this early."

I smile and shrug. "I guess your knee is all good now."

"It is. I told you it would pass with a little rest."

I roll my eyes. "Yeah, you did a whole lot of resting this week."

"I'll be doing a hell of a lot more tomorrow. No use coddling myself and making it harder in practice."

"You know you could probably take a few more days if you wanted. Tell your coach what happened. I bet he'd rather see you sit out for a few days than risk hurting yourself worse."

"I don't much imagine that Coach wants to see me at all, but I can't stay away any longer. This week was torture."

I frown. Not liking that I had a part in making his week so miserable.

He crosses the room to me and says, "You know what else is torturous? That shirt." He skims the palm of his hand up my sheer sleeve and over to place a finger on the top button. Slowly, he drags that finger down the line of buttons on my top. "Every time you wear one of these, all I can think about is tearing it open. It's so damn tempting."

I swallow and his hand stops at the top of my shorts, where my shirt disappears under the high waistband. He's shirtless and sweaty, and I want to be worried about him ruining my shirt like he said he wanted to, but all I can do is stand here.

Trying for a subject change, I say, "Why aren't you downstairs? A bunch of your friends are already here."

"I didn't feel like hanging out."

"Oh. Well, I can go then. Let you get back to your, um, push-ups."

He takes hold of the extra material on my shirt where it's tucked in. He doesn't pull or push, just holds on.

"I didn't say I didn't feel like hanging out with *you*."

When he's satisfied that I'm not going anywhere, he releases the material and says, "Let me take a quick shower. You can wait in here if you want."

I remember the last time I saw him right after a shower. I nearly let him go down on me in his kitchen, and he *would* have if his roommates hadn't showed up. I'm not sure what will happen if he comes back all wet and toweled to me alone in his room, but I know it's probably something that I don't want to happen with all his friends downstairs.

"That's okay. I'll just wait for you in the living room."

He looks disappointed, but doesn't comment. I start to leave but he moves into my space, crowding me against the door. I tip my chin up and try not to look nervous.

"Someday you should wear one of these shirts you don't mind me destroying."

"I like my clothes."

"I like the idea of tearing them off you."

"You're crazy."

He leans closer, caging me between his arms on the door. He dips his head down and trails the tip of his nose up my neck to my ear.

"You make me that way."

He makes me a little crazy, too.

He lets me escape then, but not before placing a sinfully hot, open-mouth kiss over my pulse point. I hear him laughing as I scurry down the stairs, and he closes himself in the bathroom.

Down in the living room, I recognize Silas's two roommates, Stella, and the couple who picked us up from the sheriff's office, Carson and his redheaded girlfriend. There are two more guys with the couple, one with curly blond hair and the other wearing a beanie even though it's August. There's another guy on the couch I don't recognize. He's huge with sandy blond hair . . . the kind of massive guy that I've always pictured when I thought of college football. Stella is on the couch with him, and he makes her look miniature.

"Where's Silas?" Torres asks. He tries to slip an arm over the shoulder of a pretty brunette standing next to him, but as soon as he manages it, she removes his arm.

"He'll be down soon. He's just taking a shower."

Every head in the room swivels toward me.

"Got a little dirty, did he? That was fast. Tell me he at least made it good for you, Captain Planet."

The brunette next to him scowls.

She says, "If you're trying to win an award for douchebaggery, you can stop. It's a landslide victory."

Stella laughs on the couch. "I like you, Katelyn. You should come around more often."

"I keep telling her that," Torres says.

Stella kicks her heeled feet up on the coffee table. "That explains why she hasn't been here."

Torres throws a chip at her. She picks it up from her stomach where it landed and pops it into her mouth with a smile.

I like the way they are with each other. It's what I imagine siblings are like. There were other kids in my foster home, but it was so strict there, we never got a chance to find this kind of easy camaraderie.

"Take a seat, Dylan." Stella gestures to the open spot on the couch on the other side of the giant dude. "Carter doesn't bite."

I sit down, and I notice some people are avidly watching the announcers' pregame talk, while others are talking among themselves. It's easy. I don't feel any pressure to be or act a certain way. I just sit back and listen to them bait and tease each other, and it feels a little like watching a sitcom from the inside.

There are plates and bowls of snacks laid out on the table, and directly in front of me is a plate of brownies that looks almost untouched.

Stella and a guy named Ryan argue over a subject that I've lost track of (I think they've probably lost track, too, and are just arguing to argue). I reach for one of the brownies because . . . *chocolate*, and I meet Carter's eyes as I sit back. He may be approaching the size of a woolly mammoth, but his eyes are friendly and he has a rosiness to his cheeks that makes him seem more approachable. I shrug unapologetically as I bite into the chocolatey goodness, and he smiles widely.

I suppose if someone has to catch me stuffing my face, the quiet guy is a good option.

The brownie tastes a little funny, like maybe it has too much flour or something, but I'm hungry, so I don't mind much. I was too frustrated and angry at the dinner meeting to do much beyond destroying my food with my fork, and now it has caught up to me.

I try a few other things at the table, and right as the game starts, Silas enters.

His hair is wet and curling slightly at the ends. The guy still does marvelous things for a pair of jeans. And when his eyes scan the room and land on me, every muscle in my body twists up tight.

The rest of the room fades, like the world is in black-and-white, and he's the only thing in color.

And I'm not just breathing, I'm seeing and feeling and hearing in a way that I'm not sure I ever have before.

Chapter 18

Silas

There's no space around her. She's sitting between Carter's bulky frame and the edge of the couch, and that just won't cut it. But I don't know how to get near her, to make an opening for me without doing something that *says something*.

If I make Carter move, that's calling her mine.

And holy fuck, just the word raises a hurricane in my chest. Terrifying and powerful and consuming. I want her with a fierceness I've never wanted anything.

Except football. Except getting out of my hometown.

And maybe that's why she's different. Maybe that's why she's the first girl who has ever tied me up in knots and unraveled me at the same time. She feels like a way out, a way to pull myself up a few more rungs on a never-ending ladder.

She's the next big escape.

I don't make Carter move. But rather than sitting down on the carpet or pulling in a chair from the kitchen like Torres did for himself and Katelyn, I make my way over beside her and sit on the armrest.

It puts me close enough that her shoulder touches my thigh, and the hand I brace on the back of the couch is in prime position to touch her hair when everyone stops fucking staring at us.

Not that that happens anytime soon.

For close to an hour, there's always at least one or two people looking at us, and it's driving me crazy. Enough that I'm ready to say screw it all and drag her up to my room, regardless of what people say.

I glare at Torres when he makes a lewd gesture and bounces his eyebrows. I'm about to go over there and snap him in half, but he looks away in a hurry.

He's not always the dumbass he pretends to be for attention.

I shift, uncomfortable and annoyed, and Dylan giggles.

I raise my eyebrows in question, and she giggles harder.

"I'm sorry. You're just so . . ." Then she does an impression of me that involves scowling and growling and flexing like a caveman, and she descends into laughter again.

"You're weird, Captain Planet," Torres calls from across the room.

I glower at him, and he turns and tries to start a conversation with Katelyn, who ignores him.

"This game is so slow," Dylan whispers to me. But her whisper is loud enough for everyone to hear. Brookes and Carson look a little annoyed, but they can deal with it. "Like I swear I looked at the TV *forever* ago, and it was bottom of the fourth with two outs, and it's *still* bottom of the fourth with two outs. I think time has stopped. Or is moving backward. Or it's flip-flopping, and we're in some weird time loop, and it just always is going to be the bottom of the fourth with two outs no matter what we do."

Everyone in the room is watching, and it's not with annoyance, but confusion.

This isn't Dylan. Dylan is composed and intelligent, and makes me feel like a complete hack in comparison. She's not really the giggly, ditzy type.

"Oh shit," Stella says from the other side of the couch. "Did she have one of Carter's brownies?"

Dylan lays her forehead against my thigh and rubs her nose back and forth a few times before settling down on one cheek and murmuring, "I'm tired."

I pick up one of the brownies from the plate in front of Dylan. One good sniff and I know it's chock full of pot. When Carter makes the shit, it's usually crazy potent. I look at Carter and ask, "Did you see her eat one?"

"Relax, man. She just had one. She'll be fine."

I don't like the way he shrugs. He's always been that guy just on the fringe. With Levi and I, we always knew we could get Carter to do whatever we wanted because he was so desperate to be counted one of us. Because of that, he's always doing stupid shit trying to prove he's cool enough or whatever. But this . . . this is not fucking cool. I suck in a breath and try to stay calm. Relatively.

"Did you tell her what it was?" He takes too long to answer. "Did you *fucking* tell her what it was?"

"She looked nervous. I figured I was doing her a favor, helping her loosen up." He doesn't say it, but I can see in his expression that he thought he was doing me a favor, too. *Goddamn it.*

Sound disappears from my ears, like those moments of fuzzy silence after a loud noise, and I want to take that stupid thick neck of his and twist it around until his head snaps off. I want to bloody his face until my heart stops beating so fast and hard.

But Dylan's head is on my leg. She's playing with a long strand of her hair above her face with a childlike wonder that makes me want to smile even through my fury.

But I know she wouldn't willingly do weed. I might have suggested it the night we met, but I know her better now. She's not your typical good girl looking to get a little wild. She likes control and order too much to cloud her head with pot. That stuff breaks down the walls and barriers in your mind, just flushes it all out. It's for people who want to let go of control, and when it's out of her system, she's going to be so furious.

Or sad. Or disappointed.

With me.

"Get out." I don't look at him as I say it. I watch Dylan playing with her hair because if I look at him, I'm going to hit him.

"What?"

"I said. *Get. Out.*"

Dylan lifts her head up, balancing her chin on my knee, and says, "What's wrong? What's going on?"

"Silas, man," Carter says. "If I had known—"

"Last warning. Get out of my house or I fucking throw you out bleeding."

McClain is on his feet then, and he's pulling Carter away, trying to talk him down. But still, the idiot tries to complain. He turns to Torres and Brookes trying to get them to let him stay.

When I stand, he shuts up fast. Then he's on his way out the door, Carson following in his wake. I almost want to follow him. I'm scared this is going to fuck up everything with Dylan before it ever gets started. And I want to take that unfamiliar fear and put it in him.

But I don't. I let the prick leave.

Dylan had flopped back against the couch when I moved, and I lean down to her now, curving my fingers over her shoulders. She squints up at me, her eyes already a little red, and she mimics my hold by placing one hand on each of my thighs.

She cracks up, like we're playing some game.

"Dylan, you're high."

"No." She scrambles up and stands on the couch cushions so that her head is a few inches above mine. Then she leans forward and rests her arms along my shoulders. "Now I'm high."

The room lets out an uneasy laugh, and Dylan laughs with them. She's so damn cute, but I don't know how to navigate this conversation, especially not with all of these people watching me.

I take her hands and say, "Come in the kitchen with me."

"Yes, food! I'm so hungry."

A few more chuckles.

She climbs down and walks in front of me to the kitchen. She sways unpredictably, like her feet are heavier than the rest of her body, and she can't seem to get all of herself to move at the same speed.

When we're out of the room I let out a sigh of relief. She moves to the counter, still swaying, and then she hefts herself up on top of it.

"Remember when you kissed me here?"

I swallow and don't cross to stand in front of her even though I want to.

"I do."

"That was nice."

I laugh. "Nice? I've told you before and I'll tell you again, Pickle. I'm not nice."

"You are, though. You have a nice smile. And nice arms. And your chest . . . it's a very nice chest."

I don't want to like her like this, not when I know it wasn't her choice, but I can't help it. I like anything that makes her want me the way I want her.

"Listen, baby. You ate a brownie in the living room before I came down. It had marijuana in it, and that's why you feel so weird right now."

"Weird? I feel fantastic. My head is kinda heavy, but in a good way, I think? I can't describe it but . . ." She smiles again, scrunching up her nose cutely. "I just . . . I feel so stinking good. Like happy. Are you happy?"

"I'm happy you're here. Little worried you won't want to be when you come down."

"Come be happy with me." She holds out her hands, and when I don't budge she flails her arms a little and insists again, "Come here."

I go. And I take her hands, determined that I won't do anything more.

"Did you hear what I said? You're high. There was pot in that brownie, and now you feel *happy* because you're drugged."

Her eyes go wide, and she pulls one hand out of mine to cover her hand as she laughs.

"Nooo. Really? Oh my God. Marijuana?"

She whispers it like it's a bad word, and I assure her, "You're going to be fine. Everything is going to seem really funny for the next hour or two, but then it should start to wear off and you'll just be sleepy."

"I can hear my heart beating."

"That's normal. It might even beat a little fast, but you're okay. I promise."

"Here," she says. She lifts one of my hands up to her neck, and presses my palm flat against her throat. She swallows and says, "Can you feel it?"

I can. It's steady and strong, if a little fast. And her skin is so damn warm. She has my hand practically wrapped around her throat, and it freaks me the hell out how much I like that. I want to push her back against that cabinet and devour that perfect mouth while I hold her there, feeling her pulse go wild against my palm.

I tear my hand back and put a few feet between us.

"Maybe I should take you home. Let you sleep this off there."

She shakes her head hard, her hair dancing around her. "No. You can't. My roommate will totally freak."

"Tell me what to do that won't make you hate me tomorrow. I don't know how to handle this."

"Let's just go hang out with your friends. That's what we were going to do anyway."

"Are you sure? We can do whatever you want. You just tell me."

"Whatever I want?"

"Yes."

She spreads her legs a little and leans back against the kitchen cabinet.

"Kiss me."

Fuck. Just . . . fuck.

"I can't."

God, if her lips weren't tempting enough already, they fucking obliterate me when the lower one curls into a pout.

"Please? I feel so good, and I want to do other things that make me feel good. Kiss me."

"If you still want that in a few hours, I'll kiss you until you forget to breathe, but not now."

She runs her hands up and down her thighs anxiously and presses her legs together. And God, it's torture.

But I don't want it to end, because I'm not sure what comes next.

I can't kiss her. Or touch her. Or do any of the things that pouty lip is stirring in my imagination, but these might be the last moments I have with her.

And if she pulls me up, makes me better, her leaving might send me falling right back to the bottom.

But I'm going to enjoy being at the top with her while I can.

Chapter 19

Dylan

Silas makes me a sandwich, and I don't know why that seems huge, but it does. I stand there holding the plate blinking up at him, and he's so gorgeous.

That thought keeps popping up every few seconds like an announcement on loop.

Dear World . . . In case you missed it, Silas Moore is jaw-dropping, mind-blanking, word-fumbling gorgeous.

And he made me a sandwich.

I think that means I'm winning. At everything.

Or maybe that's the marijuana. It makes me feel like everything I do is awesome.

Hopping off the counter? Someone give me an Olympic medal because that took talent! Walking without giggling? GENIUS. I would frame this sandwich (if sandwiches were frameable) as evidence of how amazing I am except that I'm so freaking hungry.

He asks me if I'm sure I want to go back in the living room, and I nod. I keep nodding until it gets too hard to nod and walk and carry my awesome sandwich at the same time. Everyone looks at us when we go back, but I'm having to focus so much on keeping my plate steady that I don't care.

I do care when Silas goes to sit in the middle of the couch where the big guy had been. Because that puts him by Stella.

"Middle!" I call out. Then I put down my plate on the coffee table and squeeze past him to plop down on the middle cushion. He smiles and shakes his head at me, then sits on my other side.

I pull my feet up on the cushion next to me and lean my shoulder against Silas. I feel Stella watching me, so I go a step further and pull his arm up and around my shoulders.

It doesn't even occur to me that he might not be fine with that until he tenses up. Maybe he doesn't want his friends to know about whatever this thing is. Maybe this thing is all in my head. Maybe it's just sex. Or talking about sex or whatever.

He leans forward, and I'm afraid he's going to stand up and move somewhere else, but he just picks up my plate and balances it on my knees where they rest partially atop his thigh. He settles his arm fully across my shoulders, and I'm either seriously falling for this guy or I've got a really good idea why so many people become potheads.

My sandwich tastes so good I actually moan out loud. And I don't even care that a few of his friends laugh. It's that good. Silas's hand tightens on my arm, but he doesn't laugh. I demolish the whole thing and when I'm done, I don't even remember chewing.

Silas puts the plate down on the coffee table, and when he sits back, I push myself a little closer to him, resting my head against his chest. I lay one arm across his stomach, and I feel his muscles contract and then release under my forearm. Fascinated, I place my palm flat on his abdomen, fanning out my fingers, and it happens again.

Something important must occur on the screen because there's a cheer or maybe roar. All I really know is that everyone is talking, but my heart is beating loud enough that I can't understand what they're saying. I drag one finger through the grooves on his abdomen, across one side and over to the other. Then I move a little lower and do it again. On my third trip across, his hand stops mine, pressing it down into his stomach.

His breath is ragged against my ear and he says, "You're not allowed to do that unless I can return the favor."

I wiggle my hand out from beneath his and say, "Return away."

"You still high?"

I shrug my shoulders and smile, and his head drops back against the couch with a groan. I ignore that and go back to my exploration, this time low on his belly and just a few inches above his waistband. I don't even get halfway across before he's plucked my hand away and closed his around it.

I lace my fingers with his because it seems like the right thing to do in my head, and he holds our entwined hands up in the air for a few long seconds, like he's never held someone's hand before. When I lay my head back down against his chest, he lets our hands drop into his lap and stay there.

I feel something warm and soft graze my forehead, and electricity skips up my spine. With his arm around my shoulders, my head on his chest, and my hand in his it feels like all roads lead to Silas. And all the restless energy floating through me keeps connecting to him and coming back twice as strong, like we're this closed circuit, and the longer we stay linked, the more powerful the pull between us becomes.

There's a frenzy to it, a need that reminds me of sex, of those moments when I'm chasing something and it feels just a breath beyond my grasp. It builds in me, fills me up, until I feel like I might burst.

Even so, as time passes, my head feels heavier and heavier, and it blankets the need, buries it. Even though I'm resting against Silas, there's this tickle at the very top of my neck that makes me feel like a string is there holding everything together, and it's about to snap. I shift and shift, suddenly exhausted, but unable to get comfortable.

After a few minutes, Silas grips my thighs and moves me so that he can lean against the armrest, his legs stretched out. It leaves more of my legs draped over his lap, and when I settle back down, I'm no longer laying just my head against his chest, but my whole upper body. The arm he'd had across my shoulders drops to curl around my waist. I fall asleep there, breathing in time with the lazy strokes of his fingers down my side.

My final thoughts are that I think the pot is wearing off, but the lightness it gave me, that bubbly giddiness in my belly, appears to be sticking around. Unless it isn't the pot that's making me giddy after all.

MY HAIR TICKLES my face as someone pushes it off my back and over my shoulder. My face is too warm, pressed against something even warmer. Breath skates over the back of my neck seconds before a kiss is placed there, chasing away some of the heaviness in my head.

I open my eyes, but the living room is dark, the television is off, and the crowd of people that had been here during my last memory is nowhere to be seen. Silas, though, is still underneath me, and I've shifted so that I'm practically on top of him. My head has migrated down to his stomach, my legs stretched out onto a now-empty couch, and I've got my arms wrapped around his middle.

I push myself up a few inches, unable to open my eyes all the way against the gravity of sleep.

"Sorry," Silas says. "I should have woken you up when everyone left, but I . . ." He trails off, but instead of finishing his first sentence says, "How do you feel?"

"Tired." My voice is deeper than usual, husky almost.

"Yeah, that happens."

I remember then, why exactly I'm so sleepy. I wait for some kind of feeling to unfurl in me—anger, shame, regret. It doesn't come, so I brace for panic, for fear, but there's none of that, either.

Instead, I remember Silas's face as he made me tell him exactly how many slices of ham to put on my sandwich, like he was going to be a complete failure if he put too much or too little.

"Did they win?" I ask, reaching up a hand to rub at my eyes.

"Who?"

"I don't know. Whichever team you wanted to win."

He laughs. "They did. In fact, they had an incredible last inning that you slept right through." I wipe my hand across my cheeks, checking for drool, and thankfully coming up empty.

"Oh, that's good. Sorry I missed it."

I should sit up, now that I'm awake and everything, but all I really want to do is lay my head back down against him.

"So, exactly how mad are you?" he asks.

"About missing the last inning?"

He sits up then, giving me no choice but to do the same.

"About the pot. I swear to God, I never would have let that happen if I were down here, and I promise Carter won't get within two feet of you ever again. That should never have happened, not in my house, not around my friends, and if . . . if you don't want to come back here again, I get that. I just—"

"It's okay," I tell him.

"No, baby, it's not."

Baby. I have a vague recollection of him calling me that earlier, something he's only said on a handful of other occasions, all of which involved a certain level of intimacy or teasing. It had felt generic then, like something he probably said to every girl he touched or kissed or flirted with, but it feels different now. Feels like that endearment belongs to me.

He drags a hand through his hair roughly, pausing to clench a handful in his fists. He drops his hand and lowers his chin, his eyes piercing through the floor, and says, "I'm sorry. Incredibly sorry."

I close the distance between us and kiss him. It's quick, but that earlier frenzy, that build of feeling that I had assumed was the drugs, comes roaring back to life. It's nothing more than just a brush of lips, but it feels big. *Huge.* Like I've just calmly walked off a cliff without even glancing down to see how far down it is to the bottom.

"What was that for?"

"I thought that was our thing. I apologize, you kiss me. It's only fair if it works both ways."

At first I think he's going to blow me off. He's got that air about him that he wants to beat something up, and doing it to himself is his only option. But then one corner of his mouth lifts for a scant second.

"Well, I do like to be fair."

I take that almost-smile and raise him a full-out grin. "And I like to say I'm sorry."

He tilts his head to the side and looks at me, his eyes focused. For the first time in a long time, I feel that edge of danger around him again. But it's a different kind of danger now, and it's even more potent.

"You're sure, Dylan? Tonight was . . . a big deal. I don't want you to pretend like it doesn't bother you if it does. Don't do that for me. Don't ever be what you're not for me. I'd rather you tell me how you feel up front."

I've made up my mind. It might be a mistake, and I have no clue where it's going, but maybe it's time I made a few more of those.

"*I'm sorry.* Was I not clear enough? Because if I was vague, I apologize. What I should have said is that I'm not sorry it happened. I'm sorry I did it unknowingly, and I'm sorry you spent the night stressing over how I would react, but you took care of me. And I'm not sorry for that. Not even a little bit sorry. But if you need to hear it *one more time*, I promise I'm not—"

His mouth slams into mine, and we go from zero to *oh my God* in seconds. He pushes me back on the couch and his big body settles over me. His lips are hard and demanding, and his fingers curl around my neck like he's scared I'm going to disappear. His tongue strokes every corner of my mouth, and I can't keep up, so I just bury my hands in his hair and hold on for the ride.

His weight is exquisite on top of me, like he's pinned me to this moment and neither my body nor my mind will wander while he's got control. He tugs at my shirt where it's tucked in until it comes loose, and he can slip his hands underneath to grip my waist. Our legs are tangled together, and one of his thighs rests between mine, pushing down on the perfect spot. I can feel him hard against my hip and I shift, rubbing against him. He pulls back to breathe but doesn't leave my mouth. I open my eyes, and he's staring down at me, his breath mingling with mine.

"I can't fucking—" He shakes his head and starts again, "I can't describe what you do to me. I don't have the words or even know them. There are so many things I want to do, so many places on your body I want to touch and taste, and I'm breaking apart just trying to focus on one."

I trail a hand down from his hair to curve around his neck, mimicking the way he holds me. "We've got time."

"Do we?"

I don't know how much time he's asking for or how much he's willing to give, and I don't want to have that conversation, not right now. I want to be able to enjoy this without asking questions.

"I don't have anywhere to be."

He lifts himself off me and stands next to the couch. When he offers his hand, I take it, and he leads me up the stairs to his room. He closes the door once he has me inside, and a trickle of nerves bubbles up in my chest.

I need something, *anything* to say. "I didn't expect your room to be clean."

He shrugs and reaches up to tuck my hair behind my ears.

"I've not had much in my life that is just mine. Makes you determined to take care of what you have while you have it."

"You take care of me . . . have from the night we met."

His hand pauses in combing through my hair, gripping tight. "Are you saying you're mine?"

I swallow. The intensity rolling off him is both intoxicating and overwhelming.

"I guess that depends."

"On?"

"On what exactly that means."

He cups my breast, lifting it in his hands, and squeezing just enough to make something give way in my belly.

"It means I get to touch you like this."

"You've already touched me like that."

His hand leaves my breast to smooth down my stomach and dip between my legs. He draws a finger along the seam of my shorts, pushing that hard edge against me. "It means only I can touch you here. Only I touch you, period."

I bite down on my lip and concentrate on how to say the things I need to say when I want him to keep touching me so badly.

"No one else is going to touch me there." His wandering fingers push a little harder, and I go a bit light-headed. I fight through the sensation to say what I need to. "But I can't be yours, Silas. I've spent too many years trying to please other people. I need to be my own for a little while." I don't know why, but most of my life has felt . . . conditional, like my parents and Henry and everyone else accepted me because I filled these holes in their lives. And I made sure I filled them perfectly because that was how I belonged, how I guaranteed my spot, by never failing to live up to their expectations. As long as I was perfect, they would have no need to cut me loose.

Except Henry did. And for the life of me, I can't think of anything I did wrong, and maybe that's why this all started. Because try as I might, *perfect* doesn't guarantee me anything. I can't control whether other people will want me or love me or even like me. I can only control how I feel about myself. And that's something I'm still discovering day by day.

And if I'm honest, I'm a little afraid I'm doing the same thing all over again with Silas. That I'm being what he needs me to be instead of who I am. And I have to be certain. I have to *know* for sure that what I do is what *I* want.

He says, "How about I just borrow you for the night, then? I promise to give you back. Eventually."

I laugh, and he kisses me in a way that is far from funny. His hands curve around my bottom and he pulls me up against his erection, and I know how very serious he is.

"You need to tell me now, baby. Because all I can think about is being inside you."

"No one else touches you, either?" I ask. "While we're doing whatever this is, I mean."

"If you're touching me, I won't want anyone else." That's not quite a straight answer, but he continues: "Right about now, I'll agree to anything, give you whatever you ask."

I'd expected him to play it cool, to be the confident, cocky guy that he's always been. His honesty, the desperation in voice . . . it does something to me. I run a finger lightly over the front of his jeans, following the seam in the same way he did to me. He hisses out a breath, and the hands on my backside clench.

So far, our encounters have mostly consisted of him touching me, driving me insane. Now all I want to do is turn the tables. I sink to my knees, dragging my fingers down his thighs as I go. His jaw clenches tight, and when I undo the button on his jeans, he looks up at the ceiling, muttering a few curse words under his breath. His jeans are stretched tight over the hard length of him, and I'm careful as I lower the zipper. I do it so slowly that I can hear every metal tine unhook. When I finish, Silas is breathing heavy, his fists clenched at his side.

"Baby, I need you to go a little faster or I'm gonna die before we ever get there."

I tug his jeans down, but I've forgotten about his shoes, and it takes him several seconds to kick them off with his jeans around his ankles. It's a touch awkward, enough to make me nervous that I'm going to do this wrong, that after all of this, all the buildup, I won't live up to the other girls he's been with. I'm not naive enough to think that there haven't been many. And I don't know how to deal with that. Henry and I were each other's firsts, so there was never any imbalance there.

I take a slow breath and reach up to touch him through the last barrier of material. The tip of his erection has pushed past the waistband of his boxer briefs, and I trace a finger over the exposed flesh. His eyes are darker than I've ever seen them above me. I lean forward and run my lips along the muscled V of his hips. I hover next to his waistband, gathering my courage, and when I exhale, his whole body tenses. I tuck my fingers under the fabric and exhale again, looking up at him as I do. He groans and twitches within the confines of his shorts.

"I take it back. You do whatever the fuck you want, however slow you want. I'll die and be happy about it."

I straighten my shoulders, feeling a little more confident, and I pull down that last piece of clothing.

That time in the kitchen, I'd touched him, wrapped my hand

around him, so I knew he was thick, but I hadn't been contemplating putting my mouth on him then.

I lick my lips and his hands shoot forward, but at the last second, he stops before touching me, and curls his arms up toward his chest, restraining himself.

"You pictured this?" I ask.

"God, more times than you probably want to know."

Weirdly, I think I *do* want to know.

"How many times?"

"Lost count," he breathes, his voice thick and rough.

"And when you picture it, what do I do first?"

"Jesus, Dylan."

"I don't see the point in doing something if I don't do it right. You want your hands in my hair, right?"

"God, yes."

"Then do it. Do what you want."

He does, his fingers tunneling through the thick strands and cupping the back of my head. But even though he's done as I said, he warns me, "You don't want to give me free rein here, baby."

"That's exactly what I want."

"I don't think you understand just what I want to do to you. You don't want to be mine, but if you gave me my way, I'd own every part of you. I'd make sure you could never look at or touch your own body without remembering what I did to it. I'd take and take and when you think there's nothing left, I'd take a little more. I'm okay with being selfish where you're concerned because—*shit*. Do that again."

I'd leaned forward just enough to let my lips bump against him in an almost kiss, and his whole body tensed, right down to the fingers in my hair. This time I wrap my hand around the base, and kiss the head again. When I pull away, I let my lower lip drag over his skin, and he hisses out a breath.

Gathering my courage, I say, "It's not selfish if I *want* you to take and take and take a little more."

Chapter 20

Silas

I can't resist her. I don't even really try.

It's probably too fast, too far, too soon, but I *want* to be honest with her. I want to be able to touch and taste and tease her without holding back or worrying about what she'll think.

So, I tell her what I want.

"Take your shirt off."

She sits back on her heels and bats her blue eyes at me while she unbuttons that shirt that's been driving me crazy all night. Her fingers are too slow, but I don't reach down to help her. I just watch as inch after inch of perfect skin is revealed. She shrugs it off her shoulders and lets it fall back behind her. She's wearing this lacy little thing beneath it, and when she lifts it up and over her head, I get my first completely unhindered view of her body. Her chest is small, but it doesn't even matter. Her rosy nipples are hard and perfect, and I can't resist touching her.

I drop one hand from her hair to explore all that new skin. While I do, she drags her lips back to my cock. I don't know what it is, but watching my cock bump against those lips is almost better than an actual blowjob. She looks so innocent, and it feels so damn forbidden, like I'm spoiling her in some way by touching her like that. Like she's an angel, and I'm the one to make her fall.

"Your shorts, too. Take it all off."

She stands, and I can't resist kissing her. I push my tongue past her lips, in and out, fast and hard, mimicking what I want to do to her. The material of her shorts skims my skin as they fall, and she's back on her knees before I really get a good look at her.

I'm just about to make her stand up again when her lips wrap around me and give a hard suck.

My knees actually go weak at the sight of her. I've imagined this so many times, and each touch keeps blowing my imagination out of the water. Her tongue flicks at the sensitive underside, and I have to fight not to pull too hard on her hair.

"That's it, babe. God, your lips are the most perfect thing in this world."

She pulls back a little, and then takes more of me inside. Her mouth is hot and wet and so damn good.

I direct her, telling her what to do, when to use her hands and her tongue and when to suck, and she never hesitates. But every once in a while, she does something on her own without me telling her. Just a slight graze of her teeth, a hard squeeze, a hot breath, and the surprise has me battling off the edge already.

She pushes her head down farther, until I feel the tightness at the back of her throat, and then she pulls all the way back, dragging my cock over her lips again. And I know . . . I'm going to remember the way she looks right now for the rest of my life. I will never be able to get this out of my head, and I don't want to.

"Fucking perfect," I tell her. "Your mouth is perfect, baby. That's it. Take me deeper."

She bobs her head again and I'm so close, so damn close. But I want to be inside her when I come for the first time. Because I know that's another thing I'll memorize.

I pull her up to her feet and kiss her. Her lips are slick and soft, and again I'm overwhelmed with all the things I want to do to her. I'm terrified that I'll only have this once, and I'll regret it if I don't learn everything I can about her.

Gently, I turn her around and push on her back until her upper body is laid across my bed, her round ass bent over the edge.

I smile because I knew this part of her would be perfect, too. I run a hand over her curves, and with an open palm give her a light tap. She squeaks and grips the comforter beneath her, pulling at the made bed.

"Someday, I'm going to spank your gorgeous ass, Dylan Brenner."

She looks over her shoulder at me and asks, "Not today?"

I groan because I swear it's like she's daring me.

"Not today. Today, I just want to look and touch."

I take my time with her spread over the bed like that. I alternate between light touches and kneading her skin. I bend over and place a kiss at the bottom of her spine, and she arches up against my mouth. I continue up her back, reaching underneath her to palm her breasts, and when my dick comes in contact with the hot center of her we both gasp. My hips surge forward on instinct, and I graze over her opening, dipping inside just for a moment.

I drop my forehead against her back, overwhelmed with just how fucking good that felt. I wanted to take my time. I had plans for the places I was going to kiss and lick and bite, but her hips lift seeking out mine, and my plan goes out the window.

Condom. I need a fucking condom because I have to be inside her now. I'll do all those things after, but if I don't take the edge off, don't *take her* I'm going to lose control.

Regretfully, I pull away from her, dragging a hand down her back in goodbye. I pat her ass again because I can't resist, and say, "Get on the bed, Dylan."

While she moves, I roll a condom on faster than I ever have. She sits on my bed, one knee pulled up, and the other tucked beneath it. I don't think she means to, but it hides all my favorite parts of her body.

She looks like she's been posed just to tease me with almost glimpses.

"I was going to take things slow. Take my time, but we'll have to do that later. I'm too impatient where you're concerned."

I kneel on the bed beside her, and push her knee down, spread her legs open. She lets out a slow breath and stares at the ceiling. She's nervous, and when I move between her thighs, she keeps right on staring at the ceiling.

"Dylan." She glances down at me, but she keeps her chin up, like that's what's holding her together. "You just have to tell me if you're not in this. I *can* be patient. I can slow down. I told you, it's whatever you want."

I'm telling the truth. I have to be telling the truth. I said I would give her anything, and I have to hold to that.

"I'm sorry."

I think my heart might actually collapse, just fall in on itself over and over again like a black hole in my chest that just keeps sucking in more and more and more. And soon there's not going to be anything of me left.

"Oh God," she says, her mouth dropping open. She sits up, "I didn't mean it like that. I meant like . . . I *apologize*. Not like . . . that I changed my mind. I just wanted you to kiss me, and I thought I was being cute, but oh God, I'm sorry. Please just kiss me and shut me up."

I'm so relieved I practically fall into her when I do. I burrow my arms beneath her, and wrap her up completely, crushing her naked chest against mine until she's as close as I can get her.

Her legs cling to my hips, and though I hadn't planned it, I'm right at her entrance. She moans into my mouth as I kiss her and says, "Now."

I shake my head, wanting to push her closer to the edge first.

But she's stubborn and repeats, "*Now.*" This time she lifts her hips, and I slide against her wet heat, and I swear we're pulled together like magnets because I'm perfectly aligned.

I'm ready to be just as stubborn back, to tease her, and then pull away only to repeat it all over again. If it were any other time, any other girl, I might have done that. But Dylan lifts her hips again and whispers, "Please."

And I realize something then and there.

I will never be able to turn this girl down. Whatever she wants from me, it's hers. No matter what she asks for, I'll find a way to give it to her. She may not be mine, but somewhere along the way, I ended up hers.

And as I sink inside her, I've never been more terrified in my whole life. It reminds me of those moments on the field when I know a tackle is coming, when I can see the defender out of the corner of my eye or hear him behind me, and I'm bracing for the fall. She's so tight around me, and her eyes lock with mine, and I'm so fucking gone for this girl. She snuck up on me and laid me out, and I'm not sure how I'll ever get up from this one.

I'm not sure I even want to.

I kiss her, and I swear my heart is in my throat the whole time. If the world felt big standing on that state championship field in high school, it feels unending now. Every time her mouth opens against mine, there are whole new galaxies, complete universes of thought and feeling pushing their way into my head.

And I was so wrong. Dylan isn't my next big exit. She isn't a way out of all the fucked-up stuff in my head and my past.

She's an entrance. She's the way into something bigger and better than I could ever have imagined, and for once in my life, I don't have anything to say. No dirty words to tease her or push her. I don't need to tell her what I want or ask her to do the same because it's so good just being inside her that I can't even think of anything else.

There's nothing I want more than exactly what I have.

When I pull out and push back inside, her hips rock up to meet me. Her hair is fanned out around her on the bed, and her head tips back, her eyes closed. I repeat the motion, making sure to grind against her so that she feels just as good as I do.

I lose track of time in her. Somewhere along the way, we move under the covers, and she straddles me, rocking against me with her hair swinging like I always wanted. She comes apart hovering above me, and if possible it's even more gorgeous than the first time I saw her do that.

I flip her under me again and sit back on my heels. I lift her hips up onto the slant of my thighs, and I watch myself entering her. I watch the way her body takes me, and the way she tenses and writhes each time I slide out. I press a thumb to her clit, and she's so sensitive from her last orgasm that she cries out and jerks against me.

I go slow, gliding my hands lightly over her body, waiting for her to be ready again, and I know she is when she digs her heels into my ass.

I slam into her then, hard and greedy. She stretches her arms above her head, and I follow, lacing our fingers together and pushing her hands down into the mattress.

I'm finally starting to adjust to the way my mind has rearranged itself around her, and now it seems so obvious. This was always going to happen. It's impossible not to fall for a girl like her. I'm not sure I even know what love is. It's certainly not a word I have much experience saying, let alone feeling, but I refuse to believe anything could be bigger than this, than the way I feel about her.

"Never," I tell her. "I'll never get tired of this. I need you to come for me again, baby. I need to feel you squeeze tight around me. And I need your eyes on mine."

That's the first time I've ever told a girl what I needed instead of what I wanted. It might be the first time that distinction has ever been important.

But I do need to know that the crazy things happening in my head and heart aren't all on me. I dip my head and close my lips over a rosy peak, and she arches, her stomach pressed up against mine. I'm going to spend a whole day devoted to her breasts. I want to spend days with every part of her.

I pick up the pace, and every time I push deep, she makes this tiny little sound, her lips curved into a circle. Her nails bite down into the back of my hand, her back arches, and she clenches around me. I lay my forehead against hers, and her breath pants out over my lips as her muscles contract again. Pleasure so strong it's almost painful tears down my spine, and my vision blurs as I come.

Time seems to stop, and the feeling stretches on for so long that I think I'm dreaming. That it can't possibly be real, and then her hands are on my face, pulling me down to her lips.

I spend half the night trying to lose and find myself in her all at the same time, and she keeps up with me, matches me kiss for kiss, touch for touch, and I begin to hope.

For the first time in my life, I'm thinking about what comes next, not what's hot on my heels.

Chapter 21

Silas

I wake to a pounding on my door, and I barely have time to pull a sheet up over Dylan's naked back before Torres pokes his head through the door.

"Dude, you're gonna be—whoa. Sorry, man."

Dylan wakes up and starts to roll over.

"Get the fuck out, Torres."

He closes the door with a quick snap and then says through the wood, "I was just gonna say that you'll be late for practice if you don't get a move on. Zay and I are leaving."

I look at my alarm clock and curse. I completely forgot to set it last night.

"You're late?" Dylan asks sleepily.

"Gonna be if I don't hurry."

Even so, I lean over and kiss her before I climb out of bed. She rolls over on her side to face me as I pull on a pair of compression shorts. She looks so damn good in my bed, that sheet doing nothing to hide her curves. I'm tempted to say screw practice and stay home with her.

"I'm sorry that I have to leave so fast."

She yawns and holds up one finger. "I'll owe you for that apology."

I don't realize how nervous I'd been about whether or not this would keep going, until she says those words.

"In that case, I'm very, very sorry. More sorry than I've ever been."

She laughs and ticks off two more fingers before burying her face in my pillow and stretching out her legs.

I finish pulling on the rest of my clothes, keeping an eye on the clock. I grab the last of my things and bend over to trail a hand over her cheek. She blinks up at me, and I'm fairly certain she fell asleep again in the minute since we spoke.

"Stay as long as you want," I tell her. "No one will be here to bother you."

"Is this the part where you tell me you'll call me? And I worry about whether or not you're telling the truth?"

"Stay here until I get home, and I won't have to call you. If you still want to be naked, I won't even complain."

"You're going to be late."

I kiss her again, curling a hand around her backside for a quick stroke.

"Worth it."

She laughs. "Go."

"If get laid out today because I'm too busy daydreaming about your mouth, I'll expect you to nurse me back to health again."

"Go, or I'm going to lay you out."

"Sounds fun, but let's save that for tonight."

I can still hear her laughing as I jog down the stairs. I don't even realize I've got my athletic shorts on backward until I'm in my truck and pulling out of the driveway.

My head is too full of her to care about anything else.

I HEAD TO Coach's office without being asked this time. My palms are sweaty, and my neck tight with nerves. Most of the other coaches have already left the office to get last-minute things ready, but Coach Cole is still in his office, on the phone.

His back is to me, and I hear him talking. "We will soon, Annaiss. I promise. She's finally getting to where she talks to me about things. We haven't been this good since she was a little kid, and I want to make sure we're solid before I throw another curveball at her."

I feel like a dick for interrupting, but if I don't, there won't be time to talk to him before practice.

I knock on the doorjamb, and his chair spins. His face is unreadable as he sees me, and he says without reaction into the phone, "I have to go. I'll see you tonight."

Rumor is Coach is seeing someone, a professor at the university, but Carson and Dallas have both been pretty tight-lipped about it, so I figured it wasn't true.

Guess I was wrong.

"Morning, Silas. Come in."

I close the door behind me and take a seat in the same chair where my world had been flipped upside down last week.

"Brookes tells me you had a minor injury."

Damn it, Zay. I told him to tell Coach that I was working everything out. That didn't give him license to tell Coach everything I did.

"Just a bit of a sprain, sir."

As I bounce my knee nervously, I don't let myself think about the fact that the joint is still tighter than it used to be.

He hums and nods, running a palm over the short beard he has growing in.

"He also tells me it happened while you were doing some sort of community service."

I sigh. "Something like that."

Coach stands and takes a seat on the edge of his desk. It puts him looking down at me, which doesn't help my nerves.

"I'll admit. That's not how I expected you to spend your suspension. I think it shows a lot of maturity."

It feels strange to be praised for something that wasn't my idea, something I only really did for a girl. And I don't want to lie to him because I haven't magically become a model citizen overnight. I'm still the fuckup trying to make it through the day without ruining his life.

"It was a friend's idea, really." I trip over the word *friend* because that word is too damn small for how big Dylan feels to me. "Gave me something to focus on, instead of sitting at home being angry."

He nods. "That's good. Really good, son."

Damn . . . this isn't going anything like I'd thought it would. I was prepared for Coach to still be mad, for him to send me out to run until I pass out with Oz again.

"Did it help?" he asks.

I shrug. "I don't know. It was something to do."

"And how is that sprain feeling now?"

He's asking like he cares, and it freaks me out because I know he does. He does care, and I've never had this many people in my life who care about me at once. I've never had this many people around for me to disappoint.

"A bit tight, but nothing I can't handle."

"And now that you've had some time to cool off, you have anything else you want to say about the fight with Keyon? Or with Levi?"

I miss the anger. Having it to hold on to had grounded me, had given me focus and kept me from thinking too much. I don't know if it was last night with Dylan or this whole week, but when I reach for it now, it's harder to grab, like trying to hold on to smoke. And I don't know how to answer his question (or avoid it) without that anger.

"It felt good to be angry," I tell him. "At Levi. At Keyon. At you. As long as I was angry, I didn't feel the fear."

"Fear of what?"

I scratch the back of my neck and resist the urge to pull at my hair, to drop my head down and stare at the floor.

"Screwing things up. Like Levi did. Like I have a tendency to do."

Coach laughs and moves to sit in the chair beside me. Together, we stare forward at his empty desk, at the trophies and plaques lining the wall behind it.

"I know a thing or two about you, Moore. I've read your file, all your stats from high school until now. I know you had some problems in school before you got into football. But how much do you know about me?"

I shrug. "Everything there was on the Internet when they hired you before the start of the season last year." I gesture at the awards on his wall and say, "All that stuff. Plus the schools you turned around, the programs you built up from nothing."

"We all deal with screwups in our own way. Like you working on those houses this week, I've spent my life building things up in front of me, so I'll never have to look at the ruined things behind me. It works for a little while. Worked nearly twenty years for me, but sooner or later you gotta face the thing you've spent all your energy ignoring. The anger might have felt good, might have been easier, but it would have run out eventually, son. But if you go that route, it will take everything from you before it does. Or you can do what I didn't, stop yourself from wasting decades, and face your problems now."

I swallow. Is that what I'm doing now? Facing them? Or have I just found a new way to ignore them? A new distraction in Dylan?

"It's a head game, Silas. If you stood on that field constantly thinking about all the ways the defense could take you down, you'd never gain a yard. You're a damn fine player because you know how to look for the gaps on the field, and how to push through and make one when the opening isn't there. Live the way you play ball, and you'll be just fine, I promise you that."

Live the way I play.

It seems so simple that I feel stupid, like he switched on a light I didn't know was there while I spent years stumbling around in the dark. It's still sinking in when he claps a hand on my shoulder and squeezes.

"You'll be with Gallt and the rest of the running backs for drills through the rest of camp, but when we're covering plays and scrimmaging, I'll be going with Williams. He's got to be ready to start in a few weeks. Can you handle that?"

I clench my jaw and nod because I don't really have a choice.

"Good. Now get out on the field. Coach Oz is waiting for you and the running backs. That fight counts as your second infraction, which means you and your group run. Unless you want Gallt to skin you alive, I suggest you figure out how not to get a third."

Fuck. Just how I wanted to start back to practice, by pissing everyone off.

IT'S THE WORST practice of my life. Not because I play bad. I play just fine. But Coach's understanding attitude did not stretch to the rest of the team. They were pissed. Keyon's lip is still scabbed, and I keep catching him glaring at me like he's just waiting for the perfect moment to jump me. Coach Gallt didn't like me to begin with, and his opinion of me sure hasn't gotten any better. If any of the other backs were feeling charitable, that's gone by the time we finish my punishment, *our punishment*, with Oz.

When the running is done, we do drills and drills and more drills, which wouldn't be so bad if I got to play when the drills are over, but I don't. Instead, I stand on the sidelines watching for the first time in years. Even as a redshirt, when I wasn't actually playing in games, I still got time in practice on the field. And after the mess with Levi, Coach is big on making sure we've got depth on the team. He rotates in backups and the backup backups to make sure there's always someone who can get the job done.

I don't get rotated in once, and when the final whistle blows, I can feel the familiar anger just beneath my lungs, and it's a lot easier to call it up now. Every time I breathe it's there, waiting to be let out.

But I hold it in. Hold my breath even when Williams clocks my shoulder as he walks past to get some water. It would be so easy to lay into him, and not with a punch this time. One thing that standing on the sidelines has given me is time to watch and analyze. The guy might be fast, but he's not *quick*. Give him an open field or a missed tackle, and he'll rake in the yards. But when there's just a split second to break through a hole, he misses it 50 percent of the time. And on top of that, he runs high. Instead of getting low and making himself a smaller target, he's more concerned with showing off, and it makes him easier to tackle.

So the guy can bump into me as many times as he wants, but until he fixes his pad level and gets quicker on his feet, he doesn't have shit on me.

That and the possibility of Dylan still being at my apartment when I get home are the only things that get me through practice, through the looks in the locker room, and through the final task I set for myself today.

I'm waiting outside on the sidewalk when Keyon exits the building.

He's walking with a few other freshmen, probably heading back to their dorms, and when I step up their conversation stops.

He lifts his chin and says, "Got a little smarter, did ya? Waiting until Coach ain't around?" He drops his bag, cracks his knuckles, and shakes out his shoulders.

I sigh and shake my head. Was I this much of an idiot my freshman year?

"Relax, man. I'm not coming at you." Even if he could stand to be taken down a peg or two. "Just wanted to say . . ." I twist my lips and spit out the word, "Sorry. You caught me on a bad day, and instead of brushing it off, I took it out on you."

He turns his head to the side and squints up at me. Then he looks at his friends and laughs. "Man, you're a pussy. You wanna hug it out next?"

God, I want to hit this kid so bad.

Instead, I take a deep breath and back up a few steps. "See you on the field, fish."

"You mean on the sidelines, right? Since that's the only thing you'll see for a while."

Keep walking. Keep fucking walking.

Before I even realize what I'm doing, I'm picturing Dylan— her sweet laugh, that tempting pout, her blue eyes always studying me. I picture her, and I put one foot in front of the other all the way to my truck. I keep it up through three red lights, a stop sign, and one slow-ass car that decided to drive fifteen miles an hour in a thirty-five zone.

But then I'm home and climbing the stairs and throwing open my door to a perfectly made bed and an empty room.

I crack. Wide open. It feels like my ribs have been pulled back like a wishbone, and I somehow have come up with all smaller halves. I throw my bag at the wall, but the thud as it hits isn't the least bit satisfying. I hear Brookes and Torres moving around downstairs, and I slam my door shut. Leaning my forehead against the wood, I squeeze my eyes shut tight and try to talk myself down.

I can't let this drag me down again. Football is too important. My future is too important to lose it every time something doesn't go my way.

I'm two deep breaths down when I hear a knock on the other side of the door.

"Go away, Brookes. I'm not in the mood."

"Um, Silas?"

It's not Brookes. I tear open the door so fast that her blonde hair flies up around her as if on a breeze. Her eyes widen in surprise, and I pull her up and into my arms within seconds. She squeals and wraps her arms around my neck. I close the door again behind us, and when I press her back against it, her legs wrap around my hips.

I kiss her mouth, her cheek, her jaw, her neck. I kiss absolutely every piece of her I can reach, and when I run out, I pull her legs down and make her stand. Then I drop to my knees in front of her, and push up that same sheer shirt from yesterday to drag my tongue over the soft flesh of her stomach.

"S-Silas?" she asks quietly. "Are you okay?"

Dragging her shorts down her legs, I wait for her to lift her feet so I can throw them away, then I kiss her bare hip, just above the lace edge of her underwear, and say, "I'm perfect." I drag that scrap of lace down, too, and put my mouth where I've wanted it for days. One of her hands clutches at my head and the other locks on to the doorknob, holding her steady. She moans while I taste her, and between flicks of my tongue I tell her again, "Absolutely perfect."

And I was right that day in the kitchen. With my mouth on her and her hands in my hair and those tiny gasps she makes, the whole fucking world just disappears.

Chapter 22

Dylan

This is either the worst idea I've ever had. Or the best. If the tumbling, twisting sensation behind my ribs is any indication, I'm going to say best.

Silas crosses the playroom toward me, an adorable brown and gray mottled puppy in his arms.

"This one's a fast little sucker. I nearly didn't catch him."

The puppy is a Labrador and cattle dog mix, and even as a puppy, he's almost too big for my arms when Silas hands him over to me.

"What's his name again?" he asks.

I check the pup's tag and answer, "Leo."

He scowls. "That's a terrible name. He'll never get adopted with a wimpy name like that."

I smile. "You got a better one?"

"Hell yeah. I think we should change his name to Bo Jackson."

He leans over and scratches the dog's ears.

"You just pull that name out of nowhere?"

Holding his hand up to his heart, Silas gives me a pained look. "You're killing me, baby. Bo Jackson is only one of the greatest athletes of all time. Possibly *the* greatest. And he was crazy fast." He scratches the dog's ears again, curving his large hand around the puppy's head. "Just like this dude."

My heart *might* be beating a little faster. Maybe. And I didn't really process anything he said after "baby."

I just know Silas plus puppies is a dangerously sexy combination.

"Has anyone ever told you that you're kind of sweet?"

He abandons the dog to focus his attention on me. Reaching out, he wraps my braid around his hand as he's so fond of doing, and tugs just enough to tip my head back.

"Anyone ever tell you you're fucking gorgeous?"

"You did. This morning."

He closes his eyes and smiles. "That's right. You were incredibly hot this morning. And greedy. And wet—"

I fumble with the dog until I've got one hand free and slap it over Silas's mouth.

"You're terrible. Someone might hear you."

He nips one of my fingers with his teeth, and his eyes are dark as I pull back.

I better head this off before we get a little too personal in public, and I'm no longer allowed to volunteer at the animal shelter.

I step back. "I'm going to put *Bo Jackson* in his cage. You go ahead and get the next dog we're supposed to walk."

By the time I get the little rascal in his cage and wash my hands like we're supposed to do between contact with different pets, there's a group of three college girls surrounding Silas. He holds our next walking buddy, some kind of pit bull mix, and the girls are cooing and smiling at the dog in his arms. I'm 100 percent sure their attention has less to do with the dog, and more to do with who's holding him.

I walk up just in time to hear Silas say, "You should take him home. He'd be a good guard dog. Good thing to have, especially if the three of you are living alone."

One of the girls snags the dog's tag to read his name, but Silas stops her. "Don't pay any attention to the tag. You should call him Emmitt. That's a good, tough name for a dog like him."

"Emmitt," one of the girls says, raising her eyebrows at a friend.

Fifteen minutes later Emmitt is on his way to a new home, and Silas looks smug as can be. By the time we go on the last walk of our four-hour volunteer shift, five dogs have found new homes (and new football-related names), and there's no deflating Silas's ego, so I don't even bother.

"I'm pretty sure that's more adoptions today than they've probably had the rest of the week combined. You might be the shelter's new secret weapon against prospective pet owners with two X chromosomes."

He switches the leash of our current dog to his other hand. I thought for sure when we got to the girl dogs, he'd let up on the football names, but apparently there was a famous running back named Gale, who's the namesake for the cocker spaniel we've got now.

"So what lesson was I learning today?" he asks.

I smile. "Nothing really. I was just stressed and wanted to play with puppies."

He shakes his head and drops an arm over my shoulder. "You tricked me."

I wrap my arm around his waist and say, "If it makes you feel better, you can say you were working on being compassionate."

We're too busy looking at each other, so we don't notice until it's too late that little Gale has popped a squat right in front of Silas's foot. He looks down and curses, pulling his shoe out of the puddle.

"Aw, shit. It's soaking through my sneaker."

"Maybe you should get a dog. It would probably teach you some anger management skills."

He uses the arm around my shoulder to pull me closer to him.

"Let's go back to my place. I think it's definitely my turn to teach you something."

I GASP AND then moan as Silas pushes me against the door to his bedroom. My breasts are flattened against the wood, and I can feel the muscled curves of his body against my back.

His mouth falls to my neck, and he bends slightly, so that the jut of his erection pushes into the curve of my ass.

"And . . ." I break off for a few seconds as his teeth graze my shoulder and my thoughts scatter. Then I push on. "What are you planning to teach me?"

"I'm still deciding."

Oh God. I'm terrified and eager, but both emotions are irrelevant as soon as he spins me around to face him. He towers over me, and his hands make quick work of my braid so that he can sink his fingers into my hair. He tilts my head back as far as it will go, and presses close against me so that I feel him now against my stomach.

He trails a thumb over my mouth, and on instinct I wrap my lips around it and suck.

His grip tightens, and his hips push harder against me. His thigh is fitted between my legs and presses tight against my center.

"I've mentioned that I love your mouth, right?"

I pull back and smile. "Maybe a few . . . hundred times."

He bends, licking and sucking and biting until my lips feel deliciously swollen, all while I rock myself against his thigh.

I reach between us to stroke the bulge in his jeans, and he breaks away.

"Fuck, baby. I had a plan. I was going to make you beg, make you tell me what you want."

"But?" I add for him.

"But you drive me crazy, and I can't wait to be inside you."

It's my new favorite game, making Silas lose control.

"So don't wait," I tell him.

He growls and kisses me again. I'm almost dizzy with want when he pulls away. He points a finger at me and says, "Clothes.

Off. Now." Then he darts to the nightstand, where he has condoms stashed in a drawer.

I'm bent over, trying to do away with the underwear currently stubbornly clinging to my ankle, when he returns.

Things move fast after that. His hands smooth over the curve of my ass, and I find my chest pressed to the door just like this whole thing started.

"This is gonna be hard and fast, babe. Can you handle that?"

My only answer is to reach one arm behind me and hook it around the back of his neck. He uses his foot to nudge mine a little farther apart. His fingers dig into my hips, and he pulls them back just a little so my back arches. Then he's pushing inside me, and I hold my breath.

It's different like this. Not just because we're standing up, and I'm facing away. He hits something inside me that makes my legs go a little weak, and for a few moments, I think I won't be able to stay standing.

But he holds me tight, and the door keeps me from falling forward. And just when I catch my breath, he moves. He slides back and then in, hard, and I cry out. I can't help it. And each time I think I've got it under control, he thrusts and another noise rips from my mouth before I can even think about stopping it.

And it's so good, I've forgotten how to breathe.

And I don't even care.

TEN MINUTES LATER, we're curled up naked in his bed, his big body curved around mine, and my heart is still beating fast.

"So what lesson was that exactly?"

He laughs, and I feel his chest vibrate against my back.

"That particular lesson was about the fact that your ass drives me crazy."

"Even crazier than my mouth?"

"All of you," he whispers against the back of my neck. "Every single thing about you gets to me, digs deep."

He slides an arm around my waist and up through the valley between my breast. His wrist presses directly over my racing heart, and his hand curls around my shoulder, holding me snug against him. It feels both strange and normal to be held against him like this. I would never have thought there would be any kind of intimacy after the kind of sex we just had, but with Silas . . . it just works.

Then I go and screw it all up.

"Can you answer my question now?"

He hums behind me, and his reply sounds groggy, like he's about to fall asleep even though the sun's not even down. "What's your question?"

"The question. The very first one I asked you."

He tenses behind me, and the arm he has looped around my body falls away. He rolls onto his back, and I miss the warmth of his skin against mine.

But I need to know this.

He seems like a completely different guy than the Silas I met a few weeks ago. He's happy and funny and sweet, and I haven't seen even a glimpse of the anger that got him into so much trouble.

But I'm not naive enough to think it isn't there. And I'm not doing him any favors by pretending along with him.

"I waited," I say. "I gave you time. But now I'm asking you again, Silas. What is it that scares you? What is it about Levi and your hometown and football that always puts you so on edge?"

I hear him sigh behind me, and I want to turn over to see his face, but I think maybe this way will be easier for him. Less pressure.

"I'm scared of failing," he says. "That's it. Nothing special."

"Failing?" I do turn over then because I'm calling bullshit. "And that's what you wouldn't tell me the first time I asked?"

"I'm not smart, Dylan. Or rich. Or particularly talented at anything besides football. I lose my spot on the team, I lose my only shot at a decent future. I'm sorry if I didn't want to say that to a girl I just met." He leans close and kisses me. Short. Perfunctory. Like he's trying to shut me up. "A girl whose ass drove me crazy even then."

He drags his mouth down to my neck, but I know a diversionary tactic when I see one. He's not telling me the truth. Or at least he's not telling me all of it.

I slide away and mumble, "I have to go to the bathroom." I pull on one of his T-shirts and my underwear, and I escape out of his bedroom and into the bathroom across the hall.

The bathroom where everything started.

That is, if you don't count the police station.

I face myself in the mirror, and I want to be annoyed that he still won't open up to me. I mean, I can infer the basics. He's running from his past. I just don't know why. The only thing in his life pre-Rusk he's ever talked about is football. He's not mentioned any family or friends or anything.

But even knowing that . . . I can't muster any anger over him closing me off. Because how can I ask him to deal with his past, when I, too, am so good at pretending mine doesn't exist?

Whatever I'm asking him to dig up is no doubt messy. It's probably painful. And God knows, I get the appeal of trying to leave that kind of thing in your past. I've always told myself that it was pointless to drag up stuff like that when it can't be changed.

But I think that's Silas's problem. He thinks that because it can't be changed, the way he *feels* about it can't be changed, either.

And maybe it's time I take a little of my own medicine and face the things I can't change. Maybe then I'll know how to better help him.

Chapter 23

Silas

I don't hear from Dylan for three days. She never dropped by. Never texted me about helping with some charity or nonprofit or anything. I texted her, but she never answered. By Saturday evening, two nights before we start back to school, my patience has all dried up. Life is shitty enough with football how it is, I'm not going to just let her ignore me. I decide to just show up at her apartment and make her talk to me, but the problem is I only have a vague idea of where she lives. I know the street, and I'm pretty sure about which complex it is, but I've got no earthly clue which apartment it is. So instead, I get a hold of her friend Matt, and he gives me her address.

When I leave the house that evening, I'm all set to storm over to her apartment and bang on her door until she talks to me, but I pull up short when I get to my truck.

She's already here.

She's wearing a dress that looks like an oversized men's T-shirt, has her hair braided over one shoulder, and her face scrubbed free of makeup. Leaning against my car door with her arms crossed over her middle and her hair down, she looks so subdued. Normally, she's sunshine. She's light and happy and unsinkable. Today, it's like her flame has been snuffed out.

And I realize what's happening.

She's ending this. That's why she hasn't called, why she looks so forlorn now. A warm evening breeze blows a few loose strands of hair across her face, and when she lifts her head to pull them away, she sees me. Her hands drop from around her middle, and she takes a step forward away from my truck.

My chest feels hollowed out at the sight of her. I want to soak her up after the days apart and keep my distance all at the same time.

"Hey," she whispers, and I don't so much hear the word as see it on her lips.

"Hey."

"Sorry I've not been around."

I want to cross to her, push her up against my truck, and kiss the apology right off her lips. But I don't. I plant my feet and stay exactly where I am.

"Where have you been?"

She shrugs. "Nowhere. Locked in my room, mostly."

I don't know how to do stuff like this. I've never been in a relationship. The last few weeks with her are the most serious thing I've ever had, the only relationship, romantic or otherwise, that has ever meant this much. I don't know the rules. All I know is that I've missed her, that my life seems out of balance without her.

"Dylan, I need you to tell me. Whatever it is that you're thinking right now, please put me out of my misery and just tell me."

She lifts a hand and traces the outer rim of my oversized rearview mirror.

"Can we go for a drive or something? Just get away for a bit?"

I hesitate, unsure what to think. I might not know much about relationships or breakups, but common sense says you don't go somewhere with someone if you're planning to dump them.

Even when I'm worried about what she'll say, I still can't tell her no.

"Sure. Okay. Hop in."

She doesn't go around to the passenger side. Instead she opens my door, and climbs up first. I'm surprised to see her sit in the middle seat, and it makes it a little easier to breathe around all the worry. She doesn't act like we're breaking up, especially when I climb up beside her and she loops her arm around mine when I reach for the stick shift.

"Any preference where we go?"

She shakes her head. "Somewhere quiet."

I take the highway south out of town, and take an exit for a smaller highway that leads out to some small towns between here and West Texas. I never planned to drive back that way, back in the direction of home, but off the top of my head, it's the only place I can think of to take her. Just before we hit the first small town I pull over onto the side of the highway. It's mostly ranches and farms out here, so the only lights around for miles are my head-lights. I park so that they shine through the barbed wire fence and out onto the field of green beyond us. I think for a few moments and then switch the lights off, leaving us in the dark.

"Come on."

I open my door and slide out, holding out a hand for her to join me. Then I lead her around to the tailgate of my truck and lower it.

If I were better at this kind of thing, I would have a blanket or something else so she wouldn't have to sit in the dirty bed of my truck and ruin her nice clothes.

But I don't have a blanket, and I have no fucking clue what I'm doing. So I just do whatever comes to mind. I climb up in the back and lift her up with me. I take a seat leaning back against the cab and pull her down in my lap. I'll have to be the blanket, be the thing that keeps her clean and warm.

She ducks her head beneath my chin and pulls her knees up to her chest. The cicadas are out in full force tonight, and the sound of them reminds me of heavy rain. They're so loud that I don't notice Dylan is crying until I feel her damp cheek against my neck.

"Dylan?"

She doesn't answer, and when I try to get a look at her face she keeps herself pressed tightly against my neck where I can't see.

"Baby, what's wrong?"

"I should never have asked."

"Should never have asked what?"

She shakes in my arms, and her gasped breaths are getting bigger, louder.

"I've gone all this time in the dark, and it should have stayed that way. But I thought I needed to. Thought I needed to know."

"You're scaring me, Dylan." I'm so bad at this shit. Hell, I go off and hit people when I can't handle my emotions. How am I supposed to deal with someone else's? How am I supposed to deal with her crying when every broken breath she takes feels like the slice of a knife over my chest? "Talk to me. Please."

"I'm adopted."

I tense. "And you just found out?"

She shakes her head against my neck. "No. I've always known. I was in foster care until I was nine, and then I was adopted."

It stings that I didn't know that. I should have *known* that.

But I never asked. I stopped asking questions because I didn't want her to turn around and ask me.

"Okay. So . . . what's changed?"

I feel her swallow, and she fiddles with her hands nervously until I lay one of mine over the top of both of hers.

"Wednesday," she answers. "When I asked you that question again . . . I started thinking that it wasn't fair of me to ask you to deal with your past, when I've deliberately chosen to remain ignorant about so much of mine. I'd always sworn I didn't want to know. I thought it would somehow jeopardize what I had with the Brenners, with my adopted parents. But as soon as I thought about it at your place, I knew I had to know. I *wanted* to know."

"Wanted to know what?"

"My birth mother. I know she d-died. That's why I was in foster care, but I didn't know how. On Thursday, I asked my parents, and they told me."

I run my fingers along her braid, dipping underneath occasionally to lightly stroke her neck, and I press my cheek tight to the top of her head.

"How?"

She trembles harder in my arms, and I pull her closer, thinking maybe if I hold her tightly enough, I can keep whatever is making her shake at bay.

"She was killed," she says. "Her boyfriend. He might have been my dad. We're not sure. Anyway, they fought a lot. My mother told me that, my adopted mother, but now I think I can remember. Maybe. Or maybe it's just my head filling in the blanks, but I think I remember the screaming. He was a drunk. And he hit her. He hit her all the time. But one night he kept going, kept hitting her, and he must have just snapped or something because he kept right on going until he killed her. Then when it was over, he killed himself, too."

"Oh, baby. I'm sorry. I'm so sorry."

I press my lips to her forehead, and she's still shaking so much it scares me. I've never felt so helpless in my life. I keep squeezing and kissing and touching her, but it's not enough. Nothing changes.

"I don't know why," she hiccups. "I don't know why I'm so upset. I knew she was dead already, but . . . I can't. I can't stop thinking about it. I imagine it, how it must have happened. And I imagine what my life would be like if it hadn't. And—"

She sobs harder than ever and pulls her arms tight around herself. I want her to put her arms around me, to pull me into her pain. It's ten times worse having her curling up in this ball with me on the outside.

"I imagine that life, and I'm glad, Silas. I'm glad she died, and I got adopted. How horrible of a person does that make me that I'm *glad*? I talk about helping people, about being compassionate, but really I'm selfish and awful."

She says something more, or she tries to, but she's crying so hard that I can't understand the words.

"You're not. You're not awful." I say those words again and again, but I'm not sure she hears me.

I don't know how to make it better, so I just do my best not to make it worse. I hold her. I hold her, and I know now why caring about another person is so damn scary. It's not that they won't care about you back, because that either happens or it doesn't. You live with it or you do everything you can to change it. The really scary thing is the moment you realize that for the rest of your life, you'll feel twice the pain, twice the joy, twice the fear.

Twice as helpless to control it all, too.

I think about what Coach told me . . . to live the way I play.

I don't know that it's the right thing, but I try it anyway. When a teammate is in trouble, when defenders are closing in, the best thing I can do is block for him, take the hits for him. *With him.*

"I'm glad, too," I tell her. "I'm glad you were in a home where you were safe and cared for. I'm glad you were able to grow up into exactly the person you are. So, if you're a horrible person, I am, too. But being glad for the things you have and where you are is not the same as being glad that your mother died. You're a smart girl, and you know that life isn't black-and-white like that. You can separate those two things. Same as I'm not glad I was suspended from the team, but I'm glad being suspended gave me a chance to know you. Everything in the world might be connected, but that doesn't mean the way we feel about them has to be."

It takes a while, but eventually she stops crying. She lifts her head from where she buried it in my neck and lays it on my shoulder instead. She tells me about the foster homes she remembers, and about the Brenners adopting her.

I thought I'd known who she was . . . my perfect girl who was spending all her energy trying to please and help other people. And that's in her, sure, but it isn't just other people she's trying to impress. She's been trying to convince herself that *she* belongs in that world, too.

And damn if I don't know *exactly* how that feels.

I think about telling her about my childhood, too, but I don't know if that will make things better or worse. Maybe it will show her she's not alone, that the past is chasing all of us, determined to pull us back into memories long gone and pains that should be healed. Or maybe it will make her feel worse right when I've finally got her calm.

If there's a chance she feels the same as me, then it's possible she'll take on my hurt the way I took on hers. And I don't want to do that to her . . . not tonight.

So, instead I scoot forward a few feet and lie down in the truck bed. I keep her balanced on top of me, cradled against my body, and together we stare at the blue-black sky until the world starts to feel big again.

Chapter 24

Dylan

The night before school starts back, I'm supposed to go to this cocktail party for all the deans and regents and important alumni.

Officially, I'm going on my father's invite. But Dad's out of town, so I'm using it as one last-ditch effort to drum up support to keep the homeless shelter open.

And because I'm crazy (and he asked), I'm taking Silas with me. I reason with myself that it will be good for him to be in that kind of atmosphere. He's not so great with the authority figures, and this way he can practice with me there to smooth over the rough edges.

I have no idea why he would want to go to something like this. Maybe he's worried I might break down again like last night. Or it's just an excuse to see me in a little black dress.

Probably the latter.

A small part of me (or a big part) was looking forward to ogling him, too. Silas Moore in a suit is probably a recipe for a heart arrhythmia. When he shows up in jeans and a nice button-down, I'm only mildly disappointed. It's not the suit of my fantasy, but he still looks good. Tall and broad and sinfully handsome.

And to make things even better, he's easygoing and charming. Right up until the moment we enter the party. It's in one of the old libraries on campus, and the place is all leather and rare books and glass cases.

And Silas—he's silent. Like try-to-pretend-you're-a-piece-of-the-wall silent.

He seems content to just lurk by the food table, and he looks miserable every time I drag him into a conversation. So eventually I let him do his thing, and seek out a few people I know in the crowd, answering questions about school and my parents, before casually dropping mention of the shelter into conversation.

It works for a little while, but eventually I can't stand the feeling of Silas's eyes on me as he sulks against the wall across the room.

So I politely excuse myself from my conversation with Mrs. Simon, the little old lady I've been chatting with for ten minutes. She's sweet, and she knows my father, and she could be an asset with the shelter. All reasons I should stay and talk to her, but I can't.

"Hey, McBroody," I say. "You know you don't *have* to be here if you're miserable. I can manage this alone."

He shakes his head. "I'm not leaving."

"Okaaay. Well, then can you stop glaring at everything."

His frown deepens. "Sorry."

I place a hand on his arm and lean closer. "Is that a ploy to try to get me to kiss you?"

One corner of his mouth curves up. "Maybe. Is it going to work?"

I don't bother hiding my smile, which is why I'm grinning like an idiot when someone calls my name, and I turn around to find my parents staring at me.

I blink, and when Mom's eyes flick to my hand on Silas's arm, I drop it to my side.

"Dad. I thought you were out of town."

"My meeting got pushed until next week, so your mother and I decided to attend the party after all."

"Oh." That's all I say. *Oh.*

It's Dad who walks over to introduce himself to Silas because I'm hearing this roaring in my ears, like something about to crash and burn because this was never supposed to happen. That was my one rule. I've let Silas bend and break every other one in my life, but these two worlds were supposed to stay separate.

"Richard Brenner," my father says, holding his hand out to shake.

I don't know if Silas is freaked-out by this. I can't bring myself to look at him. But he returns my father's handshake and says, "Silas Moore."

I see Mom looking at Silas's jeans, and I can just imagine what condescending thoughts are going through her head. She thinks I'm supposed to be with Henry. That we're a perfect couple, and I should just wait for him to come back around.

I should set her straight, but not like this. Not with Silas there to take half the fall. We're temporary. We're simple.

We're a series of wants and desires, and nothing else.

He is *not* the meet-the-parents type. That's pretty much asking for him to get spooked and run.

"Silas," my mother says. "How do you know our daughter?"

I answer for him. "We've met once or twice at school."

I hope they'll leave it at that. But Dad has a freakishly good memory.

"Your name sounds familiar," my father says. "Do you have any family members on the board? Maybe alumni?"

I hear Silas laugh, one of those laughs that *clearly* aren't about something funny. But I still can't look at him.

"No, sir. I'm on the football team. Maybe that's it."

Dad's eyebrows rise. "The Rusk football team?"

"Yes, sir. Running back."

Now Dad's eyebrows slam down and his lips purse together. "Right. Silas Moore. Now I remember." And from the steely look on his face, he's heard about Silas's suspension. I try not to let the panic show on my face. *Of course* Dad would have heard about that. He always knows everything that's going on at Rusk. Everything that impacts the school's reputation, and thus their ability to bring in money.

This isn't just going downhill. If I don't end this now, it will be akin to tumbling down the side of a mountain. Dad will poke and pry and pin Silas to the spot until he gets whatever answers he wants. That's how he works.

And knowing Silas, he'll fight back rather than lie down.

"Well, we were just chatting about classes, but now that you guys are here . . ." I step closer to my parents, and meet Silas's gaze for the first time. His expression is blank, almost stony. And I can't read anything in his eyes. "I'll see you around, Silas." I offer a smile and hope that he can read the apology through my eyes. I'll hang with my parents for a little while, and then feign a stomachache and come find him.

My parents turn to walk away, and I follow, but not before mouthing *be right back* at him.

I follow behind my mom, and we stand off to the side while Dad shakes hands with a few of his friends. Mom smiles and follows his lead. I just give a little wave. When Dad is fully immersed in conversation, Mom turns to me.

"Have you seen Henry?"

God, she's stubborn.

"No, Mom. I haven't."

"Really? I spoke to his mother, and she mentioned something about the two of you running into each other at that construction project you've been doing."

Crap. I wonder how much Henry told his mother. Did he mention Silas?

"Oh. Right. I forgot about that. We didn't really talk."

"Gloria says Henry is under the impression that you're already dating someone else."

Crap. So. Much. Crap.

I press my lips together and hum. "Hmm . . . nope. No new boyfriend."

She doesn't look back in the direction of Silas, but she does slant her body ever so slightly in that direction.

"You're sure?" she says.

"Pretty sure I'd know if I was dating someone, but who knows."

Her eyes narrow, and I know I'm being a smart mouth. I don't think I've ever been anything less than 110 percent respectful. I can see the moment where she decides what must have caused my bit of rebellion, and she looks back at the wall where Silas is standing.

Was standing.

He's not there anymore, and my stomach sinks.

Mom looks back at me, studying.

"I don't have time for a boyfriend," I tell her. "Classes start tomorrow, and I'm still trying to get support to keep the homeless shelter downtown open. I'm busy. Too busy for a guy."

"I thought the shelter was a done deal."

I shrug. "Done deal or not, doesn't mean I just have to accept it. I refuse to accept it."

"Darling, sometimes you have to be realistic and admit when you've lost."

"When we've lost is when it's the most important to make sure our voices are heard. So that maybe we don't lose next time."

There's a truth you learn early on in the activism scene . . . most protests are lost before they even start. We hope for change. Beg for it. But even when we know it won't come, still we stand with our signs and say our chants. Still we show up. Because to lie down and say nothing means the cause dies with us, and a little piece of *us* with it. So we chant. And we chant. And we say the same words again and again and again. Louder and louder. We do it to put words to the ache we feel in our hearts. And there's this small, innocent hope somewhere in the back of our minds that even if there's no point, even if it's a *done deal* . . . we hope that if we say something enough times, people will listen. Or that if we say it enough, it will finally make sense.

And what doesn't make sense to me in this moment? The fact that I'm standing here with my parents, pretending for them all over again, instead of finding Silas.

"Mom, I've got to go."

"What?"

"Tell Dad I said bye. And that I want to talk to him about the shelter sometime this week."

"Dylan . . ."

I don't stay to hear whatever it is she's going to say. Instead I head for the wall where Silas had been, stop, and scan the crowd. He's not by the food table. He's not anywhere I can see him. I walk through all the smaller rooms, waiting to see his head towering above all the shorter, gray-haired ones. But he's nowhere.

And when I go outside hoping to find him at his pickup, it's gone.

IT TAKES ME fifteen minutes to walk from the library to my apartment, and my feet feel like I've been treading on nails instead of just walking across campus in heels. I switch into flats and grab my keys.

On my way out, Nell asks where I'm going.

"To Silas's."

She looks up from the couch, where she's packing her book bag for tomorrow, and says, "So you're like dating him or something?"

"No. Yes. I don't know. *Or something.*"

"Don't stay out too late!" she calls out as I head out the door. "First day of class tomorrow!"

God, last year I would have been sitting on that couch right beside her, getting prepared like doomsday was coming instead of college classes. Crazy how things have changed.

I duck into my car, and I'm at Silas's house in just over five minutes. Pulling into the driveway, my headlights flash over his front porch, revealing a girl with peroxide-white hair, standing by his front door smoking.

I switch off my car and try to squint at the front porch to see the girl again, but now that my headlights are off, all I see is the orange glow at the end of her cigarette.

He wouldn't hook up with some other girl already, would he? She has to be a friend. Or maybe she's here for Torres or Brookes.

It can't have been much longer than half an hour since I saw him last. She'd have to just be a booty call to be over here that fast and . . .

And that's exactly the kind of thing that Silas could do. He's probably got fifty numbers in his phone from girls willing to just be a quick tumble and toss out the door.

Part of me thinks I should just go. Restart my car, and get the hell out of here. Cut my losses before any damage is done.

But I'm not the kind of girl who walks away. I don't keep my mouth shut when I'm upset. And I'm not about to start now just because the thought of some other girl hooking up with Silas makes me want to throw up.

I push open my door and slam it behind me when I'm out. I stalk up the driveway to his front porch, and before I can say anything she asks, "Who are you?"

"Dylan," I answer.

I almost return the question. Almost. But then I decide I don't want to know the answer. This girl is pretty, no doubt, but her clothes are skimpy, and she wears so much mascara and eyeliner it looks like there was an oil spill around her eyes. She's older than us. Not because I see any major wrinkles or signs of age, more because she looks like what someone not in college thinks a college girl looks like. When I look closer, there are other clues, too. Her hands, for instance. When I look at the cigarette she's holding, her skin is more weathered there, and it makes me look at her again through a whole new lens.

It seems so comical to think that this would be the girl Silas would call. A woman who's probably at least a decade older than us, if not more.

"Is Silas home?"

I don't know why I asked. He is. I can see his truck.

She snorts. "Oh yeah. He's home."

I cringe. I so don't want to know the subtext of whatever she just said.

I'm about to ring the doorbell when she bangs on the door a few times, hard, and yells, "*Baby!* You've got company!"

I hear the creak of the floorboards on the other side, a pair of stomping feet, and the door is ripped open while the blonde calmly takes another drag on her cigarette.

"I told you to—" Silas stops, his eyes widening when he sees me. "What are you doing here?"

I frown. I don't understand this. Any of it.

"You left. I went to find you, and you were gone."

"Yeah, well. You were busy. I didn't think I was needed."

"I told you I was coming right back. I just had to—"

"Lie about us?"

The woman beside me blows out a column of smoke and says, "Aw. Lover's quarrel. How sweet."

Silas turns on her. "Shut up. And leave. I'm not going to tell you again."

"Maybe if you learned how to talk to women, you wouldn't be fighting with her now."

"That's it. I'm calling the cops."

He pulls out his cell phone, and suddenly she shoots past me, trying to force her way inside, but Silas is too strong and keeps his hold on the door.

"You bastard! I haven't asked you for anything in your life, and you can't give me this one thing? *One thing.*"

"I told you. I don't have the money. And even if I did, why would I give it to you?"

"Because I'm your mother!"

I must gasp because Silas's gaze flicks to mine, his eyes wide like he'd completely forgotten I was here.

"Dylan, you should go."

I can't believe this girl . . . this woman who I thought might have been a hookup is his *mother.*

"Don't want your girl to see this? See you turn away your own mom?" Something in Silas snaps, and he steps forward, slamming the door behind him. He takes hold of his mom's arm and starts marching her across the lawn, toward a car parked on the street. But she doesn't stop. "You're too good for me now? Is that it? You have your new life here. Fancy school. Fancy sports. You're ready to forget all about me. You won't even know my name when you're off making millions a year playing some stupid game that you never would have played without me. I *let* you play. You could have been spending all that time after school working, making money so we had a place to live."

She rips her arm out of his grip, stumbling a few feet away in the grass.

I can't see Silas's face when he answers, but his voice sounds harder than I've ever heard it.

"You forgot about me and Sean long before I forgot about you, Ma. If you wanted to be part of my life, maybe you should have actually come back like you said you would after you dropped us off at that joke of a house."

She takes one last drag on her cigarette and then throws it at his feet. "Sean? You think I wronged you both? I'll have you know when your brother got out, he came straight to me. I was the one who took him in, who took care of him. You were too busy here to even *write* him or visit."

Silas freezes and his voice is softer when he asks, "Sean is out? I thought he had another year?"

She laughs bitterly. "Out on parole last year."

"Last year?" For the first time, Silas sounds wounded by this conversation that's been full of barbs from the moment he opened the door. "Where is he now?"

"Back inside. Decided to rob a liquor store three months into his parole."

Silas swears, and looks back at me. I can't read his expression in the dark, but I have a feeling he doesn't want me to hear any of this. This is the past he left behind, the one he refuses to talk to me about.

His mother's voice actually breaks as she says, "I know I left. I'm *sorry* about that, baby. I am. But you left us, too. If you'd been there when Sean got out, maybe he would have stayed straight."

It's a long time before Silas answers, and the tone he uses is completely unfamiliar to me. Low. Hurt. "Listen, I'm sorry your boyfriend is in jail and you don't have the money to make bail," but I can't help you. You or Sean. You'll just have to learn to take care of your own problems, like I always had to."

"Don't you look down on me. Like you're better than me when I *made* you. A better man would take care of his mother. A better man wouldn't cut ties with his family. Don't come crawling back to me when you end up like your brother, like your father, like every damn man I've ever known."

"Last chance." He lifts his phone in warning, but he sounds tired. So tired. "I don't want to call the cops on you, but I will."

"You ungrateful—"

"Goodbye, Mother."

When he starts dialing, she walks away cursing. He stands there in the yard until she starts her car and pulls away.

I wait for him to come back up to the house, but he doesn't. He stays, rigid and still. And even though he's a full-grown man, tall and broad, he looks so small to me then. Like a boy. A boy who had to grow up entirely too fast.

I go to him. And when I place my hand on his back, he tenses and jerks away from my touch. He turns, and he looks similar to the night we first met. He's not bruised or bleeding, but he's locked up tight. Angry.

"You should go."

Then he takes off, striding toward the door fast enough that I have to jog to catch him.

"Silas, wait!"

He jerks to a stop at the top of the porch stairs, and spins around to look down at me.

"You want to know what I'm afraid of? *That's* what I'm afraid of. That's what's waiting for me if I can't make football work."

"No, it's not—"

"Yes, it is. I can clean up, play nice with you at animal shelters and construction projects, but that's just me pretending. I'm always going to be the guy who wears jeans to fancy parties and who gets in screaming fights on his front lawn. My first inclination will always be to work things out with my fists. I might do my damnedest to hold it back, but it will always be in me. And I don't fit in your world. You couldn't even introduce me to your parents tonight, and that was before all this."

"I thought—I thought I was doing you a favor. I thought it would freak you out to meet my parents. You don't do relationships, and that—"

"You're right. I don't. I thought maybe I could, but it would only have been a matter of time before I was the one suffocating in your world. Let's face it . . . you and I, we don't match. Never have. Never will."

This is all spiraling out of control faster than I can keep up with. And I feel the urge to grab him, to hold on tight because I'm losing him, but it feels like I'm losing so much more. Something too big to name.

"Silas, I'm sorry. I didn't mean for any of it to come across like this. I'm sorry."

He gives me a smile that doesn't reach his eyes, and there's this racket in my chest called a heartbeat and it's so wild, so frantic I can barely hear over the sound.

"Still so damn polite."

Then he crosses to his front door, walks inside, and closes the door with a quiet, calm click.

Shutting me out.

And I don't know if breakup is the right word but it feels like that. Bigger than that actually. This time isn't like Henry. I don't feel relieved.

I feel sliced open and short of breath and . . . sorry. So very sorry.

Chapter 25

Silas

First day of school is shit. Complete and utter shit.

Everybody knows about the suspension, and they all want to talk about it, want to know what happened, and how it's going to affect the first game.

They all expect me to be riled up about it . . . to *want* to talk. But it's not the suspension that's got my head all twisted up. It's Dylan.

I couldn't sleep last night because my bed still smells like her. Can't take a fucking shower without imagining the look on her face when she came apart around my fingers that first night in that room. Even my goddamn truck belongs to her now.

All of it. She's in everything.

I realize when I show up for my first class why Dylan's name seemed familiar the night we met. The Brenner-Gibson building. Her family has a fucking *building* named after them, and I'm tempted to drop the class just for that reason.

I stick to the back rows during my classes, dressed in sweatpants and a T-shirt because I've got less than zero fucks to give about first-day-of-school bullshit. I'm in the mood to be pissed, and the world seems all too happy to give me plenty of reasons.

I head to the athletic complex to join the 11 A.M. workout, and Coach Gallt is the coach on duty. Keyon is there, too. So of course, I deal with an hour of having my nose rubbed into the fact that I'm not playing this Saturday. Or the next one.

And to make things worse . . . Dylan ends up being in my one o'clock history class. Her hair is down and straightened, and it keeps drawing my eye all through class. She's about four rows down directly in front of me, and she keeps finding reasons to look back. She stretches. Then she drops her pencil. Then she checks the clock at the back of the lecture hall. And those looks have me so on edge, I don't know whether I want to walk out or take her with me or yell at her or kiss her. I just know I can't take those eyes on me.

I managed to avoid talking to her at the beginning of class because I came in at the last minute, hair still wet from my shower after the midday workout, but she catches up to me on the way out.

The look she gives me . . . cautious and shy . . . it fucking kills me.

"Hey," she says.

I return the greeting, but keep right on walking. My next class is in the building next door, so I'm not in any hurry, but I act like I am.

"Silas, wait." She grabs my elbow and pulls me to a stop in the stairwell. I could refuse. Could pull away and keep right on walking. "Can we talk?"

I don't want to. I do. I don't fucking know.

I know she had it rough growing up, too. I get that, but she's different. She got taken away from that, and her foster homes were at least consistent. She was taken care of, provided for. She's *normal*.

I'm not. Never will be.

All I know is I'm fucking exhausted, and I don't have the energy for this. But even now . . . I don't know how to tell her no.

"Go ahead."

"I just . . . I thought we left things bad yesterday. And I wanted to talk."

"So talk."

"I'm sorry about the party." Her eyes drop to my mouth when she apologizes, and I clench my fists against the need to pull her against me. This girl . . . however she may make me feel . . . she's bad news for me. I'll never be able to live up to her standards, and I'll drive myself fucking crazy trying. Because I've figured it out . . . The shit with Levi and Keyon and everything else . . . that's because I was trying to be something I'm not, and if that party with Dylan is any indication, I've been wasting my time.

I won't go back to the Old Silas. I've got to keep my head on straight, keep my scholarship, but I'm also not changing or hiding who I am. Not for Rusk. Not for Dylan. No one. I've just got to stop being fucking ashamed of where I come from because other people will do that enough for me.

I shrug in answer to her apology. "It's fine. You did me a favor anyway. Not really my scene."

"I know it's not. But that doesn't mean I should have acted like you didn't belong. It was wrong, and not true in the slightest."

"It is true, though, Dylan. And I'm okay with that. I don't need or want to belong at places like that. With people like that."

She swallows and her eyes look hurt, and I figure she thinks I mean her. I don't . . . well, not completely. But I let her think that. It's easier that way.

"Okay then. Well, I guess that's all then. That's all I wanted to say."

But she doesn't move. And she's tangling her fingers together nervously in front of her chest.

"No, it's not. Come on, Dylan. What else do you want to say? Get it all out and then let's be done with it."

She takes a deep breath and squares her shoulders. "Your mom?"

I scowl. "What about her?"

"When was the last time you saw her?"

I feel sick at the thought of talking to her about this, like my insides are all twisted up. But no more shame. I need to own this. Have to.

"I don't know. Eight years, give or take."

I can hear her shock in the silence, and her body is so still, so rigid I can't read her. "You were thirteen?"

"Yeah. First time I got arrested was about a year after that. Also for fighting."

I'm trying to scare her off, end this conversation now, and by the alarmed look she tries to hide, I figure it's working.

"You were arrested before?"

"Twice before you. The second time they were wrong, though. They thought I stole shit, but that was all my brother. My brother who's still stealing, apparently." She sighs, and I can't help running my mouth. "This is what you wanted to know, right? How messed up I am? Go ahead. Ask your questions. I know you've got them."

She slides a little closer to me and lays her hand on my arm. I should shrug her off but I don't.

"I think you *need* to talk about it."

"No. I really don't. It's in the back of my mind all the time. Every day. It sticks to me like a shadow that's right at my heels no matter where I go or what I do. I don't need to talk about it, too."

"Maybe talking about it will help. You're so angry, Silas."

I do shrug her off then. I drag a hand over my face and laugh darkly. "Yeah. I am. But talking won't change that."

"How do you know? It might."

"Damn it, Dylan. I don't need you to fix me. I'm dealing with this shit just fine now. But my family . . . my past . . . there's no fixing that."

"So you're *just fine* now?"

"I had to stop fooling myself. I've done that. Now I'm good. I don't need to be your charity case anymore."

"Don't. I care about you. And I'm worried for you and—"

"Don't be. I said I'm fine. And now I need to get to my next class."

She takes hold of my arm and tries to tug me toward her, but I don't budge.

"You *asked* me to help. You asked me to keep things simple. I don't know why you're punishing me now for trying to do just that."

Because I was stupid enough to think we were on the same page. Stupid enough to think that even though our mouths said simple, she could see that we were anything but that.

"You just wanna fuck? Is that it?"

I give in to the arm trying to tug me toward her and crowd her back against the wall. She swallows hard and her eyes drop to my lips, and *fuck it*. I push away my thoughts and give in to the dark want in my gut.

I crush our lips together, and this kiss is not soft, not sweet. Our teeth clash, and I grip her to pull her closer to me. I pour all my frustration into her, my desperation, my fear. I want to push all those things out and pull her in instead.

She kisses me for a few long moments, but then she turns her head away, breaking contact. I kiss her cheek, her jaw, drag my teeth down her neck. She plants her hands on my chest and pushes me away a few inches. "No. That doesn't solve anything."

"So you *don't* want simple?" God, I can hear the cruelty in my voice, and I know I'm being a jackass, but it makes me feel better. Makes everything not hurt so damn much.

"I don't want you to use sex to ignore your problems. You have to talk about this. It's not healthy."

"I don't have anything more to say. Just give it up already."

"No. I won't give up on you. I don't give up on . . ."

She trails off and instead of continuing, she slides out from between me and the wall and takes a few steps back.

"You don't give up on what? A cause? I knew it. I fucking knew it."

"No, that's not it." But she takes another step back.

"Jesus, just go, Dylan. I'm done talking about this. This is one cause you're just going to have to let pass you by."

"You don't mean that."

"I do. I may have anger issues, and I might not make the best decisions, but at least I know my own fucking mind. You're too caught up in who you think you're supposed to be and how you're supposed to act that you're like a fucking shell. You might as well go back to Henry. I'm sure he'll be happy to make up your mind for you."

Hurt flashes across her face, and I know I've stepped over a line, but I clench my fists and tell myself it's for the best. I've saved myself from getting in any deeper than I already was. Because a few weeks with her pretty much rearranged my life, how I think, the way my heart fucking beats. If things go any further, if I give her any more time, there will be no coming back from that.

And if she stops and thinks about it, I'm sure she'll realize I saved her, too.

Saved her the trouble.

Chapter 26

Dylan

feel like the shell Silas accused me of being as I take a seat in the second row for Media Photography, my last class of the day.

I try to focus on school. On the things that matter. The things I can control.

The best thing about being a junior (and an overachieving one at that) is that I've got the majority of my basic requirements out of the way, so all my classes except two are within my major this semester. These are the things I love, what I want to spend the rest of my life doing.

I'm not a shell.

I'm not.

I always love any of my classes involving photography because photography isn't complicated. It's powerful and truthful and . . . *simple*. Not like words. Words can be bent and manipulated.

Pictures. I just try to keep thinking about pictures. Because if

I break down and cry in the middle of this class, I won't be able to show my face here for the rest of the semester.

Right as the professor is about to close the door and begin the usual first-day spiel, another person slips in the room. She adjusts a messenger bag slung over her shoulder and looks up for a seat.

I recognize her small frame and pretty face.

Stella.

She catches sight of me, too, and waves on her way to fill a seat at the back of the class. I try to smile in return, but my stomach sinks.

It's not that I don't like Stella. Really, I think she's hilarious and confident and cool. But that's part of the problem. She's a hilarious, confident, and cool girl who's slept with the guy who is no longer my . . . whatever we were.

So, not only does she remind me of him.

She reminds me of the fact that he's going to be sleeping with other people soon. And more than that . . . I just get the feeling that she understands and identifies with him in a way that I can't. I have to think about how he would react to certain things, sit back and try to pinpoint his motive and perspective, and she just always seems to know.

Stella walks into a room, and she's automatically everyone's favorite person. Even mine sometimes.

It's hard not to be jealous of a girl like that.

But I try. Especially when she comes up and hugs me after class.

"It's so cool that you're in this class," she says. "I figured it was going to be all stuffy, brainy, political types."

I smile.

Stuffy? Sometimes.

Brainy? Definitely.

Political? Inevitably.

That's me.

She shakes her head. "You know I don't mean you. You're awesome. I just . . . I'm only taking this because my art photography professor from last semester suggested it. I did a project about where artistic photography and media photography overlap, and ta-da! Here I am."

"That's awesome." I sound pitiful, not even remotely believable. "I'm sure you'll bring a really interesting and different perspective to the class."

"And volume. I always bring a lot of volume."

I force a smile.

"Listen," she says. "I'm meeting Dallas for lunch. You want to join?"

I've only had minimal interaction with Dallas since the night she and Carson gave us a ride from the sheriff's office. There's some kind of bad blood between her and Silas, and since I'm always with Silas, we tend to usually end up on opposite sides of the room whenever I'm around his friends.

Except I'm not with Silas anymore. If it weren't for this class, I probably wouldn't have ever seen these people again.

"Um . . . I don't know."

"Oh honey." Stella smiles at me. "I wasn't really asking. You're definitely coming."

"What if I have class?"

"Do you?"

I should lie, but I don't. I shake my head, and she says, "Great! Let's go."

I follow her to the Student Center, in the middle section of campus, and Dallas is already there at a table waiting for us. She's got a salad already in front of her that she's picking at with her fork.

"A salad? Really?" Stella asks her. "You can't even live a little on the first day?"

"If you'd seen how in shape all those girls were this summer, you'd be telling me to eat a salad, too."

Stella rolls her eyes and fills me in. "Dallas went to this super-elite dance intensive this summer, and now she's got a bit of a complex about staying competitive."

"I bet that's stressful."

Dallas throws up a hand. "Thank you! At least someone has a little empathy."

Stella throws her bag down in the chair by Dallas and says, "You say empathy, and all I hear is empty. As in . . . empty stomach, which I'm about to fix with a big, greasy slice of pizza smothered in as much ranch as I can convince the stingy checkout lady to give me. Wait." She pauses. "Make that two slices. First day back and all."

As Stella heads off to find her pizza, I opt for a chicken sandwich from one of the other food court stalls. The pizza place has a longer line, so I make it back to the table first, and Dallas asks, "So did you two run into each other outside or something?"

"No, we actually just had a class together." I hesitate before taking a seat. "I hope it's okay she brought me."

"Of course, it is," Dallas says. "Why wouldn't it be?"

I put my tray down and loop my bag over the back of my seat. I shrug and sit down across from Stella's open seat. "I don't know. We just don't know each other that well."

"Sorry about that. I'm just not the biggest football fan, so I tend to keep to myself when Carson and I go to stuff with the team."

"Oh. Okay."

"Why? Did Silas say something?"

She crinkles her nose in a way that might be distaste.

"So do you hate Silas, too?" I ask. "Or just football?"

Stella takes a seat at that moment and cuts in, "Oh, she definitely hates Silas."

Dallas points her fork threateningly at her friend and says, "Hush, you. I don't *hate* him."

Stella takes a sip of her soda as she scoots in her chair and adds, "Fine. She strongly dislikes him."

"Why?"

I don't know why I'm torturing myself, but I have to know. Dallas hesitates, and I have zero desire to pick up my chicken sandwich.

"It's nothing. It's old news, and I'm over it."

Stella turns a loud laugh into a fake, hacking cough. "Right. Totally over it."

"Did you . . ." I take a breath and push the question out. "Did you two date or something?"

Stella doesn't even bother hiding her laugh behind a cough this time.

"No," Dallas answers. "Nothing like that."

"Oh, just tell her," Stella says. "She should at least know what kind of stuff her boyfriend has gotten up to in the past. Give the girl some leverage, for God's sake."

"Oh, we're not . . . he's not my boyfriend."

Stella stops with a slice of pizza halfway to her mouth, ranch dripping off the end onto the table.

"You're joking, right? You guys are always together. You're not fooling anyone."

"I don't know what we were. It was this weird nonrelationship-relationship, but whatever it is . . . it ended. Last night."

Both Stella and Dallas stop chewing.

It's Stella who talks first. "That son of a bitch. I knew he was gonna screw this up." She turns to Dallas. "You should definitely tell that story now! That way we can all hate on him together."

"Actually . . . I think . . . I think it was mostly my fault."

Shocked doesn't even begin to describe the way they look at me.

"Long story short . . . we ran into my parents, and I lied about how we knew each other rather than introduce him. I thought he would be relieved not to have to meet them, but instead he was hurt. And then some other stuff happened, and it all just kind of snowballed, and he says we're too different. That we don't fit in each other's worlds."

"Sounds like bullshit to me," Stella says.

"It's not. I think . . . I don't know. Maybe he's right. I kept pretending like we were just messing around, but deep down I think maybe I knew he was serious. That he wanted it to be more."

"Well crap," Dallas says. "Totally didn't see that one coming."

I offer a sad smile. "Me either." And then because I need a distraction, but also have this sick need to keep thinking about him, talking about him, I ask, "Will you tell me why you don't like him? Is it bad?"

Dallas sighs. "There was just this stupid bet that my ex-boyfriend started that involved guys on the team trying to sleep with me. Silas and Levi, my ex, were friends, and Silas hit on me at a party in an attempt to win the bet."

"But you guys didn't . . ."

"God, no. I heard the two of them talking about sleeping with me, and I bolted as soon as I saw Silas with Levi. I didn't need to know about the bet to know he was bad news."

Dallas jerks and mumbles, "Ow," and I think Stella kicked her under the table.

"What she means is . . . Levi was bad news. But Silas isn't friends with him anymore."

I'm not sure if she's defending Silas to me because he's her friend or because she doesn't want me to think I made a stupid mistake.

I still haven't touched my chicken sandwich, but I'm feeling the need to wrap up lunch early anyway. I've tortured myself enough for today.

I hadn't let myself think about him actually getting serious about me. I'd just assumed it wouldn't happen. Instead, I'd been focusing all my energy on making sure *I* didn't get too serious. I've made myself write off each sweet, tender kiss, every time he called me baby, all the mornings he's pulled me in close like he didn't want to let me go.

Now it's like someone has taken the lens cap off, and I'm seeing everything from a new perspective . . . but I'm too late. Way too late.

I make some excuses and get up to leave, but Stella grabs my arm.

"You should go to the game with us on Saturday."

I shake my head. "I think that's the last place I should be."

"Oh come on. He won't even be playing. Besides, Dallas and I could use some new girl friends. We're kind of drowning in testosterone at the moment.

"I'll think about it," I tell her.

I DO END up going to the game.

Because something I'm discovering about my new nonshell self . . . I'm a bit of a masochist.

Besides . . . I've never been to a college football game. I've never been to a football game period. I go with Stella, Dallas, and Matt to a pregame tailgate party, wherein I see a lot of very drunk guys with painted chests and faces acting like idiots. I find them obnoxious, but Stella assures me it's a classic football tradition. I don't ask whether she means the body paint, the drunkenness, or the acting-like-idiots part. I assume it's all three.

When we finally make it into the stadium, the sun has set, but it's still suffocatingly hot in the bleachers while we wait. Dallas brought blankets that I don't understand until she lays them down on the hot metal seats so we can sit down without feeling like our butts are on a George Foreman grill.

And while we wait, the three of them teach me about football. And I try my best not to connect everything I hear back to Silas.

Dallas begins: "So each team has offensive players and defensive players. Obviously, the offense's goal is to score, and the defense's goal is to stop the other team from scoring."

"I think you can skip past the commonsense stuff. I'm not completely hopeless. Just tell me how to know when things are going well and when they aren't."

"Okay. Well, on offense, the team has four chances, which are called downs, to either score or move ten yards from their starting point, which clears the slate and lets them start over again with four more downs. That's called getting a first down. So, ideally, when we're on offense, we'll continue to move the ball enough to keep starting over until we're within scoring range and can run or throw the ball in the end zone. Defensively, the goal is to stop the other team from getting first downs, and we want to do it as far away from their end zone as possible. Following me?"

"I think so. So, Carson is the quarterback, right? He kind of leads the offense?"

"You got it," Dallas says.

Stella cuts in then: "Silas is a running back. He's on offense, too." I try not to wince at his name or look too eager. I think Stella is trying to get us back together because she keeps not-so-casually slipping his name into conversation.

Matt tags on: "If Coach Cole sticks to his game from last year, they'll be in shotgun with Silas, or I guess Silas's replacement, positioned by Carson ready to either take a handoff or block for him."

I hold up my hands. "Whoa. Whoa."

Stella rolls her eyes. "Shotgun? Really? You thought she'd follow that?"

"Fine. Silas or some running back will take the ball on occasion, and he either has to be fast enough to run through open holes in the defense before they catch him, or he has to be strong enough to run over the people in his way."

"Okay. Fast. Strong. Gotcha. What about the other positions?"

I want to know about Silas. I do. But I can only handle it in small doses.

They keep going, explaining the different positions and their purposes, and Stella helps me connect the people I know to their spots on the team.

"Wide receivers are typically the flashy guys. They get the big, exciting plays and catch the ball for bigger advances than Silas or Carson can usually get running. That is, if they actually manage to catch the ball. One guess which show-off you know is a wide receiver."

"Torres?"

"Ding ding! We have a winner, folks."

Dallas cuts in: "He's also one of the idiots who does his own little dance when he scores a touchdown."

"Hey," Matt says. "I like touchdown dances."

I snort. "You would."

He holds up his hands. "I will not feel guilty for enjoying the wonders of tight football pants. I also enjoy the way the cheerleaders jump up and down when we score. All in all, I'm a big fan of when we score."

Stella stands and goes to sit on the other side of Matt. "I'm watching the game with this guy. He, at least, knows how to enjoy the sport."

Dallas rolls her eyes.

"You don't like the game, right? But you come for Carson? And your dad?"

She says, "I'm getting used to it again. I'll like it more once fall rolls in and it's not so freaking hot."

I agree with her there. I keep looking at my watch, thinking about how long the game is going to be, and considering buying one of those nerdy handheld fans with a water spray that they were selling at the souvenir booths on our way in.

Time passes a little faster once the game starts. I follow the group's lead and hold up my hand in a claw shape and scream as the other team runs and kicks the ball to us. Dallas keeps up a running commentary for me, pointing out Carson as one of the big guys on the line tosses the ball back to him. In the beginning, it goes well. Torres and Brookes both make a catch each for back-to-back first downs.

(I feel so accomplished when I say "first down" out loud and actually know what I'm talking about.)

Then Carson runs the ball instead of passing, and the student section around us goes crazy. I see a few of the half-naked, painted guys down on the front row, screaming at the top of their lungs.

They start chanting something about bleeding Rusk red (which ick), but for a little while, I manage not to think about Silas, and I just have fun with some new friends.

Then on the next play Carson hands off to a shorter black guy, and he gets laid out when he tries to run through a hole. People around me wince and groan and I ask, "What? Was that bad?"

Dallas explains. "You know at the start of the play how the guy tosses the ball back to Carson?"

"Yeah."

"Because they're tossing the ball backward, they're losing yards, which usually isn't that big a deal as long as they make it past the starting point during the play."

"And we didn't that time?"

"No, we didn't. So we essentially just moved backward instead of forward, so now we have to get *more* than ten yards for a first down."

Ah. Hence the groans.

Stella leans around Matt to say, "And the dude who just choked is Keyon Williams. He's a freshman, and Silas's replacement."

For the first time, my eyes find Silas standing on the sidelines. He's not dressed in his uniform like the rest of the players, so he's not hidden behind pads and a helmet. And my gaze fixes on him, unable to look away, even when another play goes badly and Matt curses next to me.

A few minutes later, I pull my eyes away to watch the game, but they keep going back.

Silas's replacement gets one decent run, but the four after that are just like his first. They stop giving him the ball. Carson either runs it himself or throws it. But the defense seems to be coming down harder on him now that it's clear Keyon isn't as much of a threat. It's common sense, really. The defense focuses their effort on the players who are statistically the most likely to cause damage.

And as things get worse and worse, I watch Silas pace on the sidelines. He runs his hand through his hair again and again each time the offense fails.

With three minutes left in the game and Rusk behind by thirteen, people start streaming toward the exits. We stay, along with the painted guys and a few more pockets of people in the student section. Stella plops down on the bleacher with a groan. Dallas stays standing, biting one of her fingernails and flicking her gaze back and forth between Carson and her father.

Then time runs out. And we've lost.

Silas squats, resting his elbows on his knees and covering the back of his head with his hands. And he just looks so . . . small.

And I know he's feeling that way, too, and I ache for him.

Boyfriend or not, he holds a bigger piece of me than any guy ever has, and I'm not sure I'll ever get that back.

I'm not sure I *want* it back.

Chapter 27

Silas

I'm restless all night after the game.

I barely sleep. My thoughts bounce between the team and Dylan. Keyon and Dylan. My mom and Dylan. And I wonder how long this shit will last. How long will the memory of her stay under my skin, in my thoughts, in this bed?

After a few scant hours of rest, I do the only thing I know how to do to quiet my thoughts.

I pull on some clothes, do a few fast stretches, and then set off on a run. Levi and I picked this house because it's on the side of campus where all the athletic stuff is located. We're about a mile from the athletic complex, so that's where I head. I figure I can squeeze in some weights, and then run home, try to focus on the things in life I *can* control.

What I don't expect is to find the weight room already occupied on a Sunday morning after a game.

Keyon has two of the larger dumbbells and is doing lunges across the weight room. His back is to me, and for a moment I consider leaving, but instead I watch him. His head is down, and he's moving at a fast pace. He's focused. Determined.

"Your strength isn't why you can't break a tackle."

He drops the weights and whirls around to look at me.

He's immediately tense and defensive.

"What do you want?"

"For this team to win games."

Keyon scowls and waves a hand at me. "I get it. I ran my mouth and now it's your turn to give some back. Go ahead. I can take it."

"I'm not here to cut you down, man. I came here to work out, same as you. But I'm serious. Strength isn't your problem. It's your pad level. You're getting laid out because your body is too high, and you can't fight them off when they come up underneath you. Hasn't anyone ever told you the lowest man wins?"

"Do I look like an idiot? Of course I know that."

"Then why aren't you working on that instead of being in here lifting weights?"

"I am working on it. Stronger legs can stay lower longer."

"I told you strength isn't your issue. It's your head. And muscle memory. You need to get used to staying low."

"I'm trying."

I'm probably going to regret this. I don't even fucking like the guy, but I think back to how I felt watching that game, like the only thing I had left was slipping through my fingers, but I didn't have control over my own hands to do anything about it.

Seems like I'm feeling that way a lot lately.

"I've got an idea. Let's go for a run. I think I might know something that can help you out."

I grab a football from the locker room, and tell him to follow me.

Sometimes to switch things up, I run away from campus instead of toward it. So, I know the neighborhood behind ours is mostly families. Professors who want to live close to campus, grad students who are married and have kids. When I run that way, I always end up passing this park with a cool, modern playground.

Williams looks confused as fuck when our run ends up there.

"Is this some kind of joke? Hazing or something? Because if so, you suck at it."

I laugh. "No joke, man. We could have done this with some of the official stuff on campus, but I don't have a key to the equipment closet, so we're improvising."

"On what? The merry-go-round?" I step up into the playground area, deserted this early on a Sunday morning, and feel my feet sink into the soft wood chips that cover the ground. That's going to make things even more difficult for him, but that might be a good thing.

"Anyone ever make you run arches?"

He shrugs.

"They look like giant versions of those metal croquet things you hit the ball through. You know what I'm talking about?"

"Not a fucking clue."

I laugh. "Yeah, I'd never heard of it, either, when my high school coach mentioned it. It's a rich-people thing, I think. Or old people. Both probably. Anyway, they're small enough that you can't run through them upright, and they're narrow so that you have to keep your arms in close, the ball tucked tight against your body. Run through those long enough and it becomes second nature to bend your knees and stay low."

"But we don't have those."

"No, we have this." I place my hand on top of a long set of monkey bars, made for kids. I'd guess it's about five and a half feet tall, maybe a little more. Point is, it's low enough to make it hard for guys like us to run underneath at full speed. I toss him the football and he automatically holds it tight against his stomach the way we're taught. I walk to the end of one set of the monkey bars and look down the length of them. It's a little less than ten yards, so not ideal, but I think we can make it work. I decide to have him work on his feet at the same time, too.

"Let's do it like this." Slowly, I show him what to do, running beneath the bars with my knees bent and my body hunched. There are three sets of bracing on the sides of the monkey bars that also serve as miniature fireman's poles, and I use them like cones, popping out from underneath the bars to weave around one pole and then back under the bars until I weave around the next fireman's pole on the opposite side. I round one more pole, and then circle completely around the ladder at the other end of the monkey bars before ducking underneath them and repeating the same process on the way back. It's a little lower than the practice arches we have on the team, but he's not wearing a helmet or pads, so I figure that evens out the difficulty level.

He follows my lead, moving through it once at half speed to get a feel for it, and then he tries it at full speed. After rounding the second fireman's pole, he knocks his head going back under the monkey bars and drops to one knee.

He curses, and I do my best to hide my smile.

"I don't want to be a dick," I say. "But I told you that you were running too high."

"I thought you didn't want to be a dick?"

"It comes naturally. I've learned not to fight it."

"Well, if it's so easy, you do it."

He tosses me the ball, and I try not to look too smug as I walk over to the starting spot. I might be a dick now, but high-school-me was an outright asshole. That's what happens when you don't have a parent around to put you in your place: You become pretty damn certain that you know what's best about everything. Coach Cervera, my football coach the last two years of high school, had no problem showing me how wrong I was. The guy made me run arches every day until, I swear to God, I was walking around bent and hunched even outside of practice. I take a deep breath, blink to make sure my vision is completely clear, and then I speed through the course as fast as I can. My feet slip a few times on the wood chips, but I don't think Williams noticed, at least not based on the suspiciously blank expression he has when I'm done.

"Fine. Give me the damn ball."

I do smile then, tossing it like he asked.

I lose track of time while we work. Football does that to me. Dylan is the only other thing that has ever been that way. I could listen to her talk, watch her sleep, run my fingers through her hair . . . anything. I could do that all day long, and never get bored.

Fuck.

That's over. Done with.

I shake my head and focus back on the task at hand.

Keyon is now good enough that he's running the drill five times in a row before stopping, rather than just the one lap. He's still not quite at full speed, he's too unsure of himself, but he's already much better. I think the quick turns around the fireman's pole are helping to train his vision, too. It's a good start. And he doesn't need me anymore. Not for this.

As we wrap up, I tell him, "I know a couple more drills that would help if you want to meet up this week before or after practice."

He finishes out the loop he's on and says, "Wait." I hadn't even moved yet, but I raise my eyebrows in question. "Why are you doing this?"

"I told you. I want the team to win."

"But I'm your competition. What if I end up taking your spot?"

"If a few hours of drills makes you that much better than me, then you deserve to take my spot."

"You've still got to miss another game, though. What if I show you up?"

"I'm not exactly sitting on my ass doing nothing, Williams.

Besides, if you're good enough, maybe Coach will look at going to a two-back offense. You, me, and McClain? We could be pretty damn impressive, I think."

He nods. "Cool. Yeah." He holds up the football. "You need this back?"

"Nah, you keep it. You could stand to do this, oh, another thousand times."

I start jogging back in the direction of my house.

"Still being a dick!" he yells behind me.

"See you at practice, fish."

Chapter 28

Dylan

On the next game day, I agree to get lunch with my parents because I'm not sure I can handle watching another game with Stella mentioning Silas every few minutes. The masochism has to stop sometime.

But before I've even finished setting the table, I know this was a mistake. Mom has brought up Henry three times. She thinks maybe we should invite him and his parents over for dinner . . . *since I'm not dating anyone new.*

She gives me a look when she says that last thing, and I know I didn't fool her at that party.

Ironically enough . . . I no longer need to fool her. Because Silas is so beyond done with me.

There's that masochism again. Rubbing salt in my own wounds.

As we take our seats for lunch, and Mom passes around all

the perfectly plated dishes, I struggle to keep my mind off him. I struggle with all the things that used to come easy. The pleases and the thank-yous. Dad notices.

"What's on your mind, sweetheart?"

"Hmm?" I look up from the food I'd been pushing around on my plate. "Just have a lot on my mind, I guess. Sorry."

God, I never want to say that word again. Never. I'd be the rudest person ever, but if I never had to say that word *not* followed by a kiss again, it would be okay.

I tune out the conversation about some big donation Dad is trying to land for Rusk, and instead sneak my phone out underneath the table.

Phones aren't allowed during meals. It's one of Mom's rules, but I can't help it. I have to know what's happening at the game.

I don't know if they're playing an easier team or if things have changed since last week, but on my phone I watch the score climb, as I periodically pause to scoop some food off my plate so my parents don't become too suspicious. Rusk leads by three. Then ten. Then sixteen. And I find myself imagining Silas's face on the sidelines. Is he happy for his team? Or still too frustrated by his inability to play?

"Dylan? Is that a phone beneath the table?"

I drop my phone into my lap and look up at Mom. Guilty.

"Yeah. Sorry, Mom. I just had to check something."

"Are you waiting on a call?"

"No, I was . . . sorry. I'll put it away. That was rude of me."

I hear Silas in my head telling me to stop apologizing, and then

I imagine him kissing me, and it feels like my lungs are filled with water.

"What are you checking?" Dad asks.

I could lie. Say I'm waiting on an e-mail about school or the shelter or anything. But I'm so tired of lying.

"I was checking the score on the football game. Rusk is up by sixteen if you were curious."

"Honey." That one word from Mom is chastising, and I don't know if it's for using my phone at the table or for the information she's inferring after that confession.

As always, Dad gets straight to the point. "That football player you were talking to at the party. I don't want you involved with him. I'm not sure what he told you, but he's violent and troubled, and he's been suspended from the team because of it."

I don't know what to say to that because *technically* the things he's said about Silas are true. Granted, I wouldn't go so far as to call him *violent*. But he does walk that line, and I can't ignore that, can't excuse it just because I'm attracted to him.

"He's worked really hard to turn that around, Dad. I think if you asked around now, you'd hear a different story."

"Kids like him always have the same story. And it always ends up the same eventually."

Those words burn something up in me, and now I'm the one battling violence. Words like that, *people* like my father . . . they're the reason Silas feels like he doesn't fit in my world. And honestly, I'm not even sure that's the kind of world I want to be in.

"Then why adopt me?" I ask. "If you think people are only

products of where they came from and they can't change . . . why bother?"

"Oh sweetheart," Mom says, reaching across the table for my hand. "You were one of the good ones."

I pull my hand away and stand up, "*Silas* is one of the good ones. He's dealt . . . is dealing with a lot. And if you knew him—"

"I don't need to know him," my father says. "You think I haven't seen hundreds of guys like him go through that university? I'm happy to have them there, for them to get an education in exchange for the money they bring in on the team. But that doesn't mean I want him anywhere near my daughter."

I shake my head and purse my lips against the urge to cry. I can't believe I ever contributed to this, that I ever made Silas feel like any of this was true.

"You do need to know him, Dad. Because I'm pretty sure I'm in love with him."

"Don't be ridiculous," Mother says fast. "You and Henry have only been apart a month or two."

I look at her then, pause, and make sure she sees the seriousness in my face when I say, "Henry and I are never getting back together. I don't love him. I don't want to be with him. That's not going to change. Not ever."

"You're overreacting. Henry hurt you, and now you're lashing out in the best way you know how. I understand that. And this Silas is certainly attractive, so I don't blame you for getting confused."

"You think I'm confused?" I can't help but laugh. "For the first time maybe ever, I know exactly how I feel and exactly what I think. And you're not going to tell me I'm confused or wrong, not going to convince me I don't know who I am. Because I do. I *finally* do."

"No one is saying you don't know who you are." Dad cuts in. "But perhaps if you'll sit back and think—"

"I didn't know who I was," I tell them. And there's no stopping my eyes from tearing up now. "Not until Silas. Before that . . . I was whatever you wanted me to be. Or whatever Henry wanted. I was so worried that I'd lose you, that you wouldn't love me, or you'd regret taking me in, that I was too scared to be anything other than what you considered the perfect daughter. But I'm not perfect. I can't be. Not even if I was still interested in trying. And Silas . . . he was the only person to see that. To see how hollow I'd let myself become. So I *do* love him. I'm not confused or misguided. Not anymore."

Mom stands and comes around the table toward me. She cups my face in her hands and says, "We could *never* regret taking you in. You're our daughter. And we love you no matter your imperfections. I'm just worried, darling. It's not even about his issues. You know what guys on those teams are like. They break hearts left and right, and I don't want yours to be one of them. I believe that you love him. I do. I'm just not sure it's smart to get involved with a boy who may not be able to love you back the same way. I don't want you to fool yourself into thinking it can be something more permanent."

It stings. Because that's exactly what I thought. That I would be stupid to picture any future between me and Silas, but these days I'm having trouble picturing one without him. If I'd just gotten over my fears faster, listened a little more to my heart and less to my head, maybe I'd still have him now.

"I'm sorry, Mom. Dad. But you're wrong. Silas is good for me. And he deserves *so much more* than what I've given him. So, I'm going to go see if I can catch the end of his game. And I don't know . . . maybe eventually you'll be able to trust that I know what I'm doing."

Because I finally trust myself.

As I leave the house and climb into my car, I turn the radio station to one playing the game and start my trek across town.

I think about all the things I know about myself, the truths I've discovered and am still discovering.

I can be impulsive and hotheaded. I don't like dressing up or fancy dinners. I want to go to parties. Real, irresponsible parties, not dinner or garden ones or whatever. I want to meet people. All kinds of people. And I want to laugh. I haven't done that enough in life. I don't just want to help people. I want to *fight* for them. I don't want to be invisible ever again. I want to be bold. I want . . .

Silas. I want Silas so bad that I feel his name whispered in my every breath, can still feel the warmth of his touch like he's next to me, leaning across the dash to kiss me at the red light. He's lodged so deep in me that the memory of him is written on my bones, twined in my blood.

Stuck in traffic, I listen as the game winds to a close and Rusk wins by thirteen. I scream along with the fans I can hear in the background of the broadcast, and for the first time in two weeks, I take a full breath of air.

I'm going to see Silas after that game. I have to.

A QUICK CALL to Stella assures me that the team is celebrating their win at a frat party on campus tonight. I run home and pull on my favorite skirt, and I find a button-up shirt that I know drives Silas crazy. Tonight, though, I leave an extra button undone.

When I get to the party, Silas isn't there yet, but I find Stella in the living room. The celebration is already in full swing, and Stella is perched on a cute frat boy's lap, laughing. She waves me over when she sees me.

I'm so freaking nervous. What if he won't give us another chance? What if he's already moved on to some other girl? Or he's woken up and realized that he doesn't want to be in a relationship after all? God, what if his mother is still around? I don't even know how he's handling that, *if* he's handling that. He could be spiraling out of control again, and I would have been one of the things to push him to it.

"Cute outfit!" Stella shouts over the music. "Try to look like you're not about to vomit, though. Doesn't quite scream *I'm here to win you back.*"

I take a seat beside her and the frat boy on the couch, and drag my fingers through my hair. "I don't know what I'm doing. What if he blows me off? I'm not sure I can handle that."

Stella looks up at the ceiling and sighs before draining the last of whatever is in her cup. She holds the empty cup out to the frat boy with a playful smile, and he shifts her off him to go get her a refill. When he's gone, she turns to me. "How is it that I always end up being the one to give relationship advice? You people realize I'm completely antirelationship, right?"

"You know Silas, though."

She slants an eyebrow. "Not as well as you know him."

"I don't mean like that. I mean . . . you get him."

"I did before. Mostly because I think he's a lot like me. But you kinda rewrote the book, sister. I don't know. Just be honest. Don't try to make excuses. He'll hate that."

"How mad is he? Have you seen him at all this week? What's he been like?"

She shrugs. "Normal." My stomach sinks. Normal? Does that mean . . . like the old Silas? "He hasn't hooked up with anyone else that I know of, if that's what you're asking. But he's not drowning in a bottle, either. Dallas said he's been concentrating on football, helping the kid who took his place. Which *thank God*. If I had to sit through another game like last week, I would have lost it."

I should be glad that he's okay. That's what I want for him, what I've wanted for him from the beginning. But all I can think about is how I felt after Henry. I was thrown for sure because my five-year plan had just completely unraveled, but when the dust cleared, I wasn't sad. Not at all. What if that's how Silas feels?

"Aw shit. I shouldn't have told you that, right? It's freaking you out. Listen . . . Silas is no stranger to mistakes. You're gonna be fine. He'll understand."

I hear a cheer from the front of the house, and I take that as a sign that the first of the team has arrived. I take a few deep breaths, but I still feel like the ground isn't quite steady beneath my feet.

Stella's frat boy returns with a new drink, and as I stand to go in search of Silas she pipes up from over her cup. "Should plan A fail, there's always plan B!"

"What's plan B?"

"Naked apology. Works every time."

I see his roommate Brookes first, and I can't read the look he shoots me, but I'm 99.9 percent sure that guy doesn't like me. Silas says he's a funny guy, but I've never seen it. Then again, I'm usually on the receiving end of a glare.

I make my way over to stand by the stairs while people stream in. I recognize five or six guys from the team, but surrounding them are people I don't know. Girls. Guys. They're raucous and loud, and I'm willing to bet most of them are already drunk.

When Silas enters, it's mostly girls around him, but he has an arm slung around a shorter black guy. He's shaking him by the shoulders, and the guy is smiling, and the people around them are laughing and cheering, and he looks good.

He doesn't look remotely as torn up inside as I feel.

He walks right past me without even seeing me, and I think about making a break for it. I could do this another time, somewhere a little less public.

Then from the door I hear, "Captain Planet! What are you doing here?"

Torres has a girl on each arm, but he ditches them both and

jogs down the steps into the foyer to throw his arm around me instead.

He leans down to say something to me, but I don't even hear it because Silas definitely sees me now. His gaze is hard on me, on Torres, really, and I don't even think the guy realizes it.

I'm about to say something when I finally register what Torres is whispering to me, "And incoming in three, two, one . . ."

Silas says something to the player he'd been talking to and then starts in my direction.

Torres laughs. "Do I know my boy or what? You're welcome. Now, I'm gonna run before I lose a tooth."

He jogs away from me toward the kitchen, and starts singing the school fight song at the top of his lungs. Half the party joins in, and I can't hear anything over the tone deaf and the drunk. But I don't need to hear to see the way Silas hesitates now that I'm alone. He stops, looks me over briefly, nothing more than a quick scan, then turns and goes back to the crowd he left.

They move into the living room, and I stand there, my back pressed against the stair railing, trying not to react, trying not to let everyone see that I'm crumbling.

I was always scared that Silas would hurt me, but I never thought it would be like this.

Never thought I would feel invisible with him.

I stay there as the party kicks into high gear around me. I should leave. I should do something, but it's easier just to stand here, to pretend I'm as invisible as I feel.

"How much of an asshole am I if I say I told you so?"

I turn and Brookes is sitting on the stairs just above me.

"If you have to ask how much of an asshole it makes you, the answer is you're already an asshole."

He leans his forehead into his hand and gives a low, husky laugh.

"I'll take that."

"And I'll take that I told you so."

What had I told Silas? If he took me down with him, it would be because I jumped, not because he pulled me? Well, I'd jumped.

And I hit bottom.

"You need a drink, girl. Come on."

I think back to my earlier declaration of who I am. I wanted to go to parties and be bold. I wanted to meet people. Well, here's my chance.

I won't be invisible. No matter how Silas Moore looks at me. Or if he looks at me at all.

Chapter 29

Silas

assumed Dylan had already left; instead she's stolen away all my friends.

I walk into the kitchen a couple of hours later to refill my beer, and she's sitting on top of the dining room table. Brookes, Torres, McClain, and Dallas are around her, and they're watching in rapt attention as she tells a story.

I sidle a little closer, my back to the group, and hear the tail end of it.

"I don't even think. I just grab the handcuffs off Matt and snap them on the first thing I see, and the police officer is just staring at me like I'd completely lost my mind. Which I had, of course."

"Here's my question," Torres says. "What was your friend Matt doing with handcuffs?"

She laughs, this high, tinkling noise that goes straight through me.

"Matt is . . . oh God, how do I explain him? Matt doesn't have a serious bone in his body. He brought the handcuffs as a joke. I don't think he even remembered they were in his pocket."

"See," Torres continues. "I want a *thing* like that. A gimmick that's just mine. Like . . . the weird guy who always has a pair of handcuffs."

"You have a thing," Dallas says. "You can't seem to hold on to your clothing when alcohol is involved."

"I'll have you know, I am fully clothed right now."

"You're not wearing shoes." Brookes cuts in, low and matter-of-fact, and the table erupts into laughter.

I look, because I'm a fucking train wreck. Dylan's head is tossed back, her gold hair fanned out behind her, her long, gorgeous neck on display.

Torres shrugs. "So I got comfortable. What's the big deal?"

"Do you have any idea where your shoes *are?*" Dallas asks.

He thinks for a moment, opens his mouth, and then closes it.

The laughter doubles, and Dylan covers her wide smile with her hand, leans forward, and her eyes catch mine. I grab my beer and head out of the kitchen before the rest of the group catches sight of me, too.

I've just edged my way out into the living room, when I feel warm fingers graze my arm.

I turn, and she's there, too damn close for comfort, too damn far for everything else I want.

"I was wrong," she says. "But you were wrong, too."

"Is that supposed to be an apology?"

She pauses and smiles. "No, actually. It's not."

"Then what are you doing here?"

"I want to be here."

"Finally figured out what you want, huh?"

She shrugs. "Maybe I just gave myself permission to want it."

The music switches to a booming rock song, and she squeezes her eyes shut against the noise.

"Can we go somewhere and talk?" she asks.

"About?"

"Everything."

"Not sure I'm up to talking about everything."

"Silas, please."

How is it that I still can't say no to her?

"Fine. Upstairs. We'll find someplace quiet."

It's déjà vu as I follow her up the stairs, her perfect ass right at eye level, only there's twice as many stairs here as my place.

"So, tell me again. You're not apologizing?"

She slows her stride and glances back over her shoulder. "You, me, and sorrys don't typically lead to fruitful conversations."

I can't tell if she's serious or fucking with me. And I'm too impatient to wait until we're in a room somewhere to find out. I stop her at the top of the stairs, my hand curled around her elbow.

"I need you to tell me straight, Dylan. You know I don't like to talk, so what is this?"

She takes my hand off her elbow and holds it in hers.

Just then a door opens on the landing above us, a bathroom I assume, and I see Carter step out, in the middle of zipping up his jeans. He freezes for a second when he sees me, and I scowl. I don't like everyone knowing my business. And this place is too public for whatever is about to go down. And I'm still pissed about the thing with Carter and the brownies. Every time I see his face, the anger rises back up. Dylan might not be mine anymore, but I sure as hell don't want him anywhere near her.

Dylan stays silent until Carter squeezes his big frame past us and lumbers down the stairs. Then her hand squeezes mine, and she moves forward so that she's one step above me, almost eye level for once.

"I could make a big speech," she says. "I could explain how growing up in foster care, I had an idea of what the perfect life would be like, and I've done everything to chase that over the years, not realizing that none of it was real. I wanted a perfect home and a perfect future, and instead everything just felt empty. I could tell you all about how miserable I've been without you the last two weeks or how much I hate myself for ever making you feel like you wouldn't fit in my world. But you're not really the speech type, so I'll just keep it simple . . . I don't think you need fixing. And you have to fit in my world, because you *are* my world. And I know you've never really done the relationship thing, and I know I've screwed this all up so badly, and I'm sorry—"

"Shut up."

"But—"

I kiss her.

I kiss her, and her breath mixes with mine as she gasps into my mouth, and I sink my fingers into her hair. And as always with her, I just want to take and take and take, but this time I want her to do the same.

I want to give her what she gives me. I want her to feel perfect. I want her to have the good life and the good home and everything she could ever want.

She wraps hers arms around my neck, and together we stumble up the last few steps to the second floor, laughing through the missteps because neither of us is willing to stop kissing long enough to climb four measly steps.

When we get on level floor, I grip her hips and pick her up. She wraps her legs around my waist, and I lock her in close to my body, and open the door to the bathroom. I slam the thing shut and pin her back against the door. It's dark inside, and I reach out a hand to search for the light switch because all I can think about is that night in the bathroom at my place, and how badly I need to see her fall apart again. I lower my mouth to her neck, tasting and sucking and Jesus . . . how did I go two weeks without this?

"God, I missed you. So much, baby."

I finally find the light switch and flip it on.

"Silas." Her hands tug back on my hair, and I nip her collarbone in response.

But then her hands slide out of my hair, down to my shoulders, and she pushes, pushes me back.

"Oh my God, Silas. Stop."

I do as she says, even though I feel like my bones will break if I make even the slightest move away from her. I loosen my hold on her hips, and she slides down out of my arms.

A mess of emotions I can't even identify begins to swarm in my chest, then she darts around me, and it takes a second for me to hear what she's saying over the roaring in my ears.

"Stella? Stella!"

I spin, and it takes me a moment to focus, to let my world expand past Dylan and the way she makes me feel. But I can't make sense of anything because we're not in a bathroom like I assumed, but a bedroom. And if Dylan asking me to stop was a shock to my system, this just turns everything off, shuts everything down.

My eyes go to the bed, and I take in information, but it's all disjointed, fragmented, confused.

Bare, skinny legs. That's what I register first. A pair of underwear around one ankle. The pieces come slow, too slow—displaced clothes, smudged makeup, closed eyes. I do my damnedest not to zone out and see the big picture because that's not something I ever want to associate with the girl lying in that bed.

That girl is vibrant and friendly and . . . fuck.

Dylan is touching Stella's face, talking to her, but she's passed out cold. Finally, I get my feet to move, and I cross the room and pull a blanket over her so no one else will see her like that.

Then I only think in steps.

Step one. Take care of Stella.

Step two. Find Carter.

Nothing else matters right then.

I face Dylan, place a hand on her shoulder, and say, "Don't leave her side." I hand her my phone and say, "Call Dallas first. Then the police."

I turn to go, and she chokes out over short, broken breaths, "Where are you going?"

"I'll be back."

I don't tell her where I'm going because she'll only worry. But I'm positive this is the room Carter came out of when we were standing on the stairs, and I'd assumed he was fixing his jeans because this was a bathroom. My mind starts to piece together what must have happened before that, before he turned the lights out on Stella and just left her there, and I feel so goddamned angry and helpless.

I have to ask around for a few minutes, but when people see the look on my face, no one hesitates to tell me if they've seen Jake.

I find him out in the parking lot, trying to coax some other girl to go home with him, and fuck fair fighting. I haul off and slam him back into his truck.

I look over at the girl he'd been with, but she's already stumbling away back in the direction of the party.

"What the hell, man?" Carter says.

"I knew you were a fucking prick, but I didn't have any idea you'd go this low."

Carter holds his hands up. "I have no idea what you're talking about."

He tries to shove me off, but I'm not fucking budging until I'm done. "I went in the room. The room you came out of. I found her. Stella. No fucking way I let you get away with this."

"I didn't do anything," he swears, but this time he shoves me hard, and I stumble back a few feet.

"Did she go in that room with you?" I ask. "Was she even conscious or did you take her in there?"

"You can't fucking prove anything," Then he tries to leave, and I tackle him. He may be twice my size, but he goes down easy. We both scramble for a few seconds to get the upper hand, and he's the first one to throw a punch. It lands hard just on the edge of my jaw, and my teeth bang together.

I throw my elbow back hard into his midsection, and he rolls off me, gasping. I take the opening to launch myself at him and get in another good hit to his face.

But he's so much bigger than me, he shoves me off and I scramble to my feet.

"Just leave this shit alone," Carter says. "You don't want another fight on your record. We leave now, nobody gets hurt."

Fucking asshole.

"Stella doesn't count?"

"Come on, man. You know how she is."

I'm done hearing this shit come out of his mouth. I lunge again, and then we're locked together, both trying to ward off the other's hits, while squeezing in a few of our own. I get a good one to his nose, and I feel it crunch under my fist. He pushes me away while he cups his nose with his hand. Blood coats his fingers.

Sirens wail in the distance, and I see the panicked look on Carter's face.

"I didn't do anything wrong, man. I swear she was awake."

"Bullshit. Then why was she passed out when I got there? Why hadn't she fixed her clothes? If you didn't do anything wrong, why'd you leave her there like that? Why'd you turn off the lights?"

He doesn't say anything, but I can see it all unraveling in his expression. The closer the sirens get, the more desperate he is. He stops talking with his mouth then, and switches to fists.

I swing a solid blow into his stomach, and he doubles over. But I underestimate his stamina, and he comes back fast, swinging. His fist plows into my jaw, and the world jerks out of focus for a few seconds. I stumble back. Carter tries to leave, and I hurl myself at his back, sending us both down to the concrete. I can't take him in a fight like this. He's too big. So I just concentrate on holding on. I take a punch to the ribs, but I don't fucking care. He's not leaving.

My head knocks hard against the concrete a few times, but I hold on, sneaking in a few hits of my own. And we're both bloody by the time two cops pull us apart.

My mouth is busted up and it stings when I speak, but I say, "He did it. The girl upstairs . . . it was him."

Then things go a little fuzzy, and I pass out.

ONCE WHEN I was sixteen, I got knocked unconscious in a game for a few seconds after a particularly hard tackle. I remember coming to on the field, feeling like I had done nothing more than blink, and I couldn't understand why there were so many coaches gathered around me.

This is not at all like that.

I feel like I've been out forever, long enough for my body to decay, and my mouth to dry out, and the whole world to move on around me, but when I open my eyes, it can't have been more than a few minutes because I'm propped up against a nearby car, and there's a cop and a paramedic kneeling next to me.

"His eyes are open."

Then, just like that time in high school, more faces appear above me.

McClain. Brookes. Torres.

And Dylan.

I try to stand, but the world goes sideways, and the paramedic claps a hand on my shoulder to hold me in place.

"Easy. I think you might have a concussion."

"I do," I answer. I've had a handful of those in my life, and this feels similar.

"Stella?" I ask.

"She's awake," Dylan answers. "There's a cop with her, too. And a paramedic. She . . ." She hesitates, then finishes, "She doesn't remember what happened."

"Carter?"

It's the cop who answers this time.

"Mr. Carter is seeing a paramedic, the same as you."

"Are you going to arrest him?"

The look the cop gives me makes me sick to my stomach. Or that could be the concussion.

"When both of you are cleared medically, we'll get your statements and go from there."

"He did it," I say.

"Did you see him do it?"

"I saw him come out of the room."

The cop just nods. "Okay then." He nods at the paramedic and says to me, "Let this guy get you cleaned up and checked out, and we'll talk about what you saw when he's done."

In all, it takes twenty minutes for the paramedic to clean me up. No stitches. Nothing broken. I have a mild concussion, but I decline the paramedic's offer to take me to the hospital.

My statement for the police takes even less time, and when it's over, I'm left with a sour taste in my mouth because no one mentions anything about arresting Carter. All I keep hearing is that Stella doesn't remember, and Dylan and I didn't *see* anything actually take place. I tell them what he said during our fight, about me not being able to prove anything, but they only nod and write it down. They don't say he was wrong. The cops promise it's all taken care of, but it doesn't feel that way to me, not in the slightest.

Chapter 30

Silas

I sit on the bed and hunch over my knees after my morning run. I didn't sleep well. Not last night or the night before. The bed dips, and I feel Dylan scoot up behind me and lay her cheek against my back. I'm sweaty, but she doesn't seem to mind.

"You're talking to Coach this morning?"

I nod.

"Everything is going to be fine, Silas."

I shrug. Because I don't know that.

All I know is Carter is still walking free. Stella's talking about it all like it's not a big deal, like she's fine. And I got in another fight with a teammate, the same day my last suspension for fighting ended.

She scoots closer, situating her thighs on the outside of mine, and presses herself against my back.

"Whatever happens . . . you're not in the wrong here."

I sigh and scrub my hands over my face.

"It's all just so fucked-up. I thought he was a friend. He was in my house. Near you. I should have beat the shit out of him that night with the weed. I knew I should have."

"If you'd fought him then, it's entirely possible you and I might not have slept together that night. Besides, that would have been overreacting. This wasn't."

I reach for the arm she has wrapped around my stomach and lace our fingers together. "What if nothing happens to him? How could I ever play on the same team as him?"

"There are options," she says. "We'll find a way to fight it."

"Not if the prosecutor doesn't take the case."

I'd spent all day yesterday researching the laws and past cases in Texas, and our chances don't look good. Dallas said too many of the partygoers mentioned seeing Stella making out with random guys. That coupled with the fact she can't remember anything, and they're calling her an unreliable witness. She's not the only one. I'm apparently unreliable, too. Everything Carter said in the fight is hearsay, and with my record and history, no one's putting much stock in what I say.

"Even then," Dylan answers. "We might not get anything done through the court system, but there are laws in place requiring universities to govern the safety of their students. Those have been used in the past to support victims of unprosecuted cases. Stella has options. And she has people who care about her enough to fight the uphill battle."

Except she doesn't even want to fight. I saw her yesterday, and she spent half the conversation trying to get me to talk about the next game, about how I felt about finally being able to play again.

I didn't have the heart to tell her that might not be the case. She just . . . it wasn't anything she said or did, but something in her face told me that she *needed* to talk about that game. Needed to know that life would keep on going. She's too much like me. She'd rather ignore it all, pretend it's not there until the last possible moment.

And because I understand how she works, I let her do it. For now anyway. But I won't let her be like me, won't let it all build up around her until she's trapped beneath it. She'll have to talk to someone eventually. Dallas. Ryan. Me. *Someone.*

Dylan kisses my shoulder, pulling me back to the present, and adds, "You've got people on your side, too, you know. Your coach cares about you. He's not going to write you off over something like this."

I turn my head and kiss her, soaking up a little of her certainty, and then I hop in the shower to get ready to head over to the school.

"COME IN," COACH'S voice calls through the closed door.

I open it slowly, and poke my head in.

"Silas. I've been expecting you. Come on in."

Shit. Here goes nothing.

I close the door behind me and cross to his desk. I take a seat in the chair on the left because the one on the right is where I was sitting when I first got suspended, and I'm really hoping this time turns out differently.

"I've heard a lot about what happened this weekend. Why don't you tell me your version."

I do, leaving out everything about Dylan, about the fact that I was pretty damn sure I loved that girl when we stumbled into that room, and now I'm certain. I stick to the facts, and even though it could get me in trouble, I mention the brownie incident, too. I try to remain stoic as I recount everything for him, but my hands are shaking.

Stella is a good person and a good friend, and if what Dylan has told me is true, she's been working for the last two weeks to get us back together. I should have noticed when I saw Dylan sitting at that table with my friends that Stella wasn't there. Someone should have watched out for her. We all should have.

And now that what's done is done, it shouldn't be so damn hard to get someone to do something about it. Life has already been unfair enough. Stella shouldn't have to live with that too.

"You feel certain that Jake did this?"

"I do," I say. "If you could have seen his face, seen how defensive he was . . . you would too. And even if he didn't set out to do it, even if she was awake when they went in the room, an innocent person would have handled things differently. He wouldn't have left her there like that. And I know fighting him probably wasn't the answer, and it's my third strike and you have every right to kick me off the team. I hope you won't, but I've got to say, I'd rather be off the team than play a single game alongside Jake. This team has heart and strength and courage, and he doesn't deserve to taint that."

Coach is quiet for a long while. He looks at me, then up at the ceiling. He scratches at his jaw and sighs, before turning his gaze somewhere else and repeating the whole process all over again. Finally, he stands and moves across the room to the window that looks out onto an open grassy area of campus where students play games or study when the weather's nice.

"You know, when I suspended you from the team, I told you I needed you to be a leader. I wasn't sure then if you had it in you. I knew you could play, knew you loved the game. But I couldn't tell if you only cared about your own future, or the team's as a whole. Even without hearing what you just said, I knew the answer before you ever opened that door. You know how?"

I shake my head, too many emotions lodged in my throat to speak.

"First thing Carson told me Saturday night after he explained what happened was that I couldn't suspend you again. He said the team needed you. Brookes and Torres showed up at my door the next morning saying the same thing. Keyon rang my doorbell last night in the middle of dinner. He busted into my house, interrupted my date, and told me that you deserved to play. And if that weren't enough, my daughter told me in no uncertain terms that if I didn't support you, she wouldn't speak to me for the rest of the season. People love you, Silas. They respect you. They trust you, and I do, too. And I probably shouldn't say this, but I'm damn glad it was you that found Stella instead of someone else. Maybe fighting wasn't the best way to handle it, but I'm not sorry that's how it went. You shouldn't be, either. That girl . . ." He stops for a minute, closing his eyes and collecting his words. "I love Stella like she was my own. She brought my daughter out of her shell, and she's . . ." He trails off and looks out the window for a while. He doesn't say anything, but I can see him swallowing again and again, trying to keep his composure.

When he turns to me again, his expression is serious. "You're a good man, Silas. A good player. And I'm glad to have you on this team."

Goddamn it. I'm not going to get emotional in here. I'm not.

"I may not have any legal authority to address what happened this weekend, but I do have authority over my team. Jake is suspended indefinitely and pending a university investigation, will likely be dismissed from the team altogether. All I need is the athletic director's okay, and I promise you I'll get that. One way or another."

I grip the arms of my chair tightly and nod my head. "Thank you, sir. Thank you so much."

He comes around the table, and I stand to meet him when he holds out a hand. He shakes my hand, firm and quick, and it has all the softness of a cobra strike, but it's what nearly puts me over the edge.

I swallow hard, nod my head, thank him one more time, and then head for the door.

"Silas," he calls before I'm all the way out. "Williams told me about the playground. Pretty inventive idea."

I shrug. "I guess."

"I sure do hope this game works out for you, son. But if it doesn't, I think you could make a damn fine coach."

I close the door behind me with a quiet click, and I let the relief seep through my shoulders.

I swear to God, it's like the whole team decided to show up for early morning workout today. Torres and Brookes are pretending to watch game film in the lounge area right outside the office, and they pounce as soon as I'm out. Half a dozen more guys slink in from the locker room to hear me give them the news. Coach Oz and even Coach Gallt nod at me as they leave the office and head into the weight room.

It still doesn't quite feel real when I leave the athletic complex and head for my pickup so I can make my first class on the other side of campus. Then I see a familiar sleek gray number parked next to my rusty piece of junk, and Dylan climbs out of the driver's side.

The wind catches her hair, tossing it up in this golden column that catches the sun. She crosses to me quickly and huddles in close so that my body blocks some of the wind.

"So?"

"I'm still on the team. No suspension."

She squeals and throws her arms around my neck, and I lift her up off her feet so I can bury my face in the warm skin of her neck. Whatever tension was still left in me begins to melt away, and I could stay right here forever.

"I knew everything would be okay. I knew it."

"Carter is suspended, and if Coach has his way, he'll be cut soon."

She pulls back and smiles, running a hand along my cheek. "More good things."

I kiss her lightly and slowly lower her feet to the ground.

"Good things" doesn't even begin to cover it.

She grins up at me, slips out of my arms, and crosses to lean against my truck. She's wearing shorts and the same fall-off-your-shoulder shirt she wore the night we met. She gives me a wicked smile.

"What do you say to skipping our morning classes and going for a drive instead?"

"I say get your gorgeous ass in the truck and let's go."

I leave the windows down as we drive, so Dylan's hair blows across my chest and face as the wind sweeps through. But I don't mind because she's pressed tight against my side, my arm resting in the cradle of her thighs so I can switch gears.

I don't go as far out of town as we did last time, but I drive until all the houses and businesses disappear and there's nothing but green, wide-open space. When I park, I pull a blanket out from under my seat, and Dylan laughs.

"Oh . . . You're getting better at this." I lift her up into the truck bed and together we spread out the blanket.

"I do try to please."

"Now I don't have to worry about getting all rusty and dirty."

I sprawl on the blanket next to her feet, and tug her down into my lap. Our legs end up tangled, and she laughs as she tries to get situated.

"Rusty, no. But the other . . . I make no promises."

Summer is teasing its way into fall, and though it's warm out, the wind tells a different story. She presses close against me.

The sky is big above us. The countryside stretches out for miles in every direction. And neither of our lives has ever been so complicated. But I don't feel overshadowed by any of those things. Not with her in my arms.

There's still her parents to worry about. And she's got me trying to rope in more guys from the team to help with a new protest about the shelter. I mentioned to Stella that Dylan might be able to help, that maybe she could do something to draw more attention so that the prosecutor would take a more serious look at the case. But she just changed the subject.

I don't know when life stopped feeling small and started feeling too big, too much to handle, but I know it's easier with Dylan in my arms.

Me and her together . . . I believe we're big enough to face whatever comes.

Dylan

completely underestimated football uniforms.

During the first and only other game I had attended, we'd had a seat high up in the student section, so I'd only really seen these big, hulking gray and red masses. But Silas's first game back is an away game. It's only a six-hour drive, so Dallas, Matt, and I make the trip, and we snag much better seats. And oh my goodness, Silas in a uniform is just . . . I don't even have the words. And the game hasn't even started yet.

Stella said she had a big art project to work on, and I can tell by the persistent worried look on Dallas's face (and the way she keeps checking her phone) that she feels badly for leaving her behind.

Stella loves football. Or loved it.

But we have to trust that she knows her lines. And maybe she really does have a project she needs to work on, but if she doesn't . . . I don't blame her.

It takes us all a while to get in the groove of being without her, though. Matt tries to fill in, stepping up to play DJ as we drive. But the drive felt . . . just *less* without her.

"Ryan talked to her," Dallas says, after receiving a text. "He said she's really at the studio. He heard her talking to some other students."

"Good. That's good," I say.

Dallas nods. "She's strong."

"She is."

"She's going to be okay." I can't tell whether she's phrasing it as a question or a statement, so I just repeat the words back to her, and that seems to make her feel better.

Right before kick off we get a mass text from Stella.

I expect pictures! And updates! And if any of those punks suck it up, you guys better yell at them for me.

Dallas smiles, and we send her a picture of the three of us, decked out in Rusk gear, holding up our wildcat claws. Dallas keeps up a steady stream of updates for her as the game begins, and then I get sucked into watching Silas play.

I can't see his face. But I know by the way he holds himself, the way he moves . . . I know he's in his element. And I know he's happy. And I swear I'm so full of pride and joy for him that I'm about to burst at the seams. Or start crying. One or the other.

I could make an effort to understand more about the game,

to expand upon the knowledge that I learned last time, but I figure that can wait for another time. Today I just glue my eyes to number twenty-two and watch him do what he loves.

Football grounds him, and I will love football for all my days if only for that very reason.

It's strange, really, to think how quickly my life has changed. I'm still figuring out what I like and what I don't (with Silas's help, of course). And I know I won't undo a life of pretending in just a week. It will take time. Time to break the habits. Time to form new ones.

But I'm looking forward to it.

I've got new friends, new goals, new interests. It's exciting and overwhelming, but beneath all that . . . there's a calm that I've never felt before. I no longer feel the need to search for things to do, ways to ingratiate myself to people. I don't have anything to prove, not to anyone else, anyway.

And Silas . . . he's technically new, too, but it doesn't feel that way.

As I watch him move across the field, graceful and strong and fearless, I can barely remember how I felt before him. I try to think back to the way things had been with Henry, but that seems like a different life, a different me.

And everything about those memories is muted and dull.

The team has now moved across the field, and they're only yards away from the other team's end zone. I watch Carson hand the ball off to Silas and he pushes through the huddled mass of players, breaking through and crossing the white line painted onto the field, putting Rusk's first points on the board. I know it was probably incredibly difficult, all those big, bulky bodies in the way, but Silas makes it look so easy.

He's good at crossing lines. Pushing boundaries.

He pushed mine, and because of it, I can breathe.

I love Silas Moore, and I feel pretty certain that because of that, my life will never feel muted again.

Author's Note

njustice is defined as "a lack of fairness, undeserved hurt, or a
failure to respect a person's rights." For me, injustices always
seem to carry with them a certain amount of shock.

Shock that people could behave so reprehensibly. Shock that
no one stopped them. And too often, shock at the world's lack of
empathy and pursuit of justice.

It's strange, isn't it, how we can continue to be surprised by the
world's cruelty when we have witnessed it time and time again?
The first time I thought of the idea for this book, it was on the
heels of just such an unjust occurrence. I was moved by the things
I saw and read, but nothing moved me so much as people's reaction to it—the way some banded together to speak out even
when there was no changing what happened. Their only hope was
to change people's perspective, to make people notice. I created
Dylan's character that night. Jotting down a few of her thoughts
on a sticky note that stayed on my desktop until the story was
finished.

And I made a promise to myself then to notice more. To speak more. To care more.

And I make that challenge to you now. Notice injustice. Speak out against it. Care more for those who suffer it. This world belongs to all of us, and it could be you or someone you know who goes unnoticed tomorrow.

And if you've been the victim of a violation of your rights, your civil liberties, or your person, talk to someone. Ask for help. You are absolutely not alone.

The sad truth is according to statistics compiled by RAINN (the Rape, Abuse, and Incest National Network), a person is sexually assaulted in America every two minutes. Sixty percent of sexual assaults go unreported. Even fewer lead to an arrest and prosecution. In fact, they estimate that out of every 100 rapes, 40 are reported, 10 lead to an arrest, 8 make it to prosecution, 4 lead to a felony conviction, and only 3 rapists will spend time in prison. These statistics boggle my mind and hurt my heart. And when the law fails to serve justice, many young women and men turn to their universities for help. And even though 1 in 4 women are sexually assaulted during their time in college, 41 percent of colleges haven't conducted a single sexual assault investigation in the last five years, according to "Sexual Violence on Campus," a 2014 report conducted by Senator Claire McCaskill.

I could throw statistics at you all day long, but I think it's clear that victims of sexual assault are continually and heinously overlooked, blamed and re-victimized, and left without justice.

As readers, as people, we might not have the capacity to change the justice system. But as Dylan says in the book, we can change one person's perspective at a time. We can notice. We can speak up. We can teach this generation, my generation, that the way sexual assault is viewed and treated in this country is not okay, so that when it is our turn to step into the shoes of political office and criminal justice, we can continue changing the narrative from a place of power.

And more than anything, we can support. And we can empower. We can love.

We can be better.

Acknowledgments

It takes an extraordinary number of people to make a book happen. Most days I barely know which way is up or what time it is or even what month I'm currently in. But even so, I would be even more lost without my family and friends, in particular my father, who's been so helpful with hashing out the football details to keep the Rusk world as true to life as possible. Any mistakes, of course, are mine. Then there's my sister Amy, who I can always count on to read for me or give me her thoughts on absolutely anything. And my mother, who listened to me vent and rage and stress about these characters as if they were real people. In fact, she's there to let me vent and rage and stress a lot. Same goes for Lindsay: I always feel incredibly safe in sharing my words with you, and I absolutely could not do this without you. And thanks to Jen, Mer, Kristin, Bethany, Patrick, Shelly, Michelle, and more for the love and encouragement.

To Amanda, thank you for loving Silas with me, and for always challenging me to dig deeper and do more. KP—oh my Lord, what would I do without you, lady? (I'd be a nervous wreck . . . that's what I'd do.) Thanks for keeping me sane. And for caring so very much about my THINGS. To Suzie, Jessie, Molly, Kathleen, Pouya, Danielle, and everyone else who works so hard to help my books succeed—thank you! A thousand times, thank you!

Thank you to the incomparable Carmcats! I can say with absolute confidence that putting together this Rusk University Street Team was one of the best decisions I've ever made in my life. You all have challenged me and championed me and never fail to cheer me up. I feel like you know and love these characters as much as I do, and for that I will never be able to put into words my gratitude. Thank you: Alana, Amber, Amoolya, Andy, Anabel, Betsy, Christine, Danielle, Elizabeth, Emily, Ethan, Jen, Kaitlan, Katelyn, Kim, Krista, Lucy, Maggie, Megan, Momo, Sara, Stephanie C., Stephanie G., Yesi, and Yvette.

And to all the other magnificent readers and bloggers whom I've met over the last few years. Thank you for your hard work and dedication and love. Shout out to a few amazing people I've met this year: Misha in Seattle, Leah in Austin, Caitlin in Nashville, and so many more! Thanks also to Jen, Jay, Kathleen, Sophie, Monica, the Chelseas, Molly, Becca, Jamie, and the dozens of authors who keep me sane by dealing with my late night texts, blurbing my books, giving me awesome things to read, and God knows what else. And to everyone who reads these books, you rock! Bleed Rusk Red!

The Rusk University series continues . . .

What happens when a good girl creates the ultimate college bucket list and item #1 is to hook up with a jock?

ALL PLAYED OUT

Antonella "Nell" De Luca is the first in her family to go to college, and on a full ride, too. She's spent years working and studying nonstop to make the most of this chance. But now college is almost over and she's seriously lacking in friends and a social life of any kind. So, with the help of her friend Dylan, she does what she does best . . . She makes a to-do list. More specifically . . . the Ultimate College Bucket List.

Item #1 on that list? Hook up with a jock.

Mateo Torres is a wide receiver for the Rusk University football team. He's committed and works hard, but when he's not on the field all bets are off. He likes to party and do whatever insane thing pops into his head. It's not uncommon to find him dancing in inappropriate places, wearing inappropriate amounts of clothing, and just being generally inappropriate. If it's fun . . . that's all that matters. Because as long as things don't get too serious, he can avoid thinking about the ex he lost when he put football and his ego ahead of her.

Hooking up with Dylan's friend, Nell, is absolutely the last thing he should do. She's quiet and smart and innocent, and too much like the girl he spends all his time trying not to think about. But when he gets a taste of her, he's reluctant to give her up. Being around her almost feels like he's getting a do-over. A chance to do things right. And he's the perfect person to help her drop her inhibitions and complete her bucket list.

But as the list draws to a close, they'll both have to decide if what they have is real or just for fun. Life is more than just lists. And the past shouldn't rule the present. But can they figure that out before it's too late?

Spring 2015